River's End

Center Point
Large Print

Also by Melody Carlson and available from
Center Point Large Print:

Limelight

The Inn at Shining Waters Series:
  River's Song
  River's Call

River's End

The Inn at Shining Waters Series

MELODY CARLSON

CENTER POINT LARGE PRINT
THORNDIKE, MAINE

This Center Point Large Print edition is published
in the year 2012 by arrangement with
Abingdon Press.

The text of this Large Print edition is unabridged.
In other aspects, this book may
vary from the original edition.
Printed in the United States of America
on permanent paper.
Set in 16-point Times New Roman type.

ISBN: 978-1-61173-547-5

Library of Congress Cataloging-in-Publication Data

Carlson, Melody.
River's End / Melody Carlson.
pages ; cm.
ISBN 978-1-61173-547-5 (library binding : alk. paper)
1. Teenage girls—Fiction. 2. Grandmothers—Fiction.
  3. Runaway teenagers—Fiction. 4. Large type books. I. Title.
PS3553.A73257R575 2012b
813′.54—dc23
                                                    2012015288

1

June 1978

Despite tranquil blue skies and only a slight onshore breeze, the air felt chilly today. Or maybe it was just her. Anna pulled her cardigan more tightly around her as she looked out over the sparkling river. Perched on the hand-hewn log bench, she stared blankly toward the river and surveying her old faithful dugout canoe, let out a long, weary sigh. She'd gotten up extra early this morning. Planning to paddle the Water Dove upriver, she'd wanted to soak in the sunshine, breathe the fresh summer air, clear the cobwebs from her head, and gather her strength for the day.

She'd imagined paddling hard and steady upstream and finally, after her arms grew tired, she would turn the canoe around and allow the river's current to carry her back home . . . back to Clark and Lauren and the Inn at Shining Waters. But now she felt it was useless . . . futile even. She simply didn't have the strength to pull the dugout down the riverbank and into the water. Planting her elbows on her knees she leaned forward and buried her face in her hands. A praying position, and yet she had no words. Nothing left to pray.

5

Already she felt emotionally drained, and it was still early morning. How would she ever make it through this painful day . . . her beloved granddaughter's eighteenth birthday? It didn't seem possible that Sarah would've been eighteen by now.

More than two years had passed since Sarah had vanished from their lives. As far as they knew she'd run off with her boyfriend, Zane. She'd only been sixteen—just a child—and yet old for her years. Anna had tried to appear strong, hoping that eventually Sarah would return to them. In the meantime, she put her energies into working hard alongside Clark and Lauren. The three of them, connected in their silent grief, cooperated with one another as they kept the inn going and thriving, making constant improvements, increasing the business, faithfully serving the never-ending roster of eager guests.

It was for the sake of these guests, and even more so for her family, that Anna had maintained a positive outlook as she went through her daily routines. But beneath her veneer of hopeful confidence, the concerns for her granddaughter's welfare had remained in the shadows. How was it possible that Sarah had so completely disappeared? Without a word—not a single letter or phone call—the sixteen-year-old had seemingly vanished from the face of the earth. And for two years, despite her family's best efforts to locate her, Sarah was not to be found. What did it mean?

Anna's unspoken fear was that Sarah had come to serious harm . . . that perhaps she was even dead. Otherwise, she surely would've contacted them. At least, Clark had said early on, she would've contacted Anna. Because, as he pointed out, the bond between Anna and her grand-daughter had always been a strong one—symbiotic. Besides that, Anna felt it uncharacteristic for Sarah to be so selfish and inconsiderate to cut them off so completely. Even in adolescence and amidst her parents' marital troubles, Sarah had been thoughtful and mature. She wasn't the sort of person to intentionally put others through such pain and misery. As hard as it was to face it, the only logical explanation was that something had happened to the girl. Something tragic.

Still, no one ever voiced these mute terrors. Saying the words out loud would make it seem too real. So Anna and the others had clung to the hope that Sarah was alive, that she had simply chosen to separate herself from her family, and that someday she would return. But as months passed, and as one year slipped into the next, Sarah's name was spoken much less frequently. And if her name was mentioned, there was always an uncomfortable pause that followed . . . a quiet awkward moment would linger before the conversation resumed itself.

But realistically—as painful as it would be—it

might be easier if they were informed Sarah was actually deceased. At least they could properly grieve for her then. They could hold a memorial service to remember her and to celebrate the years of her life that had been so sweet . . . so innocent . . . so pure. Perhaps they might even build a monument of sorts . . . at the very least a special plaque or carved stone—they could set it right here by the river, and it would be a quiet place where they could come to think and to grieve and to remember Sarah's short but beautiful life in their midst.

Anna sat up straight now, gazing out over the river again. But in lieu of the crisp and clear diamond sparkles on the surface, she now saw a blurry watercolor image instead. It all looked murky and distorted . . . and hot tears ran freely down her cheeks. She hated to be weak like this . . . to give into this kind of sadness and despair. But it all seemed so senseless . . . so unfair . . . that a grandmother should outlive her granddaughter. It was just wrong.

She pressed her lips together, using the palms of her hands to wipe away her tears. This would not do. She had to remain strong today. As much for Lauren's sake as for her own because she knew Lauren would be especially mindful of her only daughter today. Eighteen years ago, Sarah had made her entrance into this world. And although Lauren hadn't really been prepared for motherhood, it had been a happy day for Anna. She had felt an immediate bond with her granddaughter.

As difficult as it would be, Anna was determined to pull this off. She intended to make this a good day. If any words were spoken of Sarah, they would be positive words, remembering all the sweetness that the girl had brought into all their lives . . . despite the brevity of her stay. Anna took in a slow deep breath and stood. She would be strong and of good courage. There would be time enough for tears tomorrow.

As Anna turned toward the house, she heard the sound of a boat's motor coming up the river. Pausing to listen to the rhythm of the engine, she couldn't help but remember the comforting sound of Henry's old boat. How she missed deep chortling echoing along the hills of the river. She missed Henry, too. As well as Babette . . . and so many others. Times and people had changed over the years, but the Siuslaw River remained the same, moving out to the sea, being pushed back gently with the incoming tide, always on the move.

Her people had lived alongside and loved this river for countless generations before her. Her grandmother's old stories made references to them. According to Hazel's research, the Siuslaw had been a matriarchal society. And Anna had known that it was the women who had handed down the traditions and what little belongings that were accumulated in a lifetime. Anna had always hoped to do the same, to leave a timeless inheritance for the generations that followed her, from Lauren to Sarah . . . to Sarah's descendants. But it seemed that was not meant to be. Perhaps the heritage of the shining waters was going to end far sooner than she'd expected.

Anna was nearly at the main house when she heard the boat's engine slowing down, and when she looked, it was veering toward their dock. It looked like the Greeley's Groceries boat. In an attempt to increase business, the store in town had decided to make deliveries on the river during the tourist months. Mostly, Anna supposed, because the youngest Greeley boy wanted an excuse to have a motorboat. But their groceries had been delivered yesterday, and she wasn't expecting anything else today. Cupping her hand over her eyes, she peered to see Bobby Greeley at the helm. Sure enough, he was stopping at their dock.

"Hello, Bobby," she called out as she walked toward the dock to meet him. "What are you doing out—" She stopped herself as she stared in wonder at the waiflike, dark-haired girl huddled in the back of the boat. Wrapped in an olive green woolen blanket, she looked at Anna with large, dark eyes. Sad, hollow eyes.

"Sarah?" Anna felt her heart give a lurch. And suddenly she was running down the dock.

Blinking in disbelief, she stared at the girl. "Is that you? Sarah?"

The girl nodded mutely as she stood, letting the blanket fall onto the bench behind her. "Grandma," she said quietly.

"Oh, Sarah!" Anna grabbed the rope from Bobby and hastily tied it then climbed into the boat and threw her arms around the trembling girl and began to sob tears of joy. "I can't believe it. I cannot believe it!" Now she held Sarah back with straightened arms, looking deeply into her eyes just to be certain she wasn't imagining this moment. "It really is you!"

They were both crying now, hugging each other tightly until finally Anna knew that she needed to get Sarah up to the house. She glanced at poor Bobby, who was watching with troubled eyes, as if he wasn't sure what to do about this feminine display of emotions.

"I'm sorry, Bobby," Anna told him. "I'm just so overwhelmed. This is my granddaughter, Sarah. I haven't seen her for years."

"That's okay, ma'am."

"Thank you for bringing her out to us," Anna quickly told him. "I, uh, I assume you'll just put the charges on our bill."

He nodded.

"Come on, Sarah." Anna helped her out of the boat. "Let's get you inside." She looked around the boat now. "Do you have any bags?"

Sarah simply shook her head. Now Anna studied her granddaughter more carefully. Looking painfully thin beneath a long raggedy dress of faded blue calico that reached nearly to her bare ankles, she had on worn leather sandals, and her long dark hair was uncombed and dull looking. Anna put her arm around Sarah's shoulders, holding her close as they walked up the dock.

"Is my mother still here with you?" Sarah asked quietly.

"Yes. She helps with the inn."

Sarah stopped walking. "I don't want to see her."

Anna looked into Sarah's eyes now. "Your mother has changed, Sarah, a lot. She's like a different person."

Sarah's dark eyes seemed even darker. "I don't care. I don't want to see her."

Anna didn't know what to do.

Sarah looked back to where the boat was pulling away from the dock. "Maybe I just should leave and go back to—"

"No." Anna's hold on Sarah grew tighter. "You can't leave. Not until we talk." She hugged Sarah close to her again. "We have been worried sick about you, Sarah. You have family here. We love you. And even if you and your mother had your problems, you still belong here with us. Do you understand that?"

Sarah just sniffed.

Anna looked into her eyes again. "This is your home, too, Sarah. This is your river. Clark and I . . . and Hazel . . . and your mother . . . we all love you."

Sarah still seemed unsure.

"Please, trust me, Sarah," Anna said quietly. She was desperately trying to think of a plan to ease Sarah back into their world. Her old room in the house might feel too confining, too close to the rest of them. Plus, Anna knew Lauren was already in the kitchen working on breakfast. And since the summer season had just begun, the inn was full. But then Anna remembered that Hazel's cabin, the same cabin that once belonged to Anna's grand-mother was unoccupied right now. Hazel was touring in Asia and wouldn't be home for a couple of weeks.

"I know," Anna told her. "You'll stay in The Oyster."

"Grandma Pearl's cabin?"

Anna smiled as she hooked her arm into Sarah's. "That's right. And that would make Grandma Pearl very happy!"

Some of the guests were milling around the grounds now. Some said hello and some just looked curiously at her and Sarah. She knew that Sarah looked like someone who had stepped out of a different world, almost as if she'd been living in a different era, and she knew that Sarah probably had a story to tell. And Anna certainly had plenty of questions. But not right now.

"You look tired," Anna said as she opened the door and led Sarah into the sweet little cabin.

"I am." Sarah went over to the table by the window that faced the river and, running a finger over the grain of the pine, looked out with a wistful expression.

"I want you to make yourself at home," Anna told her. "If you like, I won't even tell your mother that you're here yet. You can have a shower, and I'll bring you down some breakfast and some clothes and things. You'll eat and you'll rest and then we'll talk." She stroked Sarah's tangled hair. "Okay?"

Sarah just looked at her. Her eyes reminded Anna of a frightened doe.

Anna put both her hands on Sarah's cheeks, once again peering into those troubled dark eyes. "You are *home,* darling. This river and this inn and even this old cabin . . . they all belong to you just as much as they belong to me. Do you understand what I am saying to you?"

Sarah still looked unsure, but at least she nodded.

Anna hugged her again. "You are *home,* Sarah. At long last, you are home." She kissed Sarah's cheek then promised to return quickly with some food. And then, feeling as if she had wings on her feet, Anna ran up to the house, with each step wondering how she would share this good news.

2

Anna tried to compose herself as she went up the stairs to the house. Then, halfway up, she realized it would be impossible to keep this wonderful news from Lauren. For one thing, she couldn't wipe the deliriously happy expression off her face, and besides that she felt like laughing and singing and dancing. So she turned around and went off in search of Clark. She found him at the pump house, working on a leaking pipe.

"Oh, Clark!" she exclaimed as she threw her arms around him.

"What's wrong?" He peered at her with concern.

"Nothing's wrong. Everything's right." She quickly explained about Sarah.

"That's fantastic!" He hugged her tightly. "How is she?"

Anna's smile faded. "She looks beat up."

He frowned. "Someone has abused her?"

"No . . . not like that. She just looks skinny and scared and—oh, that's right!" She bit her lip. "I need to get some food and clothes out to her."

"What? Where is she?"

"I put her in your mom's cabin. Hazel won't be home until the end of the month, I thought she wouldn't mind."

"Of course, she won't mind. She'll be as delighted as anyone to hear that Sarah is safe."

"But Sarah doesn't want Lauren to know yet." Anna glanced up at the house. "And I promised."

"Well, you won't be able to keep that secret for long, you know."

"I know." She smiled again. "Oh, Clark, I'm so relieved—so glad to see her. And did you know —it's her birthday today."

He grinned. "Then we'll slaughter the fatted calf. The prodigal granddaughter has come home. It's time to have a feast!"

"Speaking of feasting, I need to get her something to eat. I just hope Lauren doesn't figure me out." She kissed Clark on the cheek. "This is a great day!" Then she turned and hurried back to the house, trying to concoct a plan to prevent arousing Lauren's suspicion.

To Anna's relief, Lauren was busy taking care of guests, and the house was bustling with activity. Anna managed to get a plate of food without Lauren batting an eyelash. "I'm taking this to a guest who doesn't feel up to coming to the house," Anna explained. And, really, it wasn't untrue. Although Sarah was so much more than just a guest. Anna carried the food to her room, where she hurried to gather up a few pieces of clothing—something clean for Sarah to put on after her shower. Then, with the clothing tucked beneath an arm and the warm

16

plate of breakfast in hand, she hurried back out.

The sound of water running told Anna that Sarah was still in the shower as she let herself into the little cabin. She turned the oven on low, setting the plate of food inside to stay warm. Then she opened the windows to allow some fresh air inside. Hazel hadn't stayed here since last summer. But following her Asian journey—a trip to celebrate her recent retirement from teaching —she planned to live here full time. While Hazel was in her early seventies, she still seemed younger, but Anna knew she was slowing down. She also knew that Hazel loved this little cabin, and even if it was convenient for Sarah—for the time being—it would have to be temporary.

Still, Anna moved some of Hazel's personal things out of the way, trying to make the little cabin seem as welcoming as possible to Sarah. She even ducked outside and picked some of the wildflowers growing nearby and was just putting the vase on the wooden kitchen table when Sarah emerged from the tiny bathroom addition that Clark had built for his mother so many years ago.

"Oh!" Sarah seemed surprised, securing the soronglike towel more tightly about her as her long dark hair dripped down over her bare shoulders. Anna cringed inwardly to see Sarah's grayish skin stretched tautly over her collarbone. She looked emaciated.

"I didn't mean to startle you," Anna said

gently. "I put some breakfast in the stove for you and was just airing this room out and straightening up a bit. Hazel hasn't stayed here since last August." Now Anna prattled on about how Hazel had recently retired from teaching at the university, and how she was now on a tour of some Asian countries.

"That sounds interesting." Sarah's voice sounded flat and nearly void of emotion.

Anna pointed to the clothes she'd set on the chair. "I know that dress will be too big for you, but it's clean and comfortable. There are some other things, too."

"Thank you." Still Sarah just stood there, warily watching, almost as if she wished Anna would leave.

"I thought we could talk," Anna said. "Why don't you get dressed and I'll make us some coffee and—"

"I don't drink coffee."

"Tea then?" Anna suggested.

"Only if it's herbal."

"Oh . . ." Anna nodded as she turned to open the cupboard near the stove. "Well, I'm sure Hazel must have some chamomile here somewhere."

Sarah took the clothes to the bedroom with her, and Anna busied herself making tea. For some reason, she felt like she was treading on eggshells here, like one wrong word, one misstep, and Sarah might take off running like a scared rabbit. And so, as she waited for the water to heat, Anna prayed. She prayed for Sarah as well as for the rest of them. She prayed that this unexpected reunion would go as smoothly as possible—and that no one's feelings would be hurt. Especially Lauren's and Sarah's.

Lauren had made so many mistakes with Sarah. Even she could admit this now. But her excuse was that she'd been young, too young . . . a child parenting a child. In many ways Sarah had been more mature than her mother. Still, Lauren had started to grow up after her marriage to Donald had disintegrated. She'd put aside many of her old self-centered ways, but although she was close to forty, she sometimes still acted in a somewhat childish way. However, Anna was patient with her. And sometimes she even blamed herself for some of Lauren's narcissistic tendencies. Perhaps if she hadn't abdicated some of Lauren's upbringing to Eunice it would have gone better.

Still, Anna knew it did no good to dwell in the past. Better to learn from your mistakes and move forward . . . trying not to make them again. The teakettle whistled, and Anna turned off the propane, filled the teapot with hot water, rinsed it around (as Babette had taught her to do long ago), then poured in the loose leaves and filled it again. Not for the first time, Anna was acutely aware of how so many parts of her life had been influenced by the women who had gone before her. How thankful she was for them.

Sarah emerged from the bedroom with her hair wrapped in a towel. Barefoot and wearing Anna's faded blue housedress, which hung on her like a sack, Sarah stood there in the doorway with a guarded expression, her arms folded across her front in a protected sort of way.

"Tea is ready," Anna said cheerfully. She used a dishtowel to remove the warm plate from the oven. "And here is some breakfast. Your favorite." She set the plate of hotcakes, eggs, and bacon on the table with a smile.

Sarah made a slightly disgusted look. "Bacon?"

"You used to love—"

"I do not eat the flesh of my fellow creatures."

"Oh . . ." Anna plucked the strips of crispy bacon from the plate, tossing them from hand to hand as they cooled. Then she removed a saucer from the dish cupboard and, placing the bacon on it, set it down at the table opposite Sarah's place. "Then I'll just have that." She hadn't eaten break-fast yet. No sense to waste good food. She pulled out the chair and sat down, waiting for Sarah to follow her lead.

Sarah almost seemed to turn up her nose as she gingerly sat down across from Anna and picked up her fork, and although she seemed uneasy, it wasn't long before she was gobbling up the food.

She was obviously hungry. Half-starved from what Anna could see.

Anna watched furtively as she nibbled at the bacon, wishing she'd thought to bring down more food. Poor Sarah looked like she hadn't eaten in days . . . maybe even weeks. "Can I get you some more?" she offered finally.

"No." Sarah firmly shook her head. "That's plenty."

Anna nodded. "All right . . ." Still she felt uneasy, wondering why this was so difficult. How was it possible that sweet Sarah had changed so completely . . . grown so distant . . . almost to the point of hostility?

"You know our ancestors nearly starved when they were relocated to the reservation up north," she said absently. Really, she was simply trying to think of something innocuous to say. Something safe and removed from whatever was actually transpiring in this room right now. "Your great-grandmother, Pearl, the one who built this cabin, used to tell me how hard it was for them to find food in those days." She sadly shook her head. "Some of the men were shot for going out in search of shellfish and berries, just hoping to feed their families. If you can imagine."

"The white men have always hated us."

Anna frowned. "Well, that's not entirely true."

Sarah glared at her through those dark eyes. "How can you say that?"

"Because I've known many good white men, including my own father." She smiled. "In fact, I'm married to one."

Sarah pushed her empty plate to the center of the table.

"I believe that fear and ignorance were the biggest problems in those days," Anna continued. "Fear and ignorance usually lead to intolerance. That was the white man's biggest shortcoming. And, to be fair, it can be anyone's downfall. When we fall into fear, allowing ourselves to believe falsehoods about others, we eventually learn to hate." She looked evenly at Sarah now. "But when we embrace one another's differences, when we make ourselves open to really under-standing one another, then it's not so difficult to love." She smiled. "With God's help."

Sarah studied Anna closely, as if trying to take this in. But then she shook her head. "Some people aren't worthy of our love."

"Really . . . ?" Anna waited.

"Some people need to be purged from our lives."

"Purged?" Anna considered this. "And how exactly does one do this?"

"By removing themselves."

Anna simply nodded. "Is that what you did?"

"I guess so."

Anna took in a slow breath. "Is that how you see me, Sarah? As someone you needed to purge from your life?"

Sarah's eyebrows shot up. "Oh, no, Grandma, not you. But my mother and father—they were toxic."

"Toxic?" Anna blinked.

"Poison. They were slowly but surely killing me."

"Oh, Sarah," Anna exclaimed. "I'm so sorry you felt that way. I wish you would've come to me . . . instead of running away."

"How could I come to you?" Sarah demanded. "My mother was here with you. I had nowhere to go."

"And that's why you left with Zane?"

"Zane . . ." Sarah slowly shook her head. "I almost forgot about him."

"You mean you weren't with him this whole time?"

"Oh, no. Zane and I parted ways early on. He wanted to stay stoned and follow the Grateful Dead all over the country. That wasn't what I was looking for."

"What were you looking for?"

"Peace . . . inner peace." She sighed sadly.

"And did you find it?"

Sarah looked out the window with a longing expression. "I thought I did . . . at first."

"But it didn't last?" Anna gently prodded.

Sarah just shook her head.

"Do you want to talk about it?"

"I'm really tired." She glanced toward the bedroom.

"Yes." Anna stood, gathering the dishes. "I'm sure you are. Please, just rest. We can talk later."

Sarah padded off to the bedroom, closing the door, and Anna rinsed the breakfast dishes then wiped down the counters and dusted a few things, shook out the throw rugs and finally, satisfied that she'd made the place as homey as possible, quietly let herself out.

"Who's the sick guest?" Lauren asked as Anna carried the dishes into the kitchen. The house was vacant of guests now, and Lauren was alone in the kitchen.

Anna set the dishes in the sink, trying to think of an answer.

"I heard Mrs. Lindley's having morning sickness," Lauren continued absently. "Remember how sick I was when I was pregnant with—" She stopped herself.

Anna turned to look at Lauren, seeing the tears in her daughter's eyes.

"Do you know what day this is, Mom?"

Anna just nodded.

"I—I—"

Before Lauren could finish, Anna gathered her in her arms. "It's going to be okay, Lauren. Really, it's going to be okay."

"How can you possibly say that?" Lauren finally said between sobs. "It's been two years, Mom. Two years!"

Anna put her hands on Lauren's shoulders, firmly grasping her. "Just trust me on this, Lauren. I know that Sarah is all right."

"How can you know that?" Lauren fumbled in the pocket of her apron, pulling out a tissue to wipe her eyes. "Did you have a dream or a vision or something?"

"Something . . . ," Anna muttered as she turned away, pretending to be busily putting the dishes in the dishwasher.

"Any coffee left?" Clark asked as he came into the house.

"I just made a fresh pot," Lauren told him. As she went to get him a cup, Anna and Clark exchanged glances. Anna was trying to warn him with her eyes not to mention Sarah.

"Well, I think I got the pump fixed," he said as Lauren handed him a mug of coffee. "Glad I didn't have to call Mike Watson in to help."

Now they made small talk about the pump and the weather and how one of the guests had caught a record-size salmon early this morning, and, for a few moments, Anna nearly forgot about her prodigal granddaughter. Before long, one of the summer staffers came in, asking for help with something in the laundry room and Lauren offered to go and assist.

"I take it she hasn't heard the news," Clark said quietly after they left.

"No." Anna pressed her lips together.

25

"How long do you think you'll need to keep it from her?"

"Hopefully not long. I feel so deceitful. But I don't want to hurt Sarah. She seems so fragile . . . so vulnerable." Now she relayed to him what Sarah had said to her, hoping that as she repeated the strange words, they would make more sense.

"I can understand how she might think her parents weren't the healthiest people in her life," he conceded. "But that still doesn't explain disappearing for two years."

"I have a feeling she was someplace where people tried to make her think like them. Almost as if she was slightly brainwashed."

"Brainwashed?"

"I know that sounds crazy. But it's like something in her is changed. Almost as if the light in her—remember that sparkle she used to have —as if it's been snuffed out." Anna felt on the verge of tears now. "Oh, I realize she's probably just exhausted. She was so filthy and sad-looking. And she looks half-starved. You should've seen her eating. In fact, that reminds me. I want to take some food down there, to have ready for her when she wakes." Anna got up and started to gather some fruit and baked goods and a few other things.

"I sure would like to see her," Clark said as Anna put these items in a basket.

"I know. And when it's time . . ."

"In the meantime, mum's the word?"

"Just for now." Anna went to the door. "I'll encourage her . . . but I don't want to push her too hard. Like I said, she seems so fragile right now, so apprehensive." But Anna didn't say what she feared most—that Sarah seemed so wounded and fearful . . . that Anna was worried she might run away again. All Anna wanted to do for the time being was to ensure that Sarah stayed here with them. At least long enough to make sense of what she'd experienced these past two years. And hopefully long enough for her to heal some of the old wounds that seemed to be festering inside of her now. Anna knew the river was a place of healing, but it only worked if the person was willing. She prayed that Sarah would be willing —and that Lauren would not interfere.

3

Sarah's birthday came and went without Lauren ever knowing her daughter was only just yards away. Anna wished there was another way to handle this, but she knew that if Lauren could grasp the whole situation—including Anna's concerns that Sarah might bolt—she would understand and appreciate that Anna was protecting the girl. After all, the important thing was that Sarah had come home . . . and that she was alive.

However, on the third day of Sarah's visit, even Anna was growing somewhat impatient. Seated across from her granddaughter in a well-worn easy chair, she turned the coffee mug around and around in her hands. "I really don't want to push you, Sarah," she began gently, "but I worry that you're holing up in here, keeping yourself hidden away like this . . . and for no good reason. Really, I think you'd feel better if you went outside to enjoy the river and this good weather. It's not always this pleasant in June, and you could take out the canoe and—"

"I do not want to see *her,*" Sarah seethed.

Anna knew Sarah was referring to her mother. For some reason Lauren was this obstacle that Sarah could just not seem to get past. "I wish you could trust me about this," she told Sarah for what felt the umpteenth time, "your mother has truly changed."

"Please, don't call her *my mother.*" Sarah scowled. "She is nothing to me."

"All right." Anna nodded with lips pressed tightly together. "Then what should I call her?"

Sarah narrowed her eyes.

"How about if I just call her Lauren?"

"Call her whatever you like, just keep her away from me."

"You need to understand that your . . . I mean that *Lauren* has many regrets for how she handled things with you."

"*Handled* things?" Sarah blurted. "That woman never handled a single thing when it came to me. She left the handling to everyone else. You or Dad or Grandmother Eunice or even Grandmother Thomas—all had more to do with me than my mother—I mean *Lauren.* She was not a mother to me."

Anna just nodded. "I know . . . and I'm sure Lauren would agree with you on that."

"I really don't care what Lauren would think one way or another. While I was gone, I pretended that she was dead. In fact, I told everyone that both my parents had been killed in a tragic car wreck."

"I can understand why you would do that." And, really, Anna could understand it. First of all, Lauren had all but abandoned Sarah— possibly when Sarah needed her the most. It was true Lauren had been getting over her addiction to Valium and alcohol and that she'd been on the verge of a nervous breakdown, but in Sarah's eyes it must've felt like abandonment. And when Sarah's father embarked on a scandalous affair with his secretary . . . well, it probably was simply easier to imagine her parents were dead. Less painful that way.

"Everyone felt so sorry for me," Sarah continued. "They welcomed me and made me feel at home." She looked at Anna with misty eyes. "Besides being here with you and Clark and

Hazel, that was the closest thing to home I'd ever experienced. And I loved it . . . at first."

"What changed?" Anna asked gently. She was eager to hear Sarah's entire story, where she'd been and who she'd been with, but up until now Sarah had been closed tighter than a freshly dug razor clam about the past two years.

Sarah leaned back in the old rocker, pushing her fingers through the loopholes in the knitted afghan over her lap. It was one that Anna's mother had crocheted many years ago. "Lots of things changed," she said slowly. "First of all, Aaron left. That was when it all started to go downhill."

"Aaron?"

Sarah looked out the window with a slightly dreamy expression. "Aaron was our leader. He was a truly good man. He loved God with his whole heart. And he wanted us to follow his example."

Anna was beginning to understand now. Sarah had probably been in one of the communes that had become so prolific in Oregon and California, especially along the coast. This particular phenomenon had started in the late sixties and had continued into the seventies. In fact, Anna even remembered a time when the inn had been suspected of being a commune of sorts. Of course, Anna had simply taken that in stride, and eventually the ridiculous rumors faded.

"Aaron and Misty were like our spiritual

parents," Sarah continued. "Everything they did was for our own good. Even when we didn't like their decisions, we knew they loved us. You could just feel it. Aaron and Misty were good people."

Anna just nodded.

"And for a while, everything was perfect."

"Perfect?" Anna tried not to sound too skeptical.

"Well . . . maybe not perfect. But it was good. Really good."

"I'm curious about something, Sarah . . ."

"What?"

"Why didn't you call us? Just to let us know you were all right. We were so worried about you. You were so young . . . and we had no idea what had happened."

Sarah seemed to consider this. "A condition of staying in the family was to break all outside ties. We were forbidden to contact anyone from our past."

"Oh . . ."

"But it's not like they forced us. We did it willingly," she said quickly. "It wasn't as if we were being held prisoner there." She frowned. "Well, not at first anyway."

"But later? Were you ever held against your will?"

Sarah took in a long, slow breath, folding her arms in front of her, and Anna could tell that this was her way of communicating that she'd said too much. And, really, Anna had been trying not to prod. "So . . . Aaron . . ." Anna tried again. "It sounds like he was a good guy . . . and you say he treated you like family . . . ?"

"Yes," she said cautiously.

"And Misty was his wife?"

Sarah shrugged. "We don't use those kinds of traditional words. It was very unconventional there. We were all brothers and sisters. But, yes, Aaron and Misty were together as a couple, if that's what you mean."

"How many people were in this, uh, family?" Anna asked gently.

"It varied. At the most, it was about a hundred, I think. By the time I left it had dwindled a lot. Maybe thirty or so."

"Did it dwindle because others, like you, weren't so happy there anymore?"

She nodded sadly. "Yes. After Aaron and Misty left, everything just started to change."

"Do you know why Aaron and Misty left?"

"Because Daniel took over." She looked at Anna like this should be obvious.

"Daniel?"

Sarah's dark eyes grew darker as her brows drew together. "Daniel was *nothing* like Aaron. He acted nice at first, but he turned out to be mean spirited and selfish. He treated us as though we were less than him, like he expected us to serve and obey him—simply because he was the new leader. We had always wanted to serve and obey Aaron, but that was because we loved him. But all the love left when Daniel took over."

"How long ago was that?"

Sarah looked up at the ceiling as if trying to calculate. "I don't know exactly. I guess it was in the fall. We'd just finished picking apples."

"You grew apples there?"

"No, we picked for local farmers. For money and in trade for apples. We put up a lot of apples for winter. Apple cider, dried apples, applesauce . . . we had lots and lots of apples."

"Oh."

"If I never see an apple again, it will be too soon." She sighed.

"I'm curious . . . where was this place? Southern Oregon? I know there are a lot of fruit orchards down there."

Now Sarah was getting that shut-down look again. Anna knew that for some reason she wanted to keep the location of this commune a secret. Why she wanted to protect people who had obviously wronged her was a mystery, but Anna knew she needed to respect it. At least for now. Anna's worst fear was that Sarah wasn't disclosing the location of the commune out of the fear that she might have to return to this horrible place . . . keeping it as an option in case things here at the river didn't work out. Anna prayed that it would work out.

"Well, I'm just so glad you're here." Anna

smiled at her. "I have missed you so much these past two years. You have absolutely no idea. It was like a piece of me was gone. Can you understand that?"

Sarah seemed to soften now. "I missed you, too, Grandma."

"And I have to admit that it still hurts to think you never tried to contact me . . . just to say you were alive," Anna confessed, "but I do understand. I know we sometimes do things that seem justified at the time . . . things we might look back on later, wondering if we could've done it differently." Now Anna told Sarah a bit about how it was for her when Lauren was a small child . . . how she might've done it differently.

"But I was so overwhelmed with caring for Lauren's father. His physical injuries from the war were serious enough, and he was certainly in pain, but the wounds in his mind were the hardest part. I felt I needed to protect Lauren from his outbursts and mood swings. It seemed too much for a child to witness. For that reason, Lauren was left in the care of her Grandmother Eunice . . . far more than I would have liked. However, at the time, I didn't see any other solution."

"I'm sure you did the best you could."

Anna shrugged. "After Adam died, I stayed on with Eunice. I know it was partly because I was so worn down by the years of caring for him, almost as if I'd lost a part of myself. I just didn't know what to do, how to start my life over again. And by then Eunice was such an enormous part of Lauren's life, and she'd just lost her father, it seemed cruel to take that away from Lauren as well. But, as you know, Eunice spoiled Lauren. She gave into her about everything." She sighed. "And I suppose I allowed it. Oh, I'd try to stand up to her, but it was like standing up to a tidal wave. I really should've left much sooner. But I didn't. So, to be fair, you should partially blame me for how Lauren was so immature and ill prepared for adulthood when she became your mother. It was like a child raising a child."

Sarah's brow creased as if she was trying to take this in.

"Sometimes I've thought that if I'd just had the strength to take Lauren away from there, and if I'd brought her here to the river, back when she was still a child, I think about how everything would've turned out so differently." She sighed. "You see how it's easy to blame myself and feel guilty over this. But that's when I try to remember that I did the best I could at the time. What's done is done and I simply have to trust God with the rest of it."

"I really don't see how you could blame yourself for Lauren's mistakes."

"Yes . . . but maybe it comes with being a mother. You always want the best for your children and your grandchildren." Now she smiled. "But then I have to remember that if I'd brought Lauren out here as a child, she never would've met and married Donald and then you wouldn't have been born. And that would've been very sad for me. In the long run, I do think that things do turn out for the best."

"I wish I believed that was true." Sarah pulled the afghan up over her shoulders, shivering as if she were cold.

"Maybe you will in time."

"I don't know." Sarah just shook her head. "Sometimes it all just seems so useless and hopeless." The glum expression on her face reminded Anna of her own mother so many years ago. Anna's mother had seemed to carry the weight of the world on her shoulders for so many years. So much anxiety and concern for so many things . . . it had prematurely aged her . . . and it had driven Anna away. Hopefully, Sarah would not fall into that trap.

Anna looked over at the bookshelf that was filled with Hazel's anthropology books. There on the top shelves were the notebooks that Hazel had filled with notes and stories she'd transcribed from Anna's father's notebooks. Anna got up and pulled a fat black notebook from the shelf, flipping it open to a section of old stories. "Maybe you'd like to read these," she said to Sarah. "My grandmother, as you know, went through some very difficult times, too. And I know she had some years where she was bitter about a lot of things." Anna shook her head. "And, really, she had a right to be bitter. The way the Siuslaw Indians were treated in those days . . . well, it was terrible."

"You mean when they were starved on the reservation?"

"Yes. They were pretty much treated like animals. Oh, the white men tried to make it look like it was an education program, and I suppose some of the people teaching in my grandmother's school weren't so bad. She did learn to sew. But my grandmother was a wise woman, and she discovered that forgiveness was a better path than being bitter."

"Well, that sounds all good and nice, but it might not be for everyone." Sarah pulled the afghan more tightly around herself, almost as if she was creating a cocoon. "Have you ever considered the possibility that some things are unforgivable?"

"Or maybe some things just take time." She set the black notebook on the worn pine table in the kitchen. "My grandmother's life has taught me a lot of things . . . maybe you can learn from her, too, Sarah."

They both jumped to hear someone knocking on the door. *"Mom?"* called Lauren's voice. "Are you in there?" And before Anna could get there, the door flew open and Lauren entered the room. "Oh, there you are, I've been looking all over for—" Lauren stopped in mid-sentence—her jaw dropped and her eyes grew huge as she pointed at Sarah sitting there in the rocker still wrapped in the afghan. Lauren turned to Anna, blinking with a shocked expression. "Wha—what is going on? What is—?"

"I cannot deal with *this!*" Sarah exclaimed as she leaped to her feet. With the afghan trailing behind her, she stomped off to the bedroom, slamming the door behind her.

"Sarah!" Lauren sputtered. "When did she—how did she—why didn't you tell me?" She pressed her fist to her lips with tear-filled eyes. *"Mom?"*

"It's a long story, Lauren." Anna glanced nervously at the closed door. Surely Sarah wouldn't climb out the window and make a run for it.

"How long has she been here?" Lauren demanded.

"Not long." Anna felt torn. Lauren had every right to feel hurt . . . and yet it was Sarah that worried her.

"Why didn't you tell me?"

"Sarah wasn't ready to—"

"I can't believe you kept this from me, Mom. My own daughter!"

"I'm sorry. I didn't know what else to do. I promised her—"

"Were you *ever* going to tell me?" Lauren's

voice grew louder. "Did everyone but me know about—"

"Calm down," Anna said quietly. "You'll scare her."

"I'll scare *her?*" Lauren's brow creased. "Do you know how scared I've been for her? How frightened I've been that she'd been kidnapped, tortured, murdered just like those other young girls that Ted Bundy—"

"She's safe, Lauren."

"But why didn't you tell me she was here? Did you know that I cried myself to sleep on her birthday? How long has she been here, Mom?"

"Really, Lauren, it doesn't matter." Anna was trying to guide Lauren out of the cabin now, wanting to give Sarah back her space . . . the peace and quiet she so desperately seemed to need.

"It doesn't matter?" Lauren planted her feet firmly in the doorway. "Sarah is my daughter. Don't I have a right to see her? To find out where she's been and—"

"If you love Sarah, you'll want the best for her," Anna said firmly. "For right now, she needs time."

"But I want to talk to—"

"Come on, Lauren." Anna tightened her grip on her daughter's arm. "We are leaving for now."

"But Mom!"

"No buts, Lauren." Anna locked eyes with her. "Trust me. This is for Sarah's best." Lauren was clearly angry, but she allowed Anna to escort her out of the cabin.

"This isn't fair," Lauren exploded as they walked through the open grassy area. "You've already spent time with her and I haven't even—"

"Come on." Anna continued pulling Lauren by the arm, tugging her toward the river. "Let's go where we can talk in private."

Lauren continued to sputter and fume, questioning her mother's sanity and judgment as they walked. "I really don't like this, Mom. You hiding Sarah from me like this. It's really not fair and—"

"Lauren." Anna gave her a stern look as she pointed to the bench by the river. "If you keep talking like this, how can I explain?"

"Fine," Lauren snapped as she sat down. "Go ahead. Explain."

Anna sat down next to her, slowly attempting to tell Sarah's story, but even as she explained, she knew there were too many missing pieces and unanswered questions. Finally she sighed and held up her hands. "It's just going to take time," she said sadly, "and patience."

Lauren's tears began to fall freely. "I'm sorry I got so mad at you," she sobbed. "It's just that I —I have so many emotions—running through me. I want to see my daughter—to hold her in my arms. And I want to shake her! I'm so angry! I want to demand to know why she left, why she stayed so long, why she never called."

"I know . . ." Anna nodded. "I have those same feelings."

"But you're so much more patient than I am," Lauren confessed. "How do you do it, Mom?"

Anna made a sad smile as she handed Lauren her handkerchief. "Years of practice, I suppose."

"When can I talk to her, Mom?"

"Soon I hope. But I'm afraid to push her too hard. She's so fragile . . . and I can tell she's been hurt."

"She seemed different." Lauren's brow creased.

"She has changed . . . but I think our sweet Sarah is still in there . . . somewhere."

"Does she hate me?" Lauren asked in a small voice.

"I think she's just confused."

"She has every right to hate me."

"Hatred is like poison, Lauren. Hopefully Sarah doesn't hate anyone." But even as Anna said this, she knew that Sarah was full of bitterness. Perhaps with enough time and patience, she would be able to let it go.

4

With Lauren temporarily pacified, Anna hurried back to the cabin to check on Sarah, but when she knocked on the door, calling out, Sarah didn't answer. Quietly letting herself in, she found Sarah, now dressed in her long patchwork dress, which still hadn't been laundered, and buckling up her sandals. "I have to go, Grandma."

"Why?" Anna went over and stroked Sarah's hair. "Why can't you stay here for a while? You can rest up and regain your strength. It's obvious you've been through an ordeal." She placed her hand on Sarah's shoulder, feeling the sharpness of bone through the fabric of the dress. "And you're far too thin."

Sarah looked into Anna's eyes. "I don't want to talk to her."

"You don't have to."

"But she knows I'm here now. She'll keep coming around and—"

"I've told her that you're not ready for that, Sarah. She understands."

Sarah looked doubtful.

"It's only natural that she wants to see you. She's made her mistakes, but she still loves you."

Sarah's dark eyes narrowed. "She doesn't love anyone. She never has."

Anna resisted the urge to argue this. "Please, stay, Sarah. This is your home . . . just as much as it's my home . . . your ancestors belonged here . . . so do you."

"I don't know . . ." But her features softened ever so slightly.

"If you allow it, you will find healing here."

Sarah let out a small sigh. "I'll only stay if you promise me that she'll leave me alone. If Lauren tries to talk to me, I will leave. I swear I will go and I'll never come back."

Anna wanted to protest the unfairness of this, but she simply nodded. "I'll explain your conditions to Lauren. I think she'll understand." As Anna left, she knew she'd have to make Lauren understand. But as she went into the house, her heart went out to her daughter. Lauren had made such progress these past few years. If only Sarah could see that.

"Is Lauren around?" she asked Diane Flanders. Diane was just a year older than Sarah. She and her younger sister, Janelle, had been working at the inn during the summer for several years now.

"I haven't seen her since breakfast," Diane said. "But she did mention that she was going to work on the floral arrangements today."

Anna nodded. "That's right, it's Thursday." This was the day that Lauren usually made fresh flower arrangements for the inn. Maybe she'd gone home to do that. "I think I'll run up to Babette's too," Anna told Diane. Even though Babette had passed on several years ago, they still called the house "Babette's." Lauren lived there full time, and occasionally, if the inn was full, they would accommodate the overflow guests there. But Lauren loved Babette's house and took excellent care of the gardens there. Anna knew Babette would be pleased by this.

Sure enough, Lauren's boat was gone from the dock. As was Anna's boat, but she knew Clark had taken it to town to pick up some supplies. Anna untied one of the small fishing boats, hopped in, and started the motor. Chugging along toward Babette's house, she planned what she would say to Lauren.

Relieved to find Lauren in the garden, where she was cutting purple irises, Anna decided to start right in. "I have an idea," she said brightly, "and I hope you'll like it."

Lauren tipped up her straw hat to look curiously at her mother. "What sort of idea?"

"I think you need a vacation."

Lauren stood up straight with a confused expression. "Whatever for?"

"Because you've been working hard for me for the past few years, and you haven't taken one vacation."

Lauren set the irises in the bucket of water and

frowned. "Working at the inn is not exactly hard, Mom. Some people would consider it like a vacation in itself."

"Maybe so. But I really think you deserve a vacation."

Lauren waved a fly away. "When was the last time you took a vacation?"

"We're not talking about me."

"No . . . and I can guess why you want to get rid of me."

"I do not want to get rid of you, Lauren." Anna sighed. "The truth is I will miss you a lot more than you can possibly know."

"Then don't make me go."

"We *have* to do this," Anna said firmly. "Sarah is not going to come out of hiding if she thinks you're around. And she needs to start doing some things . . . so she can get better."

Lauren wiped her hands on the front of her jeans. "I guess it's only fair."

"Fair?" Anna tilted her head to one side.

"That you should make me go in order to keep Sarah." Lauren's eyes were filling with tears again. "After all, I'm probably the reason Sarah ran away in the first place . . . and I know how much you've always loved her more than me."

"I love both of you equally," Anna insisted. "It's just that she needs me more than you do right now. Surely, you can see that."

"Yes, but it's true. You and Sarah were always

so close. Much more so than with me. I know it."

Anna stepped over the row of lavender and put her arms around Lauren. "Oh, darling, you know how much I love you, don't you?"

Lauren sniffed.

"And the truth is, I wasn't a very good mother to you when you were growing up. I was so busy caring for your father . . . and then trying to please Eunice. Oh, I know I'll never be able to make up for those days, but I always loved you, Lauren. You have to believe that."

Lauren pulled a rumpled tissue out of her pocket and wiped her nose. "I do, Mom. And I know I was a pill growing up. And a spoiled brat." She made a wobbly smile. "And I know I can still act pretty spoiled sometimes, but I am working on it."

"Of course, you're working on it, Lauren. And I'm so proud of you. And I've tried to convince Sarah of this very thing, but it's like she's stuck in the past. I think if you could just take this time off, give her a chance to move forward, I really believe she might start to come out of her shell."

Lauren shook her head. "But a vacation? Where on earth would I go?"

Anna looked past the garden and toward the house. "Actually, you could just stay here if you wanted. Just take it easy and do as you please. All I ask is that you stay away from the inn."

Lauren seemed to consider this idea. "I suppose I could plant some new flowerbeds. I've wanted to add to the cutting gardens. And I could catch up on some cleaning."

"Or just relax and read some good books," Anna suggested.

"Or catch up on my tan or get my hair done." She made a sheepish smile. "Remember when I used to care about my appearance?"

"See you might even enjoy yourself. Maybe you could go to town and take in a movie. Who knows, you might even meet a man." Anna chuckled.

Lauren grinned. "Now that I think about it, maybe I am due for a little vacation."

"Good." She felt a rush of relief. "And I'll come over here to visit and we can talk on the phone. I promise to keep you posted as to Sarah's progress. I really do think she'll come around in time. But it'll probably happen more quickly once you're completely out of the picture."

"But won't you be shorthanded without me? Will you have to hire someone?"

"Maybe . . . or maybe Sarah will have to help out."

Lauren looked unsure.

"Sarah used to be great help in the summers." Anna thought back to how Sarah had been such a natural when it came to working at the inn. Anna had never actually trained her, not like she did with the other summertime staffers, and yet the young girl had seemed to know intuitively how to make herself useful. Noticing when soaps needed to be replaced or when a porch needed sweeping. And the guests had always loved the sweet-spirited girl.

"But she's not the same, Mom." Lauren pressed her lips tightly together, as if she wanted to say more, but was controlling herself.

"Maybe she has changed, but it can be very therapeutic to work. Waiting on others is good for the soul."

She nodded. "Yes, I remember how you put me to work when I first came here. I resented it at first, but after a while, I learned to appreciate it. And now I really love the inn. In fact, I'm going to miss it a lot."

"Who knows, you might get comfortable becoming a woman of leisure."

She firmly shook her head. "Believe me, I've been down that road before, and I have no intention of going back again."

"Good." Anna patted her on the back. "But enjoy your time off just the same."

"How long do you think I should stay away?"

"A couple of weeks should be enough."

"It will feel strange not to be there. The inn is such a huge part of my life." Lauren bent down to clip another long-stemmed iris. "But I can do it for Sarah." She stood up straight, making what seemed a stiff smile. "And for you, too, Mom."

"And if you decide you want to go and do

something away from the river, I can have one of the girls come over here to tend things while you're gone."

"I think I'd rather stick around."

Anna smiled up at the quaint house. "I can understand that."

"And, if you don't mind, maybe I can paint the kitchen."

Anna knew that Lauren had never liked Babette's shell pink kitchen. She'd always felt it was too old fashioned.

"But don't worry. I'll paint it pink again."

Anna blinked. "Really? Pink?"

She grinned. "Sure, it's kind of grown on me. But it really could use some freshening up. And I'll take down the curtains and wash them and the throw rugs, too. The whole place could use a good scrubbing."

Anna laughed. "Just don't forget this is supposed to be a vacation, too."

Lauren pointed at her mother. "How about you and Clark? When will you two ever take a vacation? As I recall, you haven't gone any-where since your honeymoon."

Anna shrugged. Clark had said the same thing more than once.

"Maybe we should make a deal. I'll take my vacation as long as you agree that you and Clark will do the same." She stuck out her hand. "Deal?"

"Oh . . . I don't know . . ." Anna couldn't imagine leaving the inn. Nor could she see herself leaving Sarah anytime soon.

"Don't you trust me? That I can take care of things? What if you went somewhere in winter? Like Hawaii or Mexico?"

"You know, Clark might actually like that . . . someday." Anna grasped Lauren's hand and shook it. "It's a deal. I suppose everyone needs a vacation from time to time. But now, I should get back there. There's a delivery coming this afternoon."

"That's right, and I won't be there to receive it." She nodded. "And I know Sarah doesn't want anything to do with me, Mom, but please tell her that I love her . . . and that I'm praying for her."

"I'll do that." Anna smiled. "Just give her time, Lauren. She'll come around."

"I sure hope so."

On her way back down the river, she hoped that she wouldn't regret this plan. Lauren had been helping with so many things that Anna knew she might be slightly lost without her. Maybe Lauren was right . . . maybe Anna would need to hire more workers now. Even so, Anna knew that if Lauren's absence helped Sarah open up and heal, it would be worth it. Well worth it.

5

It took a couple of days before Sarah ventured out of the cabin, and then only at the urging of her grandmother. "We really need some help in the kitchen," she told Sarah on Saturday morning. "We're full up at the inn, and Diane has taken over some of Lauren's responsibilities. As a result, Janelle is feeling a bit overwhelmed right now. Would you mind lending a hand?"

"No, of course not." Sarah quickly stood. "You should've told me before."

"Well, I was trying to let you have some time to rest."

"I'm used to working, Grandma." She was slipping her feet into her sandals. "We were told if we didn't work, we didn't eat."

Anna almost pointed out that Sarah couldn't have been eating too well but stopped herself. "I know Janelle will appreciate it." As they walked together to the main house, Anna reminded Sarah about the Flanders girls. "You're right in between them as far as age. Diane is nearly twenty and starting her third year in college. Janelle is seventeen, with one more year left in high school."

Sarah didn't respond to this, and Anna suspected it was because she was thinking about

51

her own situation. She had run away with two years left of high school. Even now, Anna was unsure of how Sarah would make this up . . . or if she even would. Still, she knew they couldn't cross that bridge yet. It was enough that she'd enticed Sarah out of the cabin.

"Is this okay?" Sarah said suddenly, pausing to look down at her patchwork dress. "I washed it, but it's kind of wrinkly."

Anna smiled at her. "You look just fine, Sarah. Did you make that dress?" She remembered how she and Sarah used to put together odd pieces of ribbon and lace and muslin to create interesting garments.

"No, it was something Misty left behind. I was lucky to get it. Another girl really wanted it."

"Well, I was thinking we should get you some more clothes," Anna said carefully. "Some that fit you better than my castoffs."

"I don't need anything," Sarah said quickly. "Really, it's wasteful to have too much."

Anna decided not to respond to this. Better to wait a bit. One step at a time. "Janelle," she called out as they came into the house. "Do you remember my granddaughter, Sarah?"

Janelle smiled. "Yeah. I was always envious of you," she told Sarah. "Getting to live at the inn all summer."

Sarah smiled shyly. "Well, it's been a while."

Anna had already told Diane and Janelle a bit

about Sarah's situation. Not too specifically, but just enough information so that they could act natural around her and not question where she'd spent the past two years. "I'll leave you and Diane to it then." Anna plucked up a carrot wheel and popped it in her mouth. "I need to do some book-keeping in my office. Call me if you need any-thing." She had turned one of the bedrooms in the house into an office for the inn. Complete with an old rolltop desk that Clark had found in town, several file cabinets, and an easy chair, it was a comfortable place to work. But lately it had been Lauren who'd been keeping up the office work, and already Anna had gotten a little behind. But having an excuse to stay nearby while Sarah was acclimating herself to the house was handy.

However, as Anna worked, she considered the possibility of having Lauren take over the office work at Babette's house. But at the same time, she didn't want to infringe on Lauren's down-time. Even if it was a forced vacation, it might do Lauren some good.

"There you are," Clark said as he came into the office. Leaning over, he kissed the top of her head. "It's nice to see Sarah helping in the kitchen."

Anna looked hopefully at him. "Did she speak to you?"

"She did." He nodded with a somber expression.

"Does she seem greatly changed to you?"

"Well . . . yes . . . of course she's different. No doubt, she's been through a lot. But I could see a trace of the old Sarah in there, too. I think she's coming back."

"I wish she'd open up to me, Clark. It would help her to talk about whatever it was that happened. I see her struggling with so many emotions. I know she's been deeply hurt."

"Give her time."

"Oh, I am." She licked a stamp and pressed it onto the corner of an envelope.

"If anyone can bring her back, it's you, Anna."

"And her family . . ." Anna looked out toward the shining water and sighed. "And the river . . . if she'll just give us a chance."

"She came back to us, didn't she?"

She smiled up at Clark. His dark hair had turned steely gray, and the lines in his face were more pronounced than when they'd first met nearly twenty years ago, but his eyes were just as blue as ever. Not for the first time, she wondered what she'd do without him and didn't want to think of it. She found it hard to believe that he was in his mid-sixties now . . . and that sixty wasn't too far off for her either. When she was with Clark, she felt young somehow.

Suddenly she remembered the deal she'd made with Lauren and that she'd been so busy that she hadn't even mentioned it to him yet. She quickly told him about the suggestion. "But it's probably a silly idea," she said finally. "Business seems to pick up a bit with each winter. I hate to lose that momentum."

She wasn't surprised that he thought a winter vacation was a great idea. "I'll see if I can find us some brochures on Hawaii," he promised. "I heard there's a travel agent setting up a new business in town. Maybe I'll give him a call next week." He looked at his watch. "But it's lunchtime now. May I escort you down to the dining room?"

With her arm linked in his, she let him lead her outside and down the stairs. It had been Clark's idea to build a separate dining room a couple of years ago. Connected to the main house by a covered walkway, he'd also added a dumbwaiter elevator for getting things down from the upstairs kitchen where most of the cooking still took place. But the separate dining room was also equipped with a small kitchen that guests were allowed to use as well. All in all, it had been a good addition to the inn, and today the roomy space was bustling with guests.

Wearing Anna's blue and white gingham apron, Sarah was helping Janelle and Diane serve the tables. "Look," Anna whispered to Clark. "Sarah is smiling."

He nodded. "She's coming around."

Anna felt a small wave of relief. It seemed that work really was a good form of therapy for Sarah.

And the Flanders girls were probably wholesome influences as well. Responsible and hardworking like their parents, the two sisters were also very involved in their church. As Anna sat down at her usual table, she remembered a time when she'd almost resented Diane and Janelle. Having them around had made her miss Sarah even more—wishing that her granddaughter was working for her instead of the Flanders girls.

Oh, she'd known it was perfectly ridiculous, and she really did love and appreciate the two sisters, but she also knew that grief and loss affected one's thinking. However, she reminded herself, her time of grieving was over. Their worst fears over Sarah had never materialized. She was home and safe. Now if only Sarah could return to her old self and spirit . . . life would be nearly perfect.

On Monday, Anna insisted on taking Sarah to town in order to shop for some clothes. "But I don't want any clothes," Sarah argued as they climbed into the boat.

"I understand," Anna said as Clark eased the boat away from the dock. "But I really do need you to help me around the inn this summer. And that means you need some work clothes."

Sarah sat in the back of the boat, folding her arms across her front and making the same expression she used to wear as a child, on those rare occasions when she didn't get her way with Anna. It was almost amusing. However, Anna was curious what was behind Sarah's strong resistance to getting new clothes. She could appreciate that Sarah loved her patchwork dress, since it had belonged to her friend Misty.

At the same time, Anna remembered back when Sarah had loved creating new clothes—and she'd been quite clever at it, too. Anna wondered what had squelched that enthusiasm. She decided to gently pursue an answer. She moved to the back of the boat, sitting down next to Sarah. "I was just thinking about that summer when we did tie-dye," she began. "I think you were about ten. Do you remember how we started out by experimenting on Clark's old T-shirts? Some of them looked pretty silly at first, but then we slowly improved our technique."

"I used some of those old T-shirts as night-gowns when I was little," Sarah added. "In fact, I even wore some of them in high school."

Now Anna brought up some of the other projects she and Sarah had worked on together. "You were always so talented at designing clothes," she said carefully. "Do you ever get the urge to sew anymore?"

Sarah just shrugged.

"You know, instead of only buying ready-made clothes, we could get some fabric and patterns if you like."

Sarah's eyes flickered with a glimmer of interest. "Is that secondhand shop still around?"

"I'm sure it is."

"Do you think we could look there?"

"I don't see why not."

And so, after Clark dropped them off on the dock, they went directly to the secondhand shop and Sarah seemed almost like her old self as she meticulously went through the racks, examining one item after the next as if searching for treasure. She found a number of interesting pieces, and Anna didn't question any of them. After that, they went to a regular clothing store where Anna insisted on getting Sarah some blue jeans.

"I don't know if I will wear those." Sarah fingered the denim with a creased brow.

"Why not?"

Sarah frowned. "Women aren't supposed to dress in men's clothing."

"What?" Anna studied Sarah closely, wondering if she'd heard her correctly.

"It's in the Bible or some other religious book," Sarah said in a flat tone. "Women are not to wear men's clothes. It's wrong. Women are supposed to look like women, not men."

Anna blinked. "But these jeans are made for women." She showed her the tag. "And if you work in the garden or go fishing, you'll probably want them."

Sarah just shook her head.

"Well, I'm getting them anyway," Anna told her. "Just in case." She also picked up some T-shirts, although Sarah looked unenthused about them as well. Did she think they were sinful, too? Anna wondered if Sarah had been somewhat brainwashed at the commune. What sort of people were they?

"Maybe you'll want to transform these pieces into something else too," Anna said as they exited the store with their purchases. "But at least you'll have something to wear to work in besides your patchwork dress."

"Can we still go to the fabric store?" Sarah pointed across the street with what seemed a small spark of enthusiasm.

"Absolutely," Anna gladly agreed. And for the next hour, they shopped for fabric and trims and ribbons. And it almost seemed that Sarah was enjoying herself. Finally it was time to meet Clark at the dock. He and Anna exchanged looks as they boarded the boat loaded with all their bags. "Looks like you girls had successful shopping," he said as he helped stow their purchases.

"We really did," Anna told him. "And Sarah's going to work on some new creations."

"Can't wait to see that," he said cheerfully.

Soon they were heading upriver, but Sarah seemed back in a sullen mood again. Anna made attempts at small talk, but Sarah was not responding. They were about halfway home when Sarah turned to Anna with a worried expression. "Do you think it's evil to look pretty?"

"Evil?" Anna repeated. "To look pretty?"

"Isn't vanity wicked?" Sarah tried again. "And wanting to be pretty is like vanity, right? So is it evil?"

Anna was trying to think of a response when she suddenly thought of her grandmother. "You remind me of my grandmother," she told Sarah.

Sarah looked confused. "Huh?"

"My grandmother was creative like you," Anna explained. "She was very good with her hands, and she liked making pretty things with beads and embellishments, like the native cape that's hanging in the living room. Do you think that's pretty?"

Sarah nodded.

"And I remember my grandmother telling me that we should imitate the birds and flowers."

"What do you mean?"

"She knew that Jesus had said we should be like the birds and flowers in that we shouldn't worry about clothes and food because God provides for us. But my grandmother took it a bit further. She used to say that we should imitate the birds and flowers by wearing colorful clothes, pretty like petals and feathers. She said that was like complimenting God on his fine workmanship. Because we were imitating God's creativity."

Sarah's mouth twisted to one side as if she was mentally chewing on this. "So you don't think it's wicked to look pretty then?"

"Do you think birds and flowers are sinful?"

"No, of course not."

"Yet they are pretty. So why should people be any different?"

"I don't know . . ." Sarah looked down at her patchwork dress, fingering a section of floral fabric.

"And your dress is pretty," Anna told her.

Sarah looked up with troubled eyes. "This dress caused a fight and Daniel said that it was because of vanity. And that vanity is wicked. And wickedness must be punished."

Anna thought she didn't care much for this Daniel fellow. "But you still wear this dress," she said quietly. "Do you think that means you're wicked?"

Sarah shrugged.

"I think I would define wickedness the same way I define sin. It's doing something that hurts you or someone else or doing something that comes between you and God."

"Like vanity," Sarah said.

"Well, I guess I'd have to agree that vanity isn't a good thing sometimes. Especially if people get too caught up in outward appearances." Anna remembered how Lauren and Eunice used to be sometimes. She certainly didn't wish that for Sarah. "I don't think too much focus on one's self and one's appearance is healthy."

"Do you think it's wicked?"

"I suppose it could be if it hurt you or some-one else," Anna admitted. "Now I have a question for you, Sarah. Do you remember how you used to feel when you created a special piece of clothing?"

Sarah nodded slowly. "Yeah . . . I felt pretty good."

"You enjoyed creating something pretty, didn't you?"

She nodded again.

"Did that seem wicked or evil to you?"

"No . . . I guess not."

Clark was slowing down the engine and easing the boat up to the dock. Anna wanted to say more, but at the same time, she wanted to be careful not to say too much. She knew that Sarah was processing a lot right now . . . and Anna didn't want to interfere with it. All this talk of wickedness and vanity was very illuminating. The commune Sarah had left behind obviously had some strange religious roots.

Anna had heard stories of various communes where "spiritual" leaders would concoct their own brand of religion in order to keep the members under their control. Anna suspected that Daniel had been a leader like that. It sounded as if he'd used portions of religious teachings to shackle his followers, to ensure that he kept the upper hand. He'd probably kept a pretense of caring for them but had actually crippled them instead.

Like a wolf in sheep's clothing. Anna was so thankful that Sarah had escaped from that place. Now if only she could escape the twisted thinking as well.

6

Anna had reason to feel hopeful during the next week. Sarah was not only good help around the busy inn; she seemed to be happier, too. But as the weekend rolled along, Anna realized that Hazel would be home on Monday.

"I thought you might like to move back into your old room," she told Sarah on Sunday morning. They were cleaning up after breakfast.

Sarah frowned. "My room in the house?"

Anna gave the table a last swipe. "Yes, because Hazel will be back from her trip tomorrow."

"And she'll want the cabin back," Sarah said glumly.

"You used to love your room in the house," Anna reminded her. "I remember how you'd run to it with your bags and—"

"When I was a child."

Anna wanted to point out that Sarah wasn't much more than that now but knew she'd take that as an insult. "I wish we had an available cabin," Anna told her. "But we're full up clear into

September." She knew that Clark had been considering building more cabins back toward the woods, but she'd felt they had more than enough on their hands already. Now she wished he had time to build just one more. "There's room at Babette's house," she said tentatively.

"You mean where Lauren stays?"

Anna nodded as she dropped the washrag into the bucket of sudsy water. "There's a nice spare room there and—"

"You want to shove me off onto Lauren now?" Sarah looked at Anna with wounded eyes.

"No, I wanted you to move back into your own room. But you don't seem to want that."

Sarah swept the last of the debris into the dustpan then dumped it in the trash. "Maybe I don't belong here." Anna went over to her, placing a hand on her shoulder. "Of course, you belong here, Sarah. This is your home." She waved her hands. "Someday it will all be yours, for you and your children and grandchildren and—"

"I never want to have children," Sarah said sharply.

Anna frowned. "Why?"

"Because this world is a horrible place to bring children into."

Anna looked out the window toward the peaceful river. "I happen to love this world, Sarah. You used to love it, too."

"That was before I knew how much evil there

was in it." With a grim expression, Sarah carried the broom and dustpan to the kitchen.

Anna followed her in, emptying the bucket of water into the sink. She rinsed it out then turned to look at Sarah, carefully planning her next words. "I don't understand all that happened while you were living at the commune," she said, "but I worry that some of the things you learned there may have been wrong."

Sarah pressed her lips together. "I'll admit that Daniel taught some things that sounded wrong, but not Aaron. Aaron was a good man. He was very close to God."

Anna really didn't want to argue about this. Mostly she wanted to resolve the question of where Sarah would stay once Hazel returned. "So . . . do you really have a problem with your old room?" she asked.

Sarah shrugged. "I'll move back to my old room. Hazel can have the cabin." But something in her tone still sounded hurt.

"I want to ask Clark about building some new cabins," Anna told her. "Then you could have one of your very own. Just like Hazel."

Sarah seemed to brighten at this. "How long would that take?"

"I'm not sure exactly. Probably a month or so. But you could ask Clark." She turned off the light in the kitchen. "I can help you move your things into the house, if you want."

"That's okay. I don't have much."

"And I'll ask Diane to give it a good cleaning before Hazel arrives. I think she's not due until late in the afternoon. I thought we could have a little welcome home party for her. You know she's retired from teaching so she'll be living here full time from now on."

Sarah just nodded.

"And I'll ask Clark to get started with a cabin as soon as possible," Anna told her.

"I told Janelle I'd help her in the kitchen this afternoon," Sarah said. "I better go."

Anna wanted to tell her one more thing, but she just couldn't force the words out. Not yet. She wanted to gently warn Sarah that Lauren was due to return to work in a few days. Anna had tried to talk Lauren into taking a third week off, but she'd insisted that she missed the inn and everyone . . . too much to stay away. "I'm already counting the days, Mom. I'm homesick," she said sadly. "I've painted and cleaned and gardened, and I want to come back to work at the inn. Please, don't banish me for another week."

"You're not banished, Lauren. Of course you can come back. It's just that it'll be a bit of a challenge. For Sarah, I mean."

"I'll try not to cross Sarah's path," Lauren promised. "I'll probably be in the office most of the time anyway. I'm sure there's plenty to catch up on in there."

"Yes, and Sarah is doing better." Anna told her about some of the clothes Sarah had created. Of course she didn't mention Sarah's anxiety about wearing jeans. And, really, what did it matter if she only wore dresses? "But you need to understand that she's still not the same as before. I can tell she still needs time . . . to work things out . . . and to heal."

"And I won't force her to talk to me," Lauren assured her. "I've thought this whole thing through, and I'm beginning to understand her feelings. Honestly, I don't want to make things worse for her. I've messed up enough where she's concerned. I realize this."

"Good." Anna sighed. "And somehow we'll get through this, Lauren."

With so much going on at the inn, caring for the multitude of guests, planning a little welcome home party for Hazel, Anna didn't have time to be overly concerned about Sarah and Lauren's upcoming reunion—and when worries assaulted, she simply prayed them away.

Sarah got settled in her old room, and although she didn't seem very happy about it, she didn't complain either. Then, while Clark took the boat downriver to fetch Hazel, they set up an old-fashioned tea party upstairs, complete with the good china, silver, and fresh flowers. Anna even made Hazel's favorite lemon bars. But Hazel's best surprise when she came into the room was discovering that their long-lost Sarah had been returned to them. With tear-filled eyes, Hazel hugged the girl for several minutes. "I've dreamed of this day," she told her. "I knew you'd come back."

"I stayed in your cabin while you were gone," Sarah told her. "I hope you don't mind."

"Not at all." Hazel patted Sarah's cheek happily. "It's a good place to come home to."

"And I read some of the stories you wrote . . . the ones from my great-great-grandmother." She smiled shyly. "I like them."

"I like them, too," Hazel sighed loudly. "Oh, it's so good to be home." She glanced around the room. "Where's Lauren?"

Anna couldn't help but notice Sarah's countenance darken at the mention of her mother. "Lauren is enjoying a much-needed vacation," Anna said quickly. "But she'll be back on Thursday. Or perhaps you'll want to go visit her at Babette's house."

Clark jumped in, changing the subject by asking Hazel about her travels, and, as a result, she began foraging through her bags. Pulling out interesting and varied artifacts and souvenirs, she enthusiastically explained where she'd found them and what they were used for.

"Oh, yes, I have something for you, Sarah. I didn't know at the time I got it that it would be for you." She dug down into a bag, finally pulling something wrapped in white paper. She peeled off the paper to reveal something silky and red. "But I know it's meant for you now." She handed it to Sarah. "It's a kimono. Go ahead, try it on."

They all oohed and ahhed over the elegant golden bird embroidered on the back of the beautiful garment as Sarah modeled the kimono for them. "Thank you, Hazel. I will treasure it always."

At the end of the day, Anna felt hopeful. With Hazel back in their midst, it seemed that Sarah might actually be turning a corner in her recovery. Sarah and Hazel had always hit it off, and after dinnertime Sarah sat and drank coffee with Hazel on the upper deck, enjoying the older woman's tales of adventure in the mysterious Orient. Not only that, but Anna thought Hazel's presence might help distract Sarah when Lauren returned. In fact, while she was getting the coffee things set out for tomorrow morning, Anna decided to completely disclose the touchy situation to Hazel and enlist her help if needed.

"Did Mother look all right to you?" Clark asked, as they were getting ready for bed.

Anna stopped brushing her hair and peered at him. "What do you mean?"

"Well, she was animated and happy to be home, but she seemed a little gray to me."

"Gray?"

"Her complexion seemed a little ashen." He frowned. "Unless I imagined it."

Anna thought about it. "She did look a bit weary. And, certainly, traveling at her age must be tiring."

"She was awfully happy to get home. You should've seen her eyes light up when she saw the dock and the inn."

"I'm so glad she's home, Clark. I didn't realize how much I'd missed her."

"It was wonderful seeing her and Sarah together."

Anna nodded, setting her hairbrush down. "It really gave me hope." But as they got into bed, Anna knew that she'd be watching Hazel more closely tomorrow. Perhaps she was unwell. But Anna knew that the river air could change that . . . as well as some herbal teas and good wholesome food. If Hazel was ailing, it wouldn't be long until they'd get her well again. Like Anna's mother used to say, she'd be "right as rain."

Anna woke early in the morning. Feeling happy and energized, she turned on the coffee, set out some things, then decided to take her canoe out. The river was misty and quiet, and other than a few fishermen, she had it to herself. Paddling upriver, she felt strong and hopeful. Life was good and getting better.

Oh, the inn was a bit demanding this time of year . . . and sometimes, like before Sarah returned to them, she felt a little overwhelmed by the work that went into keeping it running smoothly. But on days like today, silently slicing through the water, watching the sun beginning to break through the mist, observing a blue heron standing majestically in the reeds by the river, spotting an osprey diving into the smooth surface of the water and emerging with a silvery fish . . . all of this was why she loved it here.

Remembering how lonely Lauren had sounded yesterday, she decided to paddle a bit further up and pay her a visit. Hopefully she'd have coffee on. After tying the canoe next to Lauren's boat on the dock, Anna reached her arms skyward, stretching her spine, and taking in a deep breath.

"Hello," Lauren called from the house up above. Still wearing her bathrobe, she waved down to Anna. "Come on up!"

Anna hurried up the path to the house, admiring the gardens as she went. It was obvious that Lauren really had been busy. "The place looks great," Anna told her.

"Come inside and see the kitchen!" Lauren exclaimed.

Anna always felt Babette's presence in this house, and as she saw Lauren's improvements— fresh shell pink paint, the white cabinets freshly scrubbed, and—even new white lace-trimmed curtains on the window above the sink, Anna knew Babette would approve.

"The old curtains fell apart when I washed

them," Lauren explained. "But I made these myself. They're actually old pillowcases that I just opened up. Do you think they look okay?"

"They're perfect," Anna said. As they sat outside drinking coffee, Anna told her about Hazel's arrival. "And I think she'll come over to visit you."

"Oh, I hope so. It's been so lonely."

"And Sarah really came to life when she was talking to Hazel." She told Lauren about the red kimono.

"I'd love to see it."

"You will," Anna assured her. "In time." She finished her coffee. "Speaking of time, I better get back. As you know, we're full up, and I noticed quite a number of guests had signed up for breakfast this morning."

Lauren frowned. "Sometimes I wonder if the time will come when we'll have to stop offering meals."

Anna sighed. "I know what you mean, but the family dining appeals to so many. I hate to think of quitting."

"I know, Mom, but it's so much work. And most of the cabins have kitchenettes. Plus there's the barbecue area Clark built. Not to mention the public kitchen in the dining room. As we get older, we might want to consider making it easier."

Anna laughed. "Who has time to get older, darling?"

Lauren chuckled. "Well, you never seem to get older, but some of us might."

Anna kissed her on the cheek. "We're as young as we feel, right? And today I feel so happy that I must still be in my twenties."

Lauren let out a little groan as she stood and rubbed her back. "Well, I spent yesterday afternoon weeding an old flowerbed out back, and I feel like I'm about a hundred years old today."

"Don't forget you're on vacation," Anna reminded her.

"And don't forget you promised to take a vacation, too," Lauren called as Anna started back down the hill.

"Don't worry. Clark is already looking into it." She waved. "Have a good day. And don't forget to take it easy."

"You too, Mom!"

As Anna let the river current help her down-river, she thought about Lauren's suggestion about the dining situation at the inn. On some levels, it made sense. Certainly, they didn't make much money off serving food. And it was a lot of work. Plus, like Lauren had pointed out, they had made enough improvements that guests could easily fix their own food if they were so inclined. However, it was a bit of a trip into town, and not all the guests felt comfortable operating boats without help. In all fairness, it wasn't exactly easy for guests to bring in or go out for provisions. How could they fix meals without access to food? *Unless* . . . Anna stopped paddling as the idea materialized in her head—unless they put in a store.

A store! Suddenly Anna flashed back to her childhood, back to a time when her parents had run the only store on the river. Situated in the lower part of the house, their little store had served so many people, from locals to tourists. She remembered how fun it had been to have customers coming and going from their dock, sharing the latest news, purchasing what they needed, and sometimes even trading for items. Especially during hard times. Anna couldn't believe she hadn't considered this before. Of course, it made perfect sense—the inn needed a store! She paddled harder now. She couldn't wait to tell Clark this idea.

7

"That's a great idea," Clark told Anna as they ate breakfast upstairs in the house. Since it was Hazel's first morning back, they'd decided to dine up there instead of in the busy dining room.

"If I might make a recommendation," Hazel set down her coffee cup, "I think it would be nice if you sold some of your herbal remedies there, too. And what about finding someone to make Babette's soaps and lotions? You still have all the old recipes, don't you?"

"Of course. In fact, Lauren has expressed interest in doing that. But I've kept her so busy helping to manage the inn . . . well, there just hasn't been time."

Hazel frowned. "Becoming too busy at the inn seems to defeat its original purpose, Anna."

Anna sighed. "Yes . . . I remember the time when we longed for more guests. Now I sometimes find myself longing for some peace and quiet."

"Even the winter season isn't as slow as it used to be." Clark shook his head. "I'm not sure what the answer is."

"Raise your rates?" Hazel suggested.

"Oh, I hate to do that." Anna reached for another strip of bacon. "Our faithful old regulars would probably stop coming if we increased the rates. Even this idea of not serving meals is a bit unsettling."

"Perhaps you change this into a bed and breakfast."

"A bed and breakfast?" Anna tried to imagine this.

"They're all the rage on the east coast and some European countries," Hazel continued.

"That's not a bad idea," Clark said. "It might make the transition easier. Perhaps starting with the next season, or the new year, you could increase the rates slightly but include breakfast in the cost. By then we'd have the store up and running and time to better equip the kitchens so that guests really would want to do their own cooking."

"And people could still use the dining facilities and public kitchen," Anna added. "In case they wanted to eat family style in a large group."

"And just think how much easier it will be on you and the staff," Clark said.

"What will be easier on the staff?" Sarah asked as she came into the room, setting a basket of blueberry muffins on the table. "These were leftover from breakfast."

So, Anna told Sarah about the idea of opening a store and discontinuing meals. But Sarah didn't seem to like this plan. "What about Janelle and Diane and the rest of the staff?" she asked. "What will we do for work then?"

Anna laughed. "Oh, there's always plenty of work to go around."

"I don't know . . ." Sarah slowly shook her head.

"Someone will need to mind the store," Anna said.

"And we might need another fishing guide." Clark grinned at Sarah. "Speaking of fishing, I wondered if you'd like to go out with me tomorrow morning."

Sarah looked at Anna. "Would it be okay?"

"It would be fine." Anna smiled. "And hopefully you'll catch some salmon. We're due for a salmon bake night."

"A salmon bake sounds lovely." Hazel sighed wearily. "But if you'll excuse me, I have a lot of sorting and unpacking to continue with."

"Are you feeling okay, Mom?" Clark peered curiously at her.

"Just feeling my age, son." She slowly pushed herself to her feet. "I'm afraid that trip really wore me out."

Clark stood, too. "How about if I walk you back to your cabin?"

She gave him a grateful smile. "You're a good boy."

He linked his arm in hers. "And you're a good mother."

Sarah and Anna began to clear the table, but Anna could tell by Sarah's expression that she was worried about something. "You know my parents used to run a store downstairs," she said as they rinsed dishes. "I grew up helping out in there. It was really quite fun. I'll bet you'd enjoy working in the store once we get it set up."

"Would it only sell food?" Sarah asked.

So Anna told her of Hazel's suggestion that they carry other things as well. "And perhaps we should carry those sorts of things that guests sometimes forget."

"Like toothbrushes and shampoo?"

"Yes. We'll have to start making lists of all the items we'd like to have. Maybe we should ask the guests for suggestions too."

"I guess it could be sort of fun," Sarah admitted. "Maybe you could have T-shirts printed up with the inn's name on the front."

"That's a good idea." Although Anna didn't want to see guests going around looking like billboards, she did like that Sarah seemed to be getting into the spirit of things. "And we'd have to be sure the T-shirts were tastefully done. Maybe you could help with some design ideas."

"Yeah." Sarah nodded eagerly. "Maybe something with a canoe."

They continued chatting as they cleaned up the kitchen things. Janelle and Diane came back up to start prepping some things for lunch. "Can I tell them about the new idea?" Sarah asked Anna.

"Sure." Anna dried her hands. "Like Clark said, I don't think we'll start implementing it until next season. Although it might be fun to get the store up and running to see how guests respond to it."

As Sarah began explaining the idea for the store, Anna went down to look for Clark. He was just coming out of his mother's cabin, but he looked worried. "Is something wrong?" she asked.

He scratched his head. "I'm not sure, but I get the feeling that Mom isn't well."

"She did seem awfully tired. But I'm sure she's just recovering from the trip."

"Probably. And she didn't really seem sick. Just tired."

"We'll make sure she gets plenty of rest," Anna assured him. "Maybe I'll have Sarah bring her lunch to her cabin."

"Good idea." He pointed over to the open area near the dock by the river. "Speaking of ideas, what do you think of locating the store right there?"

Together they walked down to this area, planning how the store would be situated. "I thought we might even make half of it into a boat rental store. And we could even sell swimwear and fishing poles and bait and things."

Anna nodded. "And perhaps we'll want to sell sandwiches in the store. That wouldn't be too difficult for staffers to make. That way if someone was going fishing, they could grab a lunch to take with them."

Clark put his arm around her. "I can't believe we didn't think of this a long time ago."

She looked out over the river. "I suppose at one time I would've been concerned that it was too commercial."

"But your parents ran a store," he reminded her.

She nodded. "I know. But I really wanted the inn to be a peaceful place . . . a place for healing as well as for recreation."

"And it is." He pointed to a father and son out in a canoe. "Look at Mr. Williams and his boy.

He told me it's their first vacation since his wife passed on. He said it's been very good for both of them."

"The river is restorative."

He turned and looked into her eyes. "But only if we don't burn ourselves out on it, Anna. If the success of the inn makes us too tired to enjoy the river, then what are we left with?"

She smiled up at him. "I know . . . those were my exact thoughts this morning. But I think we're finding our path."

"I'll start working on some plans for the store today," he assured her.

"And a cabin for Sarah, too?" she asked hopefully.

He frowned. "I can only chase one rabbit at a time, but I'll do my best."

She glanced back to the house. "I suppose she's adjusting to being back in her room. Maybe it's not such a priority, Clark. You decide what's best."

As the next couple of days passed, Anna was relieved that Clark continued to focus on plans for the store. Busy attending to the guests and feeling almost as if they couldn't keep up this hectic pace, she was tempted to place a help-wanted ad in the newspaper. However, she'd been letting Lauren handle the hiring the past several years, and, knowing Lauren would return tomorrow, Anna decided to just wait. Besides, having Lauren back meant more hands . . . less work. Perhaps they wouldn't need to hire anyone after all.

"I wonder if you should see a doctor," Anna said to Hazel on Thursday morning. Hazel had made her way to the main dining room for breakfast, but she still didn't seem her usual self. "Do you suppose you picked up a bug on your last trip? Some kind of exotic flu?"

Hazel waved her hand. "The only exotic bug I'm suffering from is old age, Anna. I might as well get used to it. Time and tide wait for no man . . . or woman either for that matter." She attempted to laugh, but it was unconvincing.

But Anna wasn't so sure this was truly old age. And whether it was Clark's suggestion from a few days ago or simply a fact, Anna felt that Hazel seemed unusually pale and suddenly wondered if she might be having some kind of heart problem. She pressed again for a doctor's visit, but since Hazel adamantly refused, Anna decided to search out some herbal remedies.

Perusing through the notebook that she and Babette had begun compiling long ago, partly from her grandmother's knowledge and partly from what Babette had learned over the years. After a bit, Anna discovered that hawthorn berries and rosemary were both helpful, as well as a number of other things like garlic and ginger. And so she concocted some tinctures and teas and took these over to Hazel's cabin.

"Certainly, I don't want you taking all these together," Anna warned. "But I thought you might try the hawthorn tincture first." She explained how to mix it with water or tea. "See how you feel and whether you think it's helping or not."

Hazel studied the small bottle and smiled. "I always said you were a natural healer, Anna. Just like your grandmother. And come to think of it, I haven't been feeling too frisky lately. Maybe this hawthorn will do the trick. Anyway, I'm happy to try it. Thank you for taking the time for this."

"I'll do some more research," Anna promised. "But right now I need to go tend to some office work and return some phone calls."

"It will be good when Lauren comes back," Hazel told her.

Anna nodded. It would be good . . . at least on some levels. She just hoped Sarah was ready for it. Or, at least, that Lauren would remember her promise to avoid crossing her daughter's path. And really, that shouldn't be too difficult if Lauren stayed in the office. No doubt, there was plenty to be done in there.

Anna was only mildly surprised when Lauren showed up on Wednesday afternoon. "I thought you were coming in the morning," Anna told her as they stood in front of the dock.

"I am coming tomorrow," Lauren stated as she reached to remove a box from the boat. "But I picked strawberries this morning, and I thought I should get them to you while they were still good." She glanced up at the inn. "Besides, it's officially been two weeks since you kicked me out of here."

Anna frowned. "I didn't kick you out."

Lauren made a slightly sheepish smile. "I know, Mom, but it sort of felt like it." She handed the box to Anna. "The berries are coming on really good this year."

Anna sniffed the fragrant red berries and smiled. "Thanks. These do look delicious. But, really, you could've called. Someone would have picked them up."

She shrugged. "I was heading to town anyway. My last day of vacation, I thought I should do something fun."

Anna noticed that Lauren was dressed a bit nicer than usual now. "You look lovely, dear. I hope you have a wonderful time."

Lauren shrugged. "I'll get back to you on that." She looked longingly back up at the inn again. "I never realized how much I love this place until you banished me, Mom."

Anna felt bad again but didn't say anything.

"Sorry, Mom." Lauren patted her on the back. "And don't worry, I'll be on my best behavior tomorrow."

"Thanks for bringing these," Anna called over her shoulder as she turned away with the berries.

"And have fun in town!" As she carried the box to the house, Sarah met her on the stairs.

"Was that Lauren?" Sarah asked with a frown.

Anna held out the box. "Yes. She had these lovely berries. She's on her way to town."

Sarah narrowed her eyes. "Does she come back to work tomorrow?"

Anna simply nodded. "You want to put these in the kitchen for me?"

"Okay." Sarah's voice sounded flat again. Anna wanted to question her on this, to ask why Sarah was so bitter against her mother—and how long was it going to take her to get beyond it? But there was too much to do right now. In fact, she'd been tempted to grab Lauren and insist she come back to work immediately. But seeing the darkness in Sarah's eyes told Anna, she was still not ready. And that's when Anna remembered something.

"Sarah," she said suddenly. "I found something for you the other day."

"What?" Sarah asked.

"It's in the house," Anna said as she followed Sarah up. "I found it when I was looking for some of the herbal journals. It belonged to my mother. Your great-grandmother."

"Is it very old?" Sarah asked with interest.

"Well, it's not terribly old." Anna knew how Sarah appreciated antiquity. "I think my mother got it a few years before she passed away. But it's probably close to thirty years old by now." Anna went into the office where she'd stashed the small leather-covered Bible the other day. "And it's very special." She reached up to get it from a high shelf. "And I think your great-grandmother would want you to have it. In fact, I'm certain of it, Sarah." She reverently handed Sarah the well-worn Bible.

Sarah's brow creased as she smoothed her hand over the cover. "Oh."

"I don't actually remember my mother being terribly interested in the Bible or God when I was growing up," Anna admitted. "My grand-mother had her own faith, but my mother had seemed . . . well, almost stoic."

"What's that?"

"Very strong in herself. Almost as if she didn't need religion. But I think as she aged, she changed and softened a lot." Anna smiled. "I know you'll take good care of her Bible."

"Yes. Thank you for trusting me with it. I'll put it in my room now."

"And if you like, we could read some of it together. Maybe talk about it."

Sarah just nodded. "I'd better get back to work."

"Do you mind taking Hazel her lunch again today?" Anna asked as the office phone began to ring. "I'm afraid she's still under the weather."

"Not a problem," Sarah said, sounding more like her cheerful self again.

"Thanks, sweetie." Anna turned to answer the phone. She wished Lauren was here to do the office work, but she reminded herself that it was worth it. She was so glad that Sarah was home, that she seemed to be settling in. Even if it was going to be rough going for a while, especially when Lauren returned. At least Sarah was here . . . and safe. Yet at the same time, Anna had a nagging feeling she might be steering her boat straight into a gale. Hopefully everyone would hang on tight!

8

Lauren came to work on Thursday, and several hours passed without a single incident between the estranged mother and daughter. True to her word, Lauren had been nearly invisible, even eating lunch in her office. Besides that, Sarah had now settled firmly into a routine. She stayed so busy, Anna felt perhaps her concerns had been for naught.

"Lauren and I have decided that you need to take the afternoon off," Clark informed Anna as she was helping to clean up after lunch.

"What?"

He nodded firmly. Removing the washrag she'd been using to give the dining room tables a good scrubbing, he dropped it in the bucket. "Go freshen up if you need to, and then we're heading out."

"But where are we go—"

"Nowhere fancy. Just grab a jacket and walking shoes. Okay?"

She studied him a moment then nodded. A break actually sounded delightful. Soon they were on her boat with Clark at the helm and the river breeze blowing through her hair. "This is nice," she told him as she looked out over the water as he headed the boat downriver. "Are we going to town?"

"Not exactly."

She smiled at him. He obviously had something up his sleeve. Well, she didn't really care where they went. Mostly it was good to be on the river . . . and with Clark. She glanced toward the back of the boat but didn't see any fishing gear. Although there was a picnic basket, which was interesting since it was still only mid-afternoon. But maybe he planned to be gone during dinner. Not that she minded. She didn't. As much as she loved the inn and her guests there, she was getting a bit tired of the pace. Perhaps that was the price of success, but perhaps it was also a sign that something needed to change. Maybe her idea of opening a store and putting an end to mealtimes would be just the ticket.

"Lauren and Sarah seemed to be getting on

okay," Clark said as he rounded a bend in the river.

"You mean because they have succeeded in avoiding each other?"

He chuckled. "Yes. I know that can't go on forever. But I feel confident they'll work things out. They're both reasonable people . . . most of the time."

She let out a loud sigh. "Well, I don't want to think about that now."

He nodded. "Sorry. I didn't mean to bring that up today. This afternoon is supposed to be about us."

She slipped an arm around his waist, leaned into him, felt the firm strength of his body, the buoyant rolling of the boat, and for a moment, she imagined it was nearly twenty years ago . . . when they'd first met . . . and fallen in love. So much had changed since then, and yet they were still the same. It was reassuring. Their love was strong and sustainable . . . like the river.

To her surprise, Clark piloted the boat beyond the town docks and was heading toward the bridge. "Are we going out to the ocean?" she asked curiously. "I know you and Sarah had good luck fishing the other day, but it seems a bit late to—"

"No, we're not going fishing," he said.

She looked up at the bridge. "I still remember when this was built," she told him. "I was a teenager at the opening of it, back in 1936. The bridge was the biggest thing that had happened to our town in my lifetime. My parents were so excited about it. They thought it would help business at the store."

"Did it?"

"Oh, yes. It helped businesses everywhere. I guess you could say it put us on the map."

"And that was a good thing?"

She shrugged. "Mostly good . . . you know in the way growth and progress can be good . . . and bad." She turned back to see the river before them now. "Kind of like the jetties, they opened up the ocean to more fishermen . . . according to my grandmother that was both good and bad."

As he continued on down the river, her curiosity grew. But she decided not to question him . . . just let it play out. He obviously had some kind of plan. Finally, they were getting close to the end of the jetty, and Clark pulled into a short dock.

"Our final destination?" she asked as he helped her out.

"Not exactly," he said as he tucked a folding camp chair beneath one arm.

Laughing at this unexpected sense of adventure, she let him now lead her up the hill and through some blackberry bushes and brambles where someone had hacked a rustic trail. Without questioning, she continued to follow him on and up until they were standing on a high piece of ground.

"Look," he told her, sweeping his arms all around.

Catching her breath, she looked all around. "You can see the ocean and the river from here," she said happily. "It's beautiful."

"It's the river's end and the ocean's beginning," he said happily. "And I just knew you'd like it."

She nodded. "I do like it."

"Now, if you'll wait here, I'll go fetch our things."

"Let me help," she said quickly.

"No." He unfolded the camp stool, setting it up on the crest of the hill. "You just sit here and relax. Enjoy the view!"

"Okay." She sat down and looked out over the beautiful vista. So much blue! Varying shades, one blending into the next. She could barely see the line between the ocean's horizon and the sky. Serene, peaceful, calm. She took in a long breath, filling her lungs with fresh sea air, and then slowly she released it. Yes, this was just what she needed.

After several minutes, Clark returned with the picnic basket and the other camp stool. He was slightly out of breath, and she rose to help him. Once again, she remembered they were getting older.

"Would you like the full tour?" he asked eagerly.

"The full tour?"

"Of the property?"

She shrugged with uncertainty. It seemed quite nice right here. "Sure. Is there more to see?"

He took her hand. "It's not a large piece. Just a bit more than an acre." Now he led her around the brushy area, walking along the property lines as best he could make out according to the corner posts that someone had set up. She wondered why it mattered and why he seemed so enthused. Surely, he wasn't considering purchasing this property. More likely, it belonged to a friend in town. Perhaps someone looking for some building advice.

"I figure a septic tank could go in there," he told her. "Since it's the least rocky spot. And over there, where you were sitting, would be the perfect spot for a house."

Now she wondered if the property owner had talked Clark into building for him. Clark used to build houses. But he'd given that all up when they'd married. He'd seemed happy to be her partner, and he'd been invaluable when it came to building up the inn.

But was it possible that he was getting an urge to build something bigger than a cabin or even a store now? Something more impressive and challenging perhaps? And, for whatever reason, this hurt to consider. Did he really plan to tackle a project like this? For Clark to take time away from the inn to build for someone else . . . well, what could it possibly mean?

Still, she said nothing regarding her feelings as she continued to follow him around. Apparently, he'd given a lot of thought to this property and how to best optimize it. She did her best to listen as he talked about the placement of rooms and observation decks and the size of windows, how to get the best views, the best sunlight, where he would build a glass wall to block the ocean breezes. But like the breeze, it mostly went right over her head, floating away into the clear blue sky.

She knew it was selfishness on her part, but all she could hear was that Clark was choosing someone else—someone to build a lovely home for—choosing someone's needs over hers. Where would the inn be without Clark? Where would she be?

By the time they returned to their camp chairs, Anna felt close to tears. On one hand, she could understand his enthusiasm for a project like this. It was so unlike the buildings he'd been working on at the inn. The little cabins were sweet, but they were all quite small and fairly rustic. Plus, they were all nearly identical. How much of a challenge could that have been for him? She knew he'd built some lovely houses in his time. Why wouldn't he want to do it again? Especially before he was too old. She wondered why he hadn't mentioned a desire to do something different long before this. Perhaps she could've prepared herself for it.

Yet, at the same time, she knew that most men his age were retired or planning for retirement. Oh, certainly, Clark was young for being in his mid-sixties. But even so, Anna couldn't grasp what had motivated him to take something like this on. What did it really mean? Was he unsatisfied with their life? With her?

Busy laying out the plaid picnic blanket, Clark removed items from the picnic basket, carefully setting them out. It was actually quite a lovely scene, almost photogenic, as he set out a bottle of Chianti, a chunk of cheese, a couple of apples, and a loaf of bread that he must've sneaked from the kitchen this morning. Despite her angst, she couldn't help but feel amused by this. "Did you bring a book of verse as well?" she asked in a slightly teasing tone.

His eyes twinkled. "Only the verses that are written on my heart."

"This is all very lovely, Clark." She studied him as he uncorked the bottle. "I don't know what to say."

"You can start by telling me what you think of this property." He poured her a glass of wine and handed it to her with an expectant expression.

"Well, I . . . uh, I don't know where to begin."

His brow creased as he filled the second glass. "What do you mean?"

She looked around the property and sighed. "It's obviously a beautiful place to build a beautiful home. I've no doubt that someone will love it very much."

"But not you?" He frowned. "You mean you don't like it?"

"Of course, I like it, Clark. It's an amazing view."

"And you don't think a house . . . like I described . . . would be perfect here?"

"Yes. It sounds perfectly lovely." She looked down at her glass, seeing the reflection of a lone cloud floating over its surface.

"But you don't really like it?"

She looked back up at him. "I guess I'm just curious, Clark. Who are you building this house for?"

He brightened. "For us, darling. Did I forget to mention that tiny detail?"

She blinked. *"For us?"*

"Yes." He chuckled. "At first I thought I'd just surprise you with the house."

"Surprise me with a house?" She was shocked.

"Yes. I imagined sneaking out here and building a house, you know over the course of the next six months or so. And then one day I'd bring you out here and show it to you—and hand you the key."

Anna felt more than a little confused. "But who owns this land?"

He grinned. "I do. Or, I should say, we do."

"How is that possible?"

Now he explained how he'd been in town discussing plans for the store with a building official when someone told him about this piece of property for sale. "So I came out to see it and fell in love. I made an offer and it was accepted."

Anna was dumbfounded. "And you bought it? Just like that?"

He nodded eagerly. "I got a great deal, too. Another guy was interested so I had to move fast. But when I told the owner mine was a cash offer, he couldn't say no."

"You did all this without even discussing it with me?"

Now he looked slightly dismayed. "You don't like it, do you?"

"Oh, Clark." She stood now, walking as she talked. "It's a beautiful piece of land. But I just don't get it. Why would you do something like this—something this big without even asking my opinion on it?"

"Because I knew you'd love it?"

She took a sip of wine, trying to gather her thoughts. She didn't know why she was reacting like this. Really, it was a sweet gesture. But for him to leave her out of it . . . well, it just didn't sit well.

He came over to stand next to her. "I wanted to surprise you, sweetheart."

"Oh, I'm surprised . . . all right."

"Are you mad?"

She turned to look into his eyes. She didn't want to hurt him. But at the same time she felt hurt. "I'm not mad, Clark. Just confused . . . and, well, I'm hurt that you left me out of the decision."

He let out a long sigh, turning away from her. And now she knew that she'd hurt him, too. "It's a beautiful piece of property, Clark, but I don't understand how we can possibly use it . . . and another house. I feel like we have our hands full already."

He turned and looked hopefully at her. "That's just it, Anna. I thought this could be our little getaway spot."

"But I don't see how . . . I mean, how can you possibly have enough time to build this house? And to build the store too? And there's Sarah's cabin as well. Not to mention the daily maintenance at the inn. It just feels impossible to me."

He shrugged. "Maybe it doesn't feel impossible to me."

She wanted to question him on the expense too. How could they possibly afford this? Sure, the inn was prospering, but they were putting almost everything back into it. And there were taxes and bills and other expenses. Some of the cabins were already getting old and in need of updates and improvements. Especially if they wanted the kitchens to be more efficient for when they discontinued meal service. How could he possibly manage to do it all? For that matter how could she? Really, it was overwhelming.

"I can see I've frustrated you with this," he said solemnly. "Maybe we should just forget about it."

"Or maybe we should discuss it further," she said.

But already he was tossing out his untouched wine, repacking the picnic things, and just like that, they were loaded up and heading back down the steep hill. Without speaking, he set the basket and camp stools in the boat then helped Anna in as well. Soon the motor was going full bore, and Clark directed the craft straight up the river, barely slowing down for the speed limit as they went beneath the bridge and then on toward home. At this rate, they would be there in time for dinner. And Anna could help as usual. Not that she wanted to. Why had he done this?

The dinner hour passed awkwardly. Clark said only a few words to Anna. On top of that, Hazel was quieter than usual and still looked a little under the weather. Perhaps worst of all was how Sarah seemed to be treating Lauren. As Sarah helped Janelle and Diane serve food in the dining room, she went out of her way to avoid her mother, and if she had to be near her, she gave Lauren the most chilling looks. It was as if Sarah was seething inside.

Anna wondered how it was possible for a

young person to be filled with so much hatred. Even as a child, during those years of sadness and neglect, Sarah had never been bitter like this. What could've brought it on at this stage of life? As Anna helped clear the table, she wondered if it might be related to the time Sarah had spent at the commune. She knew that Sarah had been taught some strange things. Was it possible she'd been taught to hate as well? And, if so, how could Anna help her get beyond it? Bitterness never helped anything . . . or anyone.

Anna watched as Clark helped his mother up from the table. Supporting her arm in his, he slowly walked her out of the dining hall. Such a good son and such a good husband, too. Why had Anna reacted so negatively to his "surprise"? She wished she could go back and do the afternoon differently. But at least she could straighten this out with him.

Always when they'd had disagreements in the past—and those had been few and far between —they would smooth it out before bedtime. She had no doubt this misunderstanding would be worked out as well. As Anna set a stack of plates on the counter, she noticed Lauren motioning to her from the other side of the dining room. Seeing that Sarah was preoccupied with loading the dishwasher, Anna discreetly went over to see what Lauren needed.

"Can we talk?" Lauren asked quietly.

"Outside?" Anna moved toward the door.

"I don't know what to do," Lauren said as she closed the door behind them.

Anna pointed down to the dock. "Why don't I walk you down to your boat?"

"Sarah is so angry at me, Mom," Lauren said sadly. "I can feel the hatred pouring from her."

"I know." Anna sighed. "I noticed it too."

"I'm sure *everyone* noticed it. What am I going to do?"

"I don't know." Anna pulled her cardigan more tightly about her. "I suppose it's just going to take time."

"Yes, you've said that, but how long is it going to take her to get over this? And in the meantime, what if it's making the guests uncomfortable?"

"Oh, I don't think they really pay much attention to—"

"I saw Mrs. Phillips staring at us tonight, Mom. I'm sure she knew something was wrong."

"Well, Mrs. Phillips has been coming here for years, Lauren. She's quite perceptive, and I'm sure she knows nearly as much about you and Sarah as I do."

"But earlier today, when you were gone, Sarah and I had a little run-in. I'd gone to get some towels for a guest, and Sarah was in the laundry room. She started yelling at me, saying she was already taking care of it. And I'm sure the guest heard everything."

"Oh . . . well, guests must understand that we're only human."

"Maybe so . . . but I just feel so bad, Mom. This is supposed to be a place of peace and healing . . . and here Sarah and I are spoiling everything for everyone."

Anna thought about this. Originally, this inn was supposed to be a place of peace and healing. But it had become so popular and busy in recent years . . . sometimes she wondered if she'd lost that initial vision. Was it really a place of peace and healing now? And, if not, how was she going to get it back?

9

Clark was late coming to bed, but Anna waited up for him, apologizing as soon as he came into the room. "I don't know why I reacted so negatively," she said finally. "It's a beautiful piece of property, an amazing view. I think it's just that I'm feeling overwhelmed . . . and everything at the inn feels as if it's going faster and faster . . . and then there's Lauren and Sarah's troubles . . ." She shook her head to think of how disturbed Lauren had been this evening.

"And there's Mom."

"Your mother?" She peered curiously at his eyes.

"I'm worried, Anna. She really doesn't seem to be herself."

"Did you encourage her to see a doctor?"

"I did, but as she told me—her excuse for never going to the doctor—she doesn't have a physician in this town."

"Then she should get one." Anna wondered which of the local doctors might be best for Hazel. "I'd be happy to help her tomorrow."

"The fact is that my mother has never been overly fond of the medical profession. It goes back to before I was born. I don't even know the full story."

Anna frowned. "Maybe I can do some more research on herbal remedies for her. I wonder if the hawthorn helped . . . or if she's even been taking it."

"You'll have to ask her about that." Clark yawned sleepily as he unbuttoned his plaid shirt. "And as far as that property goes . . . well, I was giving it some thought, Anna. I really shouldn't have tried to do that deal behind your back. I mean I thought it was going to be a wonderful surprise for you. But it seems I was wrong about that. I'm sorry."

She laid her dressing gown on the back of the chair. "I'm the one who should be sorry, Clark."

He came over and wrapped his arms around her, looking intently into her eyes. "All I want is what's best for *both* of us," he said quietly. "I

101

want us both to be happy. And maybe it's not too late to get out of that deal."

"You mean buying the property?"

"Yes. I'll talk to the seller and see if the other party is still interested. Maybe we can work something out that will please everyone."

She sighed. "It did sound like it'd be a lovely house, Clark."

He nodded, stroking her hair. "But even the loveliest of houses would be worthless if we weren't both happy in it . . . together."

She couldn't agree more.

The morning dawned foggy and gray, and a chilly breeze was blowing in from the west. Even so, Anna noticed that several of the guests had already set out in the fishing boats. Hopefully, they would have a good day even if the weather was less than summerlike. Anna had taken great care to be honest in the inn's brochures, advising guests that Oregon coast weather could change abruptly. She'd advised guests to bring clothing suitable for all sorts of conditions. And today looked like one of those days.

As Anna was opening a new can of coffee, Sarah emerged from her bedroom. "Good morning," Anna said pleasantly.

Sarah returned the greeting in a slightly gruff voice.

"Everything okay?" Anna stuck the measuring

cup into the fresh-smelling coffee, trying not to be too obvious as she studied Sarah's glum expression.

Sarah shrugged.

"Anything you'd like to talk about?"

"Not really."

Anna put the lid back on the can and turned to face Sarah. "I know that you and Lauren are having a tough time," she said gently. "Is there anything I can do to help?"

"You mean besides sending Lauren on another vacation?" Sarah said in a slightly sarcastic tone.

"I'm sure that sounds good to you."

"I don't see how you can stand her, Grandma."

"She's my daughter."

Sarah narrowed her eyes. "Yeah, well, I'm her daughter, but that never seemed to make much difference, not to her."

Anna reached out to put a hand on Sarah's shoulder, looking into her eyes. "I know Lauren has hurt you, Sarah. I'm sure she's hurt you even more than I realize."

Sarah softened slightly. "Yeah, that's true."

"But it will only hurt you more if you continue to let this bitterness control you. It will eat away at you, and eventually it will poison your spirit."

"What am I supposed to do?" Sarah asked in a defiant way. "Pretend like she never hurt me, like she didn't ruin my life, like she didn't ruin my dad's life?"

"No, you can't pretend things away," Anna told her. "But you can forgive her."

"How?" Sarah demanded. "How can I forgive all *that?*"

"With God's help."

"What if Lauren doesn't deserve to be forgiven?" Sarah stepped away from Anna. "What if she's not really sorry?"

"She is sorry—"

"She might act like that around you. She might be able to make you believe she's changed. But I'm not falling for it. And even if she is sorry—what difference does that make to me now? It doesn't undo all the damage she's done in my life." Sarah held out her hands in a helpless way. "It might make Lauren feel better if I pretended to forgive her, but it doesn't change anything for me."

Anna took in a slow breath, searching for the right words. "I'm not saying this for Lauren's sake, Sarah," she said carefully, "I'm saying it for yours. You need to forgive Lauren, not for pretend, but for real, and you need to do it for yourself."

She shook her head negatively. "I don't want to forgive her. I want her to be accountable for her mistakes. I want her to suffer the way I've suffered. God will repay evil for evil, and I want Lauren to get what she deserves. It's like karma."

"Is that what they taught you?"

"Who?" Sarah scowled.

"The leaders at the commune . . . is that what they believe?" She kept her voice even and calm —much calmer than she felt. "Did they teach you that God is a cruel taskmaster, that he will punish—?"

"God *does* punish," Sarah insisted. "It's in the Bible or the Koran or one of those books, Grandma. It's better to suffer harsh punishment and repent from wickedness than to escape punishment and go to hell."

"What about forgiveness?" Anna said quietly. "I know that's in the Bible. Maybe we could look it up together—"

"Forgiveness is earned by repentance," Sarah said stubbornly. "And Lauren has not earned forgiveness. Not from me anyway, not yet." She shook her head. "I doubt that she ever will." And without saying another word, Sarah turned and stormed out of the house.

Anna stood there for several minutes, just trying to wade through Sarah's confusing tirade of words. All this talk of earning forgiveness, repaying evil for evil . . . what kind of people taught such twisted doctrine? And was it only to keep vulnerable girls like Sarah under their control? At least Sarah was free of all that now. Physically anyway . . . it seemed it was going to take much longer to become spiritually free. But time and love and patience could work wonders.

Anna knew this personally. And she had plenty of all three of those for her granddaughter. Now if only she could convince Lauren to do the same. Maybe all three of them could sit down and study the Bible together. It certainly couldn't hurt.

"Anna?" Clark's voice sounded different as he came into the house. "Can you go and stay with Mom?"

"Sure. What's—"

"I'm going to call the hospital. I think it's her heart."

"Oh dear!" Anna rushed past him. "I'll go right now." Then she remembered something. "One of our guests—in cabin eight—Dr. Schwartz—should I see if he can be of help?"

"Good thinking." Clark was already on the phone as Anna hurried down, nearly running into Lauren who was coming up the exterior stairs. She grabbed Lauren by the hand, quickly explaining. "You get Dr. Schwartz while I go to Hazel," she said breathlessly. "Hurry!"

Anna ran to Hazel's cabin. Not even knocking on the door, she let herself in, finding Hazel still in bed. "How are you, dear?" Anna asked gently, taking in the old woman's pale countenance.

Hazel looked at Anna with fearful eyes. "Not so good."

"Have you taken the hawthorn?" Anna asked.

106

"Hawthorn . . . ?" Hazel seemed confused.

"Remember the tincture I made? It's for the heart."

She just shook her head. "I . . . I suppose I forgot."

So Anna went in search of the little brown bottle. Finding it, she could see it was almost completely full. She quickly stirred a teaspoon full into some water and took it to Hazel, helping her drink it. She had barely finished when Lauren and Dr. Schwartz, wearing only his trousers and undershirt, came bursting in.

"Where is the patient?" he demanded.

Hazel's eyes grew wide. "Who are—?"

"He's a doctor," Anna told her. "And a guest."

Already he was by Hazel's side, taking her pulse and looking closely into her face and asking her questions.

"Let's give them some space," Anna told Lauren.

Back out in the front room, Anna explained how Hazel hadn't seemed well for days now. "Clark is calling the hospital."

"I didn't realize it was this bad," Lauren said.

Clark came into the cabin now. "The hospital is sending an ambulance to the dock, and I just arranged for Greeley's son Bobby to get the guys upriver with a stretcher and oxygen. We think it'll be faster than trying to take the road. The medics will get Mom into our boat and tend to her as I take us downriver where the ambulance will be waiting." He glanced at the closed bedroom door. "Is she ready?"

"Dr. Schwartz is with her," Anna said.

Clark frowned. "Maybe I'll run down there to meet Greeley's boat and make sure ours is gassed up and ready to go."

"Good idea." Anna locked eyes with him. "Everyone is doing everything possible, Clark. She's in good hands."

He nodded quickly. "I know."

Anna started gathering some blankets after Clark left. They would need to keep Hazel warm on the river. She turned to Lauren. "Maybe you should go back to make sure everything is going okay for breakfast," she told her.

"Yes, I doubt there's much I can do to help here." Lauren frowned. "And feel free to go to the hospital with Hazel, Mom. I can handle everything at the inn while you're gone."

Anna made a weak smile. "I know you can. Thanks."

"And I'll be praying for Hazel. And I'll ask others to as well."

"Thanks."

Anna tucked the blankets more snugly around Hazel's shoulders as Clark piloted their boat downriver, like a floating hospital, filled with medics, Dr. Schwartz, and the stretcher. Anna thought Hazel's coloring looked slightly better, perhaps as a result of the oxygen mask . . . or was it from the hawthorn? Anna would need to tell the hospital doctor about that, just in case it would present a problem with any other medications they might want to give Hazel.

She held Hazel's hand, warming the cool fingers in her own. "You're going to be okay," she said gently.

"So much bother," Hazel labored to say, "for an old lady."

Anna smiled down on her. "You are a greatly loved old lady."

Hazel closed her eyes, and Anna silently prayed. Hazel might be old, but they were not ready to lose her. Not yet. Especially with the problems brewing between Lauren and Sarah. Anna felt she needed Hazel's wisdom and strength more than ever now. *Please, God, do not take her from us,* she prayed. *Help everyone to help this dear woman . . . please, heal her . . . make her well. We need her.*

Anna looked up to the front of the boat where Clark was pushing the boat to the fastest speed that was safe on the river. She knew he was feeling the stress of this as much, maybe more, than she was. Besides his son, Marshall, Hazel was Clark's only living relative. They had always been close. Anna knew that his concerns for his mother would be intense. *Please, God!*

Although it had to be one of the fastest trips she'd ever experienced into town, it still seemed like hours before the medics were finally loading Hazel's stretcher into the back of the ambulance. Clark and Anna ran to the car they kept parked in the side lot of Greeley's Groceries and were soon on their way.

"All things considered that wasn't such a bad trip," Clark said as he drove through town. "I think it was faster than the road. Not to mention smoother."

"I can't believe that in all these years of running the inn, we never had to do something like that before," she said.

"There was the time when the Miller boy broke his arm," Clark reminded her.

"Yes, but we didn't have medics come out."

"And no ambulance."

"I guess we've been fortunate."

Clark blew out a loud sigh.

"It's going to be okay," she told him.

"I hope so."

"Everyone is praying for her, Clark."

He just nodded.

By the time they were able to see Hazel, she seemed a little better. Again, Anna remembered the hawthorn, quickly explaining to the doctor attending to her what she'd given Hazel.

He frowned. "Hawthorn?"

"It's an herbal remedy," she told him. "It's good for heart and circulation problems."

"Oh . . . ?" He wrote something down on his clipboard.

"I just thought you should be aware."

"Yes . . . well . . ." He nodded briskly. "It does appear to be heart. Perhaps angina. Or possibly something more. We'll be running tests." He looked at Clark now. "You're the son?"

"Yes."

"You'll need to fill in the paperwork for insurance and such. At the front desk." He made a stiff-looking smile. "And there's a waiting room out there." Now using an authoritative voice, he called over to the nurse who was standing nearby. It seemed that Clark and Anna were being excused.

"We'll be in the waiting room," Anna told Hazel, pausing to gently squeeze Hazel's hand. "Just rest and do all you can to get well again, dear. Everyone is praying for you. We need you."

The sides of Hazel's mouth turned up ever so slightly.

"Don't try to talk." Anna released her hand. "Just rest. We'll see you soon."

10

After a long day at the hospital, Clark and Anna finally felt comfortable about leaving the hospital. Reassured that Hazel's condition had stabilized and relieved to see her able to take some food at dinnertime, they decided it was probably time for them to return to the inn. Lauren had assured Anna that all was well when they'd spoken by phone earlier, but Anna knew that this was a busy time of year and, that their absence would put more stress on the staff.

"Don't worry about me," Hazel told them as they were saying good-bye. She glanced over at the night-shift doctor who had just examined her. "If I had my way, I'd be going home with you."

"We just want to observe you a while longer," the doctor said kindly. He was an older gentleman with what Anna felt were much nicer bedside manners than the previous physician. "It appears to be stable angina," he explained. "But we just want to be sure you're all right and that the angina medication is helping before we release you to go home."

Now Anna told him about how she gave Hazel hawthorn earlier. "I did mention this to the other doctor, and I expect it would be out of her system by now . . . but I did want you to know . . . just in case it was a problem with the angina medicine."

His eyes lit up. "Yes, hawthorn was just the right treatment," he said. "In fact it's much gentler and safer than digitalis." He peered curiously at Anna. "Are you an herbal healer?"

"She most certainly is," Hazel said quickly. "Her grandmother knew a lot of the old herbs and how to use them."

"And I had another friend, too." Now Anna told him about Babette.

"I knew Babette," the doctor said. "I met her shortly after I set up my practice in town. Wonderful woman."

Anna nodded. "Yes, I still miss her."

"You kids go on home," Hazel told Clark and Anna. "I can tell I'm in good hands now." She grinned at the doctor.

Clark leaned down to kiss his mother's forehead. "I'm so glad to see you feeling better, Mom."

"So am I." Anna nodded.

"Suddenly I realize that I'm hungry as a bear." Clark patted his midsection. "And I'm sure they've finished dinner at the inn by now."

"You take Anna out for a nice dinner," Hazel insisted. "Enjoy a night out."

He grinned. "I think we'll do just that."

Anna had such a sense of relief and hopefulness as they exited the hospital. Despite the long and stressful day, she wasn't even tired. The chilly fog had completely burned off, and the air out-side was now warm and moist, with only a slight breeze coming in off the ocean. A perfect evening.

"I do feel a bit guilty," she admitted as they went into the restaurant. "Like we should be back at the inn to help out."

"They'll get by without us," he assured her. "And this makes up for yesterday's fiasco."

She frowned. "What fiasco?"

"My unfortunate picnic plan. Remember?"

"Oh, yes." She shook her head. "Was that really only yesterday? It seems like so long ago."

"A lot's happened since then." He smiled as he pulled out a chair for her. "I'm just so glad that Mom is okay."

"And even though it was a trying day, I think it was well worth it," Anna said "to get her to be seen by a doctor."

"Although it sounds like your home treatment might've worked too."

"If she'd been taking it." Anna put a napkin in her lap. "I have a feeling we'll have to stay on her when she comes home, Clark. We may need to remind her to keep up with her medications."

"I'll talk to her about that," he promised. "And now let's just enjoy this evening."

That is exactly what they did, taking their time over dinner, then enjoying a walk down by the docks and finally, slowly making the trip upriver by the light of the moon. "I forgot how beautiful the river is at night," Anna said as she pulled one of the blankets more snugly around her shoulders and leaned into Clark. "Very romantic."

He chuckled. "Guess I'll have to take you for more moonlit boat trips."

"I guess so." Of course, as she said this, she wondered what the likelihood of that would be. Usually they were busy in the evenings, cleaning up after a meal, preparing for a bonfire session or tending to business. Once again, Anna had to question whether the inn had gotten too big and too busy. Was this really what she'd dreamed of back when they'd started this?

As soon as Clark docked the boat, Anna could tell that their magical evening was over. "Go ahead and go inside," he told her. "I still need to tend to the boats and get everything ready for morning."

She offered to help, but he wouldn't hear of it. And so she went on up to the house where the lights were still on and Sarah was sitting in the living room with a frustrated expression. "How is she?" she demanded as Anna came inside. She was obviously very worried about Hazel.

Anna quickly explained about the heart condition. "But she's stabilized now," she told Sarah. "And hopefully she'll get to come home soon."

"What made her have a heart problem?" Sarah's eyes were filled with concern.

"I don't know for sure," Anna admitted.

"I've heard that stress can give people heart attacks," Sarah said. "Do you think she was stressed out by something here?"

"Maybe . . . or maybe it's just her age . . . and being worn out from her travels." She touched Sarah's cheek. "I really don't know. But please don't worry about her. I'm sure she's going to be fine now."

"I hope I haven't stressed her out." Sarah's brow creased. "I know I haven't been exactly easy to live with lately."

Anna smiled. Did this mean Sarah was trying to move beyond her bitterness toward Lauren? Perhaps these concerns over Hazel could be a wake-up call—a reminder that life is too short to be angry at someone you should love. "I'm sure we'll all do whatever we can to make Hazel comfortable and at ease when she comes home," she told Sarah. "And trust me, Hazel is very eager to get back to the inn and her little cabin. She would've gladly come home with us tonight if the doctor had allowed it."

Now Anna asked about how things had gone at the inn during their absence. "I felt badly for not being here. Did that make it hard on anyone?"

Sarah shrugged. "Well, it was pretty crazy and busy all day. But I guess we took care of it. I didn't hear any of the guests complaining."

Anna hugged her now. "Thank you, Sarah. You have no idea how much I appreciate your help around here."

"I'm glad someone does."

Anna wondered what this was in reference to but, worried that it was probably Lauren, decided not to pursue it. "And you know that, just like always, you'll be paid for your work here," she told Sarah. "If you like we can keep a portion of it in an account for you like we've done with the other kids, in case you want to use it for college."

"College?" Sarah looked surprised. "How do you expect me to get into college when I haven't even graduated from high school?"

"I've been meaning to talk to you about that." Now Anna explained about how she'd heard that Sarah could take a test and get a diploma that was equivalent to a high school degree. "I think it's called a GED," she said. "Would you like to do that?"

Sarah frowned. "I don't see why."

Anna tried not to look too surprised. "Well, maybe you'd like to think about it some." She glanced at the clock. "It's getting late, and I'm sure you're worn out from a long, hard day."

Sarah just nodded.

"Goodnight, darling. And thanks again for helping out today."

Sarah said good night, but something about

117

her expression made Anna feel slightly uneasy as she got ready for bed. Had Anna said something to offend her? Was it the suggestion about college? Or was Sarah still out of sorts over Lauren? Whatever it was, it would have to wait until morning. Anna was too tired to figure it out tonight.

The house was quiet when Anna got up the following morning. That wasn't so unusual since it was still quite early, although Clark was already up. Probably out at the boathouse helping the guests who planned to go fishing today. Anna dressed, then got the coffee in the house started before she went down to the dining room to lend a hand there as well. She didn't always help with the meals, but it would be her way of repaying her staff for their extra efforts yesterday. Although it wasn't even seven, Diane was already fast at work. "You're an early bird," she told her.

"I thought it wouldn't hurt to get ahead of the game," Diane said cheerfully. "Yesterday felt kind of like a mad marathon."

"Well, Clark and I will try to make up for that today."

"How is Hazel?"

Anna gave her the report from last night. "But Clark plans to call the hospital around eight to see how she's faring."

"We've all been praying for her."

"I know Hazel is appreciative."

"So . . . did Sarah tell you about yesterday?" Diane cracked an egg, dropping the contents into a big mixing bowl.

"Just that it was pretty busy."

"She didn't mention anything about Lauren then?"

Anna leveled the scoop of coffee then peered curiously at Diane. "What about Lauren?"

"Well, I don't want to sound like I'm tattling. But Sarah and Lauren got into another little spat. To be fair, Lauren was trying to be patient with Sarah, but it just kept escalating."

"Oh, dear." Anna dumped the scoop of coffee into the basket and sighed. "I suppose there were guests around when it happened?"

"There were a few. It was about an hour before dinner, and you know how they like to mill around in here."

Anna just nodded grimly.

"Anyway, after it was all said and done, Lauren attempted to do some damage control. I mean she'd tried to keep things calm during the argument. And she did apologize to the guests afterward. Sarah had stormed off by then."

"What were they fighting about?"

"It started out over Sarah's idea for rearranging the tables. It was actually kind of a good idea, but the timing wasn't so great. I mean we were barely keeping our noses above water as it was. There really wasn't time to rearrange tables in here."

"Yes . . . I can understand that."

"Lauren tried to explain that it would have to wait and Sarah just flew at her."

Anna could imagine that.

Diane lowered her voice. "And Sarah told Lauren that she'd been working at the inn practically her whole life and that she knew more about it than Lauren did. Of course, that got Lauren's hackles up. I mean she works pretty hard for you, too."

"Yes . . . she does."

Diane glanced around the deserted dining room as if to be sure no one could hear them. "Then Lauren told Sarah that everyone needed to work together just now. Especially seeing how Hazel was so sick at the hospital. Like everything was already pretty stressful."

"That's true." Anna finished filling the big coffee urn with water.

"And I suppose Lauren was just tired or fed up by then because she said something that I think really cut into Sarah. I'm sure it's why Sarah stormed out."

Anna came over to where Diane was still cracking eggs by the stove. "What did Lauren say?" she asked quietly, almost afraid to hear.

"Lauren said that Hazel's heart problems were probably a result of all the bickering that had been going on lately. She told Sarah that the inn was supposed to be a place of wholeness and healing and if Sarah didn't get her act together, maybe the inn would be better off without her."

"Oh!" Anna's hand covered her mouth. "She said that?"

"Something like that." Diane sighed.

"Oh, dear."

"In Lauren's defense, she kind of took it back almost as soon as she said it. But it was too late. That's when Sarah stormed off. She didn't even come back to help serve dinner so it really was a little crazy then."

"Oh, my." Anna wondered why Sarah hadn't mentioned this last night. Probably she was embarrassed.

"But at least Sarah came back after dinner. She was real quiet, and I could tell her feelings were still hurt. But she did more than her part cleaning up. Fortunately, Lauren was gone by then. I'm sure she felt terrible for losing it like that. But we were all a little on edge yesterday."

"That's understandable. Hopefully today will be better."

Now Janelle came into the kitchen. Greeting Anna, she tied on her apron and inquired about Hazel. Anna filled her in as she hurried to finish setting out the plates and silverware.

"I already told her about the spat between Sarah and her mom last night," Diane quietly told her sister.

"Yes." Anna wiped her damp hands on a towel.

"And I'll see what I can do to help smooth things over."

"Sometimes it's hard having family working together," Janelle said sympathetically.

Diane laughed. "Yeah, Janelle and I sometimes fight like cats and dogs. But we usually try to do it at home."

"And we don't even fight that much any more," Janelle said defensively. "Not like we used to anyway."

"Hopefully there'll be no more family feuds around here either." Anna exited the dining room. She had no idea how she'd handle this. She certainly didn't want to make matters worse. And yet, she didn't want to sweep it under the rug either.

Checking her watch, she knew Lauren should be arriving within the next fifteen minutes. Perhaps the best plan would be to meet her at the dock and discuss it down there where there'd be no chance for Sarah to overhear them.

When she got down to the dock, she could tell that Clark was perplexed. "Is something wrong?" she asked.

"Probably not." He frowned at the boats still secured to the dock. "Just that we're missing one of the fishing skiffs."

"Missing one?"

"Well, there's one gone. It was here last night but gone this morning. And no one seems to have checked it out."

"Oh." She shrugged. "Probably someone decided to go fishing and simply forgot."

He nodded. "I suppose. But I've tried to make it so easy for everyone. The sign-up sheet on the side of the boathouse is in plain view. The sign stipulates that all boats must be signed out, for safety's sake."

"Well, I'm sure you'll figure it out." And with no one about to listen, she took the opportunity to explain about the conflict between Lauren and Sarah yesterday. "Sarah didn't say a word about it last night," she said finally.

"Maybe it wasn't such a big deal," he suggested.

"According to Diane it was." She glanced out on the river, spying what looked like Lauren's boat making its way toward them. "I plan to talk to Lauren about it now."

"I'm sure you won't make her feel too badly about it."

"That's not my intention. I just want her to take the high road with Sarah. It seems only fair that Lauren, being the mother and the adult in the situation, should have to be more mature. And maybe she'll have to learn to bite her tongue where Sarah is concerned. At least for a while." She peered at Clark. "Do you think that's too much to ask?"

He shrugged. "I don't think so. And maybe you should tell her that. But, like you've told me before, it's not like you can control Lauren. Either of them for that matter, Anna." Now he excused himself to go over to the boathouse in order to assist an elderly gentleman who was wrestling with a life jacket.

Anna walked down to the end of the dock now. Attempting to clear her head and center herself, she took in a slow, deep breath. She often utilized the peaceful calm of the shining blue river to steady herself. Watching the slowly approaching boat, Anna silently asked God to lead her as she prepared to lovingly confront her daughter. She knew that she should be Lauren's example in this situation. She also knew that Lauren still had a lot to learn about mothering—particularly a grown child, which was usually a bigger challenge than with a juvenile. Even so, Anna was determined to handle what could be a sticky and potentially explosive situation with patience and serenity.

11

"I know you're right about this, Mom." Lauren's voice sounded tight and slightly high-pitched. But, to her credit, she'd listened patiently while Anna had asked her to try to keep her conversations with Sarah private and away from the curious ears of guests. "But I think you should speak to Sarah, too. It felt like she wanted to pick a fight with me. How do I just walk away?"

"I do plan to speak to her." Anna glanced back up at the house. "But I just feel that you, being the adult, will have to take the lead with her. And sometimes you do need to just walk away. I know Sarah can make it difficult for you, and sometimes you'll just have to take a deep breath and disengage. Take the high road, Lauren."

Lauren nodded with a somber expression. "I'll try to."

Anna smiled at her. "I know it's not easy, darling . . . but hopefully with time and patience and plenty of love, Sarah will be able to move past these problems."

Lauren frowned. "Sometimes I wonder if she wants to move past them. What if she gets some twisted sense of pleasure from the conflict?"

"Oh, I don't think so . . ."

"I don't know . . . sometimes she reminds me a lot of her great-grandmother."

Anna blinked. "Of Eunice?"

She nodded grimly. "Sarah has a mean bite when she wants to."

"She's been through a lot."

"Maybe . . . but believe me, Mom, the girl isn't always sweetness and light. Not like you and Clark sometimes believe her to be. I've seen her dark side."

Anna sighed. She didn't want to argue with Lauren, but she felt she was wrong about this. Sarah certainly wasn't perfect, but anyone who'd been through the struggles she'd been through had the right to some problems. Hopefully, they'd be surmountable ones. Anna intended to do all within her power to guide Sarah beyond this rough spell.

"Anyway, I'll try to keep my mouth shut," Lauren said as she reached for a tin can containing freshly cut lavender, handing it to Anna while she retrieved another that was full of Shasta daisies. "And how is Hazel? Should we send some flowers to her?"

"That's a marvelous idea." Anna nodded as she sniffed the fragrant lavender. It always reminded her of Babette. "Perhaps you could put a bouquet together for Clark to take when he goes over after lunch. I haven't heard how she's doing yet today, but he plans to give the hospital a call this morning."

It wasn't until Anna returned to the downstairs dining room to help with the post-breakfast KP that she found out that Sarah hadn't come down to help at all this morning. "Is she sleeping in?" Diane asked. "Or sick?"

"I don't think so." Anna frowned as she swiped the long wooden table. "But maybe I should go check on her just in case." She finished with the table then went back into the house and quietly tapped on Sarah's door. When she didn't answer, Anna knocked louder, calling her name. Finally, she quietly opened the door to see that Sarah's bed was neatly made. Everything looked the same as usual with nothing out of the ordinary. Her clothes and personal items were still there. And yet . . . something didn't feel right.

Was it possible that Sarah was still feeling out of sorts from last night? Had her feelings been so badly hurt that she was off by herself, licking her wounds? Perhaps she'd taken a long walk. Or maybe she'd taken Anna's canoe out. Anna couldn't remember if it had been down by the boathouse or not.

"Have you seen your daughter this morning?" Anna called in to where Lauren was working at the desk in the office.

"No. I figure she's avoiding me." Lauren made a sheepish smile. "And it's mutual," she said quietly.

Anna nodded. "Yes, that's probably a good thing." As she left the house, Anna decided to check in the laundry room. Several machines were operating, but Sarah wasn't down there either. Nor was she in the garden or the bathhouse or anywhere that Anna could see on the grounds. Finally, Anna remembered that Hazel's cabin was temporarily vacated—of course, that was probably where Sarah had holed up. As Anna walked toward it, greeting guests along the way, she recalled how she sometimes used to hole up there herself as a teenager. She had always loved Grandma Pearl's little cabin, even back when it was quite rustic. Sarah loved it, too. And perhaps one day, if Hazel was willing to relocate into one of the nicer more modern units, the old cabin could become Sarah's own special place as well.

But no one answered when Anna knocked on the door, and, when she went inside, everything looked slightly rumpled and in disarray, exactly the same when they'd hurriedly left it yesterday. Hoping that Hazel might be coming home today or tomorrow, Anna decided to straighten things up a bit, as well as to change the linens and open the windows. Satisfied that all was in good order, she returned to the laundry room with a basket of Hazel's clothes and linens.

"Do you mind seeing to these?" she asked Janelle, who was now folding towels. "They're Hazel's."

"Not at all."

"Have you seen Sarah?" Anna asked hopefully.

Janelle shook her head. "Not this morning."

Anna felt a tiny spike of worry as she walked down to the boathouse. Oh, she knew it was premature . . . but Sarah had run off once before . . . what if she'd done it again? First, Anna checked to see if the Water Dove was in its place, but seeing that it hadn't been moved and was dry, she went off in search of Clark to see if he knew where the missing girl had gone.

But Clark was on the phone when she went into the house. His voice sounded intense, and she could tell he was talking to someone at the hospital and so she waited.

"How is she?" Anna asked as he hung up the phone.

He frowned. "I'm not sure. It sounded as if they don't want to release her for a few more days. Do you think it's a bigger concern than just the stable angina that the doctor told us about yesterday? Something more serious?"

"I don't know, but I'm sure that the various types of heart problems aren't always easy to diagnose. Maybe it's best for them to carefully observe her for a while. Just in case it is more serious."

He nodded. "Yes, that's probably wise. And hopefully she'll be able to rest there." He smiled at Anna. "Plus that alleviates you from the burden of caring for her while she recovers."

"Hazel is not a burden," Anna pointed out.

"Yes, but it's so busy here. You don't need one more thing to worry about."

"Speaking of worries . . . have you seen Sarah?"

His brow creased. "Come to think of it, I haven't."

Anna bit her lip.

"Something wrong?"

"I don't know. Probably not. But no one has seen her this morning."

He tipped his head to one side. "You know, I still haven't figured out who took the missing skiff. Do you suppose Sarah went out? Perhaps early this morning?"

"I suppose she might've gone out fishing." Anna felt this was unlikely. Sarah knew how busy they were. Would she really take off like that? Without telling anyone? Anna remembered the time Lauren had gone out on the river in a time of emotional crisis, and how they'd all gone searching for her . . . and although it had been a close call, Lauren had been fine in the end. The river was usually gracious in that way. It usually threw its victims back. Besides that, Sarah was a good swimmer.

"That's probably it. Sarah went fishing." He made a forced-looking smile. "She does enjoy it. And the trout have been plentiful lately."

Anna was not convinced, but she tried not to show it.

"Don't worry, darling, I'm sure she'll turn up."

"Yes . . . I'm sure she will too." But even as she said this, she wondered. What if the fight with Lauren had pushed Sarah over the edge? What if Lauren's strong words about upsetting the peacefulness of the inn had cut too deeply? Sarah had always been sensitive . . . so conscientious she was sometimes overly protective of the inn and the guests. What if Lauren's accusations had alienated Sarah even more? Instead of feeling like part of this family, a part of the heritage of the river . . . Sarah might even perceive herself as an outsider with no right to be here.

Worse yet . . . she might be hurt deeply enough to want to leave. What if she had decided to go back to that horrible commune? Anna cringed to think of the doctrine they'd foisted upon her granddaughter. Really, it seemed nothing short of brainwashing—and mental, if not physical, cruelty. Surely, Sarah wouldn't go back for more of the same. Would she?

Suspecting that Sarah had taken the missing boat, Anna decided to run up and down the river. "I'm taking lunch with me," she informed Clark as he helped her with the boat. "Maybe I'll find her and we'll enjoy a little picnic together."

"Do you want me to come?"

"No." She set the basket in the back of her boat then climbed in. "We're already short-handed. And you still need to go check on your mother. We can't keep up this pace, Clark. We need to hire more help."

He nodded as he untied the rope, tossing it into the boat. "You're right. I'll remind Lauren to place an ad."

She started the engine. "I'll head downriver first and ask at Greeley's. Then back up to Mapleton."

"Good luck."

She forced a confident smile as she put the boat in reverse and waved. It wasn't a bad plan . . . unless Sarah really didn't want to be found. Anna didn't want to think about that. The surface of the water was ebb tide smooth and glassy. The few fishing boats here and there looked settled in with poles out and lines cast. Some of the fishermen were already enjoying lunch. She waved at the ones she knew, trying not to show the disappointment that none of the boats contained her missing granddaughter.

As Anna continued guiding her boat down-river, she prayed. First for Sarah's safety and then for Sarah's heart. "Bring her back to us," she said quietly, "and back to herself . . ."

She docked the boat, then, while carefully checking the boat slips for the skiff, made her way into town. She inquired at Greeley's, particularly with Bobby who usually kept track of the river traffic, but it seemed that no one had seen Sarah or the skiff.

"Something wrong?" Bobby asked her curiously as he walked outside with her.

Anna wasn't sure how much to say but then remembered a time when Bobby and Sarah had been on friendlier terms—back before Sarah had gone to live at the commune. "I'm not sure," she admitted to him. "I think Sarah might've been upset by something. Perhaps that's why she left."

He nodded with a sympathetic expression. "She's been different ever since she came back."

"Yes. She was staying in a rather strange place."

"That commune?"

Anna was surprised he knew this but reminded

herself it was a small town and news traveled fast. Sometimes this was good . . . sometimes not.

"I had a friend who was at the same place," Bobby told her. "He left last winter, but he knew Sarah, and he told me a little about it. Pretty weird stuff, if you ask me."

"Really?" Anna felt a rush of hope. "Is your friend still around?"

He shrugged. "I'm not sure. I haven't seen him for awhile."

"Because it might be helpful to talk to him," Anna said eagerly.

"His name's Jim Viceroy. His folks are in the phone book. If he's still around, he's probably living at home."

"Thanks." Anna repeated the name in her head several times.

"And if I see Sarah anywhere, I mean around town, I can give you a call."

She thanked him again. "Another thing, Bobby, if you know any reliable kids looking for summer jobs—we're looking for more workers at the inn."

He nodded. "I'll get the word out."

Anna felt a smidgeon of hope as she turned back up the river. Knowing the name of someone who had been at the same commune could be very helpful. Especially if Sarah had gone back there. Why she would go back there was mystifying, but Anna knew it was a possibility. She pushed the boat a little harder going upriver, only slowing down when she spotted a fishing boat and knew they wouldn't appreciate her wake.

She paused at her own dock just to make sure Sarah hadn't come home. "No sign of her or the boat around here," Clark told her.

"Same thing downriver. But I got a good tip from Bobby Greeley." She filled him in on Jim Viceroy. "And I mentioned we're looking for some more summertime help. So maybe you should hold off on the ad."

He nodded. "I'm just getting ready to go see Mom."

Anna put her hand on her forehead. "That's right. I nearly forgot about Hazel. Maybe I should've run in to see her too while I was—"

"No." He cut her off. "Mom would want you to put your energy into finding Sarah. That's your top priority."

Just then, Lauren hurried down to the dock. She had a bright bouquet of flowers in her hands. "This is for Hazel," she breathlessly told Clark. "I forgot to give them to you."

He nodded. "She'll love these."

Lauren looked at Anna. "Any luck?"

Anna filled her in. "But I still want to go up to Mapleton."

Lauren bit her lip with a worried look.

"I'll try to make it a fast trip," Anna told her. "I know we're shorthanded."

134

"Don't worry about that," Lauren assured her. "I'm letting the office work go so I can help out in the kitchen. And Clark actually helped us with laundry. Really, Mom, we're all right. You just keep looking for Sarah, okay?"

"I'm doing my best." Anna put the boat into reverse again.

"That boat has to be on the river somewhere," Clark called out.

Anna nodded, but she wasn't completely sure of this. It was something she was trying not to consider, but Anna and Clark both knew if the boat wasn't on the river, there was another place it might possibly be—the ocean. Everyone knew that if you continued on past Florence, beyond the bridge and through the jetties, there was only one place left to go. And that little river skiff wouldn't last long out there.

But as she headed on upriver, she didn't want to think about that possibility. Not yet, anyway. Instead, she prayed. With all her heart and soul, she prayed. And as she prayed she got a very strange sensation that others were praying with her. As odd as it seemed, it felt as if all the other river people—the ones who had passed—were agreeing with her prayer. She could feel her grandmother and her mother and father and even Babette . . . so strongly . . . as if they were all praying for Sarah's safety, too.

She made it to Mapleton without seeing the

skiff anywhere. Anna's rationale for looking up here was that Sarah might've come up here if she wanted to get a ride toward Eugene. Anna knew that Sarah had hitchhiked to get back to them. And it was highly likely she would hitchhike to get away as well. But with no sign of the boat, Anna was unsure. Just the same, she docked her boat and went to the post office to ask around, but no one appeared to have seen a dark-haired teenage girl looking for a ride.

Disheartened, Anna guided the boat back toward the inn. Her stomach rumbled, and she knew she should have some lunch, but the idea of food . . . when Sarah was out there some-where, possibly in great danger, or at the least hungry . . . well, it was just unappealing. It seemed so unfair that Sarah came home to them only to stay such a brief time. Why, oh, why hadn't they been able to hold onto her better?

12

Thoughts of Sarah taking the little skiff beyond the river's end . . . and out into the ocean . . . filled Anna with an ice-cold fear. So much so, that she called the hospital and, in hopes of finding Clark, asked to be connected to Hazel's room. "Oh, I'm so happy to hear your voice," she told Hazel. And, it was true, she was. "How are you feeling?"

"Well enough to be let out of here," Hazel said a bit grumpily.

"I'm sorry. But hopefully it won't be long."

"Enough about me. Did you find Sarah?"

"No . . ." Anna's voice trailed off. "But I might have some good leads. Is Clark still there?"

"Yes. Would you like to talk to him?"

"Thank you." Anna waited for him to get on, trying to think of a careful way to say this.

"Did you find her?" he asked eagerly.

"No. And I didn't find the skiff either," she explained. "And that got me to thinking . . . if the skiff isn't on the river . . . well, that leaves a couple of possibilities."

Clark cleared his throat. "Neither of them good."

"I know. Do you think she would actually try to go out to the ocean?"

"Why?"

"I don't know why, Clark." She could hear the panic in her voice. "But I don't know why she would do any of this. It makes no sense whatsoever."

"I know, I know." His tone was soothing now. "I have the big boat, and it's an awfully nice day."

"What?" Now she realized he was talking like this for Hazel's sake. "Yes, yes, it is."

"So maybe I'll do a little ocean fishing. I hear it's been good."

"And you'll look for her? For the skiff?"

"I'll bring home whatever I catch," he said cheerfully.

"Thank you," she told him. "But, please, be careful, Clark. Don't go too far. You know the skiff couldn't get far . . ."

"I promise to be home in time for dinner," he assured her.

"Do you think I should call the coast guard?" she asked suddenly. "So they can be looking for her too?"

"Not yet. Let's just see how it goes first."

"Right." She felt a lump growing in her throat.

Now Clark pleasantly told her good-bye, as if nothing whatsoever was wrong, and she hung up the phone, blinking back tears. What if Sarah had actually taken the little boat to the river's end? Was it possible that she could still be safe? Even on the calmest seas, the little fishing skiffs were far too small for the open ocean. It was crazy.

"Mom?" Lauren came over with frightened eyes. "Did you say you're calling the coast guard?"

Anna tried to appear strong. "No. Clark said to wait."

"But you're considering it?"

"I don't know."

"Do you think she went out to sea?"

Anna took in a slow breath. "I honestly don't know what to think. I searched the river and never saw the skiff."

"Maybe the skiff sunk in the river," Lauren said eagerly, "you know, sort of like I did that time? And then maybe Sarah swam to shore and she's hunkered down somewhere."

Anna nodded. "Yes, I suppose that's a possibility." But Anna knew the flat little skiffs, while not seaworthy, were not easily sunk on a calm river. Still, it seemed pointless to mention this fact since Lauren was well aware of it. "Anyway," Anna said firmly, "I know there's a lot to be done around here so we might as well get busy."

Lauren's chin quivered. "This is my fault, Mom."

Anna placed a hand on Lauren's shoulder. "Don't go there. Really, all we can do for Sarah right now is to simply pray . . . and hope for the best."

Lauren looked away. "All right."

Anna tried to conceal her anxiety as the dinner hour came and went without a word from Clark. Fortunately, no one here knew that he'd promised to be home by now. And, Anna hoped, perhaps this was good news. Perhaps this meant Clark had found Sarah. Perhaps he was with her now!

Anna jumped to hear the phone ringing. Lauren was still in the dining room downstairs, and Anna hurried to answer, hoping it would be Clark calling from town to say that they'd found Sarah and would soon be home. Instead, it was a strange man's voice. "Is this the inn down the river?" he asked in a slightly grumpy tone.

"Yes. This is actually our home line," Anna explained. "Were you calling for reservations or—"

"No, I'm calling because I think one of your boats is tied to my dock."

"A small fishing boat?"

"Yeah. And the name of the inn is on it. The one at the old Larson place, right? Where the store used to be?"

"Yes," Anna said eagerly. "Did you by any chance see a young girl with the boat?"

"You mean you've lost a kid?"

"Well, she's not a child." Now Anna described Sarah.

"Haven't seen anyone 'round here fitting that description. But you can come get your boat whenever you want."

"Of course, we'll come get it as soon as possible. Where are you located?"

"The Johnson place out past Mapleton, beyond the bridge, on the south side of the river." He described the house and dock to her.

"I didn't even think to go that far when I was searching for it," she admitted.

"You think your lost girl is 'round here some-where?" he asked. "You know the highway runs right behind my place. She might've hitched a ride up there."

"That's possible," she said sadly.

"Kids these days . . . never know what they'll do next."

"Someone will come down for the boat." She looked out the window to see it was already getting dusky. "Probably in the morning if that's all right. Thank you for calling."

"No problem. That's how people on the river used to live, looking out for one another. Not like these newcomers or part-timers who just come and go, without so much as a howdy-do."

She felt slightly insulted by his tone, as if he assumed she was a newcomer too. "I grew up on the river too," she told him. "My parents ran the store here when I was a child."

"You're Anna Larson?" he asked.

"Well, I'm Anna Richards now. Do I know you?"

"I was a little older than you in school. Johnny Johnson. Remember the big kid with the red hair and freckles? I played football."

"Yes," she told him. "I do recall you. You still live on the river?"

"Well, I left home to serve in the Pacific, and after that I lived in California. My parents passed on a few years back, and I decided to move back to their place. But everything's changed 'round here. Well, everything but the river."

"Yes, thank goodness for the river." She made a bit more small talk with him then, worried that Clark might try to call, she cut it short. "Feel free to stop by the inn sometime," she told him. "For old time's sake."

She put down the receiver and began to pace. So Sarah had made it to the Johnson place, tied up the boat, and then she'd probably gone up to the road to get a ride. Of course, that made perfect sense. She went right past Mapleton and avoided being noticed. Anna wondered how long ago Sarah had left . . . how far she'd gotten by now.

Anna went to Sarah's room and looked around. Sarah was obviously traveling light. The only thing that Anna could tell was missing was that old patchwork dress. Although it was possible that Sarah had taken a few other items of clothing as well, but most of her things still seemed to be in her closet and drawers. And Anna knew Sarah had no money since she hadn't been paid yet. How did Sarah expect to get anywhere without money? Even if she managed to get rides, what would she eat? Where would she stay?

Furthermore, why did she do it like this? Why couldn't Sarah have come to Anna, told her she was unhappy and wanted to leave? Why did Sarah feel the need to run away like that? To scare them all half to death? Anna shook her head and turned off the light. It was just too aggravating to think about.

As she went into the living room, turning the lights on in there, she remembered that poor

Clark was out there right now, possibly still out on the ocean, maybe even risking life and limb, as he searched for Sarah. Off on a fool's errand—and Anna had sent him on it! Anna went to the phone, wishing there was some way to get word to him. To tell him to come back to her and forget about the senseless search. She even considered calling the coast guard but could just imagine Clark's reaction to that. No, she knew that all she could do was wait . . . and pray.

As she waited, she busied herself with straightening the kitchen. Lauren had made a big batch of cookies for tomorrow's lunch menu but hadn't had time to clean it up yet. Anna welcomed the busywork. Anything to keep her mind off Clark out there in the ocean as it grew dark. What if something happened to him? Not only would she blame herself, but also she would miss him more than she cared to think about. With all this focus on her daughter and granddaughter recently, Anna knew that Clark had probably been neglected. Not that he complained. Clark was not a complainer. But if something happened to him . . . if she lost him . . . because she'd sent him on this fool's errand—

"Mom," called Lauren as she came into the house. "Are you in here?"

"In the kitchen," Anna called back in a tired voice.

"Clark's not back yet."

Anna wiped her hands dry on the dishtowel then sighed. "No . . ." Now she told Lauren about Johnny Johnson's phone call and the skiff.

"Do you want me to go down and get it?" Lauren offered.

"No. It can wait until morning."

"And Sarah is gone then?"

Anna shrugged, carefully hanging the towel on the stove handle. "It would seem so."

"Maybe it's just as well," Lauren said a bit bitterly.

"Oh, Lauren." Anna shook her head. "Don't say that. She's just a child. She should be here . . . with us."

Now Lauren began to cry. "I'm sorry," she said. "But I just don't understand her. I mean I realize I was a spoiled brat at her age. But I don't think I would've done anything like that. Not to you, Mom."

Anna had to bite her tongue now. Of course, Lauren couldn't remember all that she'd put Anna through during her young adulthood. Clark, too, for that matter—and he was only a stepfather. But youth, similar to old age, could impair the memory. Anna was certain of it. In fact, Anna knew that she'd put her own parents through their own sort of grief when she'd eloped with Adam and moved away from the river to live with him. Oh, she'd tried to protect them in her letters, but she suspected that they'd read between the lines. And then . . . Anna hated to remember this . . . she had rarely come home to visit. How that must've hurt them.

"We all do things we regret," she said quietly to Lauren, "when we are young and foolish. When we're older, we realize that we have to forgive our children in the same way our parents forgave us. And likewise, we often have to forgive our parents too. It's as constant as the river, Lauren."

Lauren looked unconvinced. "Well, I suppose I should go. Unless you want me to stay here to wait with you for Clark."

"No." Anna shook her head. "Clark will be fine. You know he often comes home late from an all-day fishing trip."

"Except that he hasn't been fishing."

Anna shrugged. "Who knows? Maybe he did some fishing out there."

"Oh, Mom." Lauren rolled her eyes.

"Go on home," Anna told her. "I'll call you if anything is amiss. And tomorrow will be another long day. Come on, I'll walk you to the dock. And I'll bet Clark will be rolling in."

However, Clark's boat was nowhere in sight as Anna waved good-bye to Lauren. Even so, Anna decided to stay down there, checking in some of the boats and hanging up life preservers . . . doing the chores that Clark usually did. Finally, worried that he might be trying to reach her in the house, she decided to go inside. It seemed very likely that he might've stopped by the hospital to pay his mother one more visit before coming home.

Tempted to call and ask, Anna looked at the clock to see that it was well past nine and beyond visiting hours now. Pacing back and forth in her living room, Anna wondered when she'd ever felt this frightened and lonely. Perhaps back when her mother had died and she'd come home to figure out her life and start over. But since that dark day, she'd been so busy with the inn, so occupied with family and friends . . . and Clark . . . that she'd barely had a moment to be lonely. But what if something happened to Clark? What if she lost him? She couldn't bear to think of it.

It was nearly midnight, and she was just seconds from calling the coast guard when she saw the lights of his boat coming down the river. Grabbing her jacket, she raced down to the dock to meet him. Not even waiting for him to tie up, she jumped onto the boat, throwing her arms around him and nearly knocking him over. "Oh, Clark!" she sobbed into his chest. "I've been so worried."

He stroked her hair. "I'm sorry," he said, "I looked and looked, but I couldn't find her anywhere. I really wanted to bring her back to—"

"I'm not worried about Sarah," she explained as she grabbed the rope, jumped out, and secured the boat. "About you."

He gathered some things then climbed out,

146

pulling her close to him again. "Don't waste your worries on me, Anna."

"But it was so late . . . you were out there all alone . . . I never should've asked you to do that, Clark. I don't know what I'd do without you."

They started walking up to the house, and he explained how he'd looked up and down the coastline, using his binoculars in hopes of spotting the skiff along the beach. "And wouldn't you know it." He shook his head. "Just when I was ready to call it a day—right around sunset—I realized I was nearly out of gas."

"Oh, Clark."

"So I thought about radioing for help, but that's embarrassing. So I realized I probably could make it if I waited for the tide to turn and let the incoming high tide help carry me through the jetty." He paused to open the door for them.

"But that is so dangerous." She stared at him in shock.

He nodded. "And foolish. I was actually starting to question it myself. Can you imagine what it would be like to be midway through the bar and lose power?"

"Your boat would probably be smashed to bits."

"Plus the tide wasn't going to change until midnight."

"I was about to call the coast guard," she admitted.

He grinned. "As it turned out the coast guard

cutter was out there practicing night maneuvers and those good ol' boys came to check on me."

"And they helped you home?"

He nodded sheepishly. "I'll admit it was embarrassing. But I was hugely relieved."

"Oh, my." She put some of Lauren's cookies on a plate and poured him a cup of slightly stale coffee, sweetening it up with cream and sugar.

"I told them about our missing granddaughter," he explained, "and they were quite understanding."

Now Anna told him about the phone call from Johnny Johnson. "So my guess is she went up to the road behind his house and got a ride."

"Oh . . ." Clark sighed.

"I feel so terrible that you went out there like that," Anna said contritely, "that I encouraged you to put yourself in harm's way . . . for nothing."

"We didn't know it at the time." He locked eyes with her. "And Sarah isn't nothing, Anna. You and I both know that."

"Too bad she doesn't know it."

"She does know it," he said quietly, "deep inside of herself, she must know it. Sarah is a good girl. And she's spent enough time here on the river and enough time with you to know who she is, Anna. She might be confused right now, but you know who she is . . . and you'll never give up on her."

Feeling gently chastened as well as comforted, Anna simply nodded. "You're right. Absolutely right."

13

After a restless night filled with frustrating dreams about Sarah, Anna rose early and dressed quietly. Taking time to leave Clark a note, she then slipped outside and down to the dock where she started her boat's engine and slowly eased the craft out into the main current. Keeping the engine's noise low, she headed upriver, where the sun was just coming up. It didn't take long to see she wasn't the only one out this early.

Steering away from fishermen, she slowly chugged upriver toward Mapleton and the Johnson place where she planned to pick up the abandoned skiff and tow it home. Clark had offered to do this, but she could tell by how hard he was sleeping that he was worn out from yesterday's ocean expedition. Besides with another clear sunny day, there would be guests anxious to get out and enjoy the river. He would be needed at the boathouse.

Anna continued past Mapleton, realizing that she rarely came this far up the river, although she did remember coming with her father to make deliveries a few times. She spotted the rickety-looking dock Johnny had described, and there, along with a wooden rowboat, was the skiff. She tied up her boat then got out to tend to the skiff and was just securing it to the back of her boat, when she noticed what looked like a piece of paper beneath one of the floating boat cushions. Curious, she climbed into the little boat and removed a small white envelope that said *To Grandma* on the front.

She sat down on the vinyl cushion now, feeling a lump growing in her throat as the small boat rocked from side to side in the water. She took in a deep breath as she ran a finger over the blue ink of Sarah's neat penmanship then slowly opened the envelope.

Dear Grandma,

I know you are probably mad at me by now. You should be. As hard as it is to admit this, I realize I don't belong with you on the river anymore. Even Lauren, as much as I hate her, has more right to be there than I do. Like you said, my bitterness is poison, and I can see that it's poisoning everyone. I've been told again and again that I have badness in me. I know it's true. And I know it will take more hard work, self-denial, and penance to remove it. That is what I'm going to try to do. I'm sorry that I hurt you, Grandma. You have always been good to me. You do not deserve such a worthless granddaughter.

Sorry,
Sarah

Anna's tears dropped onto the white paper, blurring the blue ink. She carefully refolded the page and was just slipping it back into the envelope when she heard footsteps approaching.

"Hello down there?" called a man's voice.

She looked up to see a slightly grizzled-looking man coming her way. With shaggy gray hair and an unshaved chin, he looked a bit scary, but then he waved. "Is that you, Anna Larson?"

She waved and nodded. "Yes. I was just getting ready to tow the boat home."

He came down to the dock, peering curiously at her. "Are you crying?"

She brushed her wet cheek with the back of her hand and nodded. "I was just reading a note my granddaughter left behind."

"Kids," he said with exasperation. "They can break your heart."

She studied his face, seeing the sadness there. "Do you have children, Johnny? Grandchildren?"

He shoved his hands in his jean pockets. "I did."

She tilted her head to one side. "You did?"

"Just one . . . a son. We didn't think we'd have any kids, but then after seven years, we got John

Junior. JJ for short. What a kid. You should've seen him throw a football." He ran his fingers through his messy hair. "Chip off the old block."

"Oh . . ." She waited, fearing the worst.

"JJ would've turned thirty next year."

Anna nodded. "He passed on?"

"Yeah." Johnny looked up at the sky.

"I'm sorry."

"Me too."

Anna stood, and with the letter in one hand, she held to the edge of the skiff and got out onto the dock then put a hand on Johnny's shoulder. "I can imagine how much you must miss him."

He nodded, pressing his lips together.

Now she told him about how they'd spent the last two years thinking that they'd lost Sarah, too. "It felt as if she'd died," she said, "and then she came back to us."

"Anyway, you know she's alive."

"Yes . . . but now she's gone again."

"At least it's not your fault."

Anna wasn't sure what he meant . . . or if he was even right.

"You see JJ went through some of the stuff a lot of the kids went through in the sixties—all that antiestablishment crap. We were down in California, the Bay Area, and I'm sure he did some experimenting with drugs—turning on and tuning out or whatever it was kids were doing. Probably still are."

"Was that how he died?"

Johnny shook his head. "I think it would've been easier if that was the way it happened."

"Oh . . ." Anna wasn't sure whether she should press him or not. Sometimes she would have sessions like this with guests, but many of them expected this sort of thing there at the inn. This was Johnny's place.

"JJ wanted to dodge the draft. He wanted money to go up to Canada. I told him to forget it. I told him to man up and face his responsibilities and went on about how I'd fought in the Pacific and how freedom wasn't really free. You know the drill." Johnny rubbed his hand over his eyes, and Anna could tell he was trying to hide his tears. "For some crazy reason, JJ listened to me—next thing we knew he was on his way to Vietnam."

"Did he die there?"

He nodded. "Didn't even last three months. Came home in a wooden box. My wife blamed me for it, and our marriage fell apart. But she's right. It was my fault. I should've let him run. At least he'd be here now."

"Oh, Johnny . . ." She sighed. "It's not your fault. You were only trying to get him to do the right thing . . . to obey the law. You didn't know how it would turn out."

His tears were flowing freely now. "I never dreamed he wouldn't make it back," he said, "after all I went through in the Pacific, I was certain

JJ would do the same, a chip off the old block."

She nodded. "I'm sure JJ knew you loved him, Johnny. And in the end, he made his own decision to go and serve. He could've gone to Canada even if you hadn't helped him. You must know that."

He tapped the side of his head. "I know it up here." Now he tapped his chest. "But sometimes it doesn't feel like it in here."

"I can understand that." Now she told him about Sarah's letter. "Something she said makes me feel as if I'm to blame. I told her something— something she misunderstood. I told her that not forgiving someone was like poison. I meant it was poisoning her, but she thought I was saying she was like poison to the people around her. That's not what I meant. Not at all." Now Anna was crying again, too.

To her surprise, Johnny reached out and hugged her. For a long moment, they just stood there crying together, and finally, they both stepped back as if embarrassed. Anna knew that it had been nothing more than two hurting people trying to comfort each other, something she often did at the inn. But for Johnny's sake, she wanted to make it clear.

"Please, come and visit us at the inn," she told him. "My husband, Clark, is a veteran, too, and I have a feeling that you and he would have some stories to exchange, Johnny."

He nodded. "Maybe I'll do that."

So she told them about the bonfires they had on Saturday nights and how sometimes there was music and storytelling. "And Clark likes to go deep-sea fishing when it's not too busy at the inn," she said as she untied her boat and hopped in. "Maybe you'd like to go sometime."

He made what seemed a hopeful smile. "Maybe I was wrong. I guess there are still some good people on the river, Anna."

She smiled back. "Yes. You can be sure of it."

Her trip downriver was one of mixed emotions. Thankful that she'd managed to make a connection with an old acquaintance but saddened at Johnny's heartache and deep loneliness. And although she appreciated Sarah's attempt to communicate and apologize in the letter, Anna couldn't help but grieve over Sarah's words. She felt as if she'd failed her granddaughter.

As Anna slowed down for the dock, she reminded herself of what she'd just told Johnny. Just like with JJ, Sarah had made her own decision. No one had forced Sarah to run away. Sarah had to know, even if it was deep down, that Anna still loved her . . . would always love her. Anna knew that blaming herself for Sarah's bad choices wouldn't help anyone. The best thing Anna could do was to pray for her . . . and perhaps contact Jim Viceroy.

Clark met her on the dock, helping her to tie off and moving the skiff out of the way. "I thought I was going to take care of that," he said as he helped her out of the boat.

"You looked so peaceful, sleeping so soundly. I thought you probably needed your rest." She patted his cheek. "And as it turned out, I think it's good that I went."

As they walked to the main dining room for breakfast, she told him about her unexpected visit with Johnny Johnson. "He's a sad, lonely man."

"Poor guy."

She smiled at Clark. "I invited him to come visit us. I told him that maybe you guys could swap war stories." As they went into the dining room, she remembered the letter still in her jacket pocket. Because it had been written to her, she wasn't sure how much of it she planned to share. Maybe none of it for now.

After breakfast, Anna looked up the Viceroys in the phone book and, finding only one listing, dialed the number and asked for Jim. "Who is this?" a woman's voice demanded. So Anna identified herself, confessing that Bobby Greeley had told her about Jim. "Bobby said that Jim might've lived at the same commune where my granddaughter stayed for a while."

"Your granddaughter was in that horrible place?" Mrs. Viceroy sounded shocked.

"Well, I'm not positive, but I think so."

"Good grief, it was bad enough having a son stay in a place like that, I can't imagine how

I'd feel if it was a girl. How old is she anyway?"

"She just turned eighteen. But she'd been gone for two years."

"You mean she was there as a juvenile?"

Now Anna explained how Sarah had run away from home. "We searched and searched for her but never found her."

"Someone should press charges against that place," Mrs. Viceroy said bitterly. "The way they mess with people's minds is despicable."

"I'm sure I agree with you." Anna twisted the cord in her fingers. "So, is Jim there? Is it possible to talk to him?"

"Oh, I thought I already told you. No, Jim's not here. He took off a couple of weeks ago. I have no idea where he's off to this time. I just hope it's not back to that place. He did mention wanting to go work on a crabbing boat in Alaska." She let out a loud sigh. "Dangerous work, I'll admit. But it seems a sight better than that awful commune. You don't think your granddaughter went back there, do you?"

"I'm not sure, but I'm afraid she might've. Do you happen to know where it's located?"

"Not exactly. But somewhere near Medford. Out on a farm. I think Jim said it was west of Medford. Or maybe I just imagined that part."

Anna thanked her for her help, giving her their phone number in case she heard from Jim.

"I'm real sorry for you," Mrs. Viceroy said

finally, "I wouldn't want any girl of mine—or a boy for that matter—stuck in that place."

Anna felt worse than ever when she hung up. Mrs. Viceroy seemed to confirm all of Anna's worst fears about that commune. But knowing its general location was something of a comfort.

"Good news," Lauren said as she came into the office where Anna had used the phone.

"About Sarah?" Anna asked hopefully.

Lauren's smile faded. "No . . . about some extra help around here. A couple of kids, friends of Bobby Greeley, just pulled up to the dock. Mind if I bring them up here to do applications and interviews?"

"Not at all." Anna started to leave then stopped. "By the way, I've discovered that the commune Sarah lived at is near Medford."

Lauren nodded. "Do you have an exact location?"

"No, but I plan to do some more calling. I'll use the house phone."

"If you find the place, I could go down there and try to get her to come home," Lauren offered. "It seems the least I can do."

Anna just nodded. "Let's cross that bridge when we come to it." But as Anna headed for the other phone, she knew that it would not be wise to include Lauren in this. If Sarah saw Lauren coming for her, she'd probably take off running in the opposite direction. For this to work, it would have to be done carefully . . . and prayerfully.

14

Anna called the Medford police first. She hoped they might have concern about some kind of criminal element and want to go have a look at the commune. But when she couldn't really give them specifics, they suggested she call city hall and speak to someone there. After several calls, she finally managed to get someone to give her some more specific directions to the commune. She wrote everything down then went off to search for Clark.

"I'm going down to get the boys now," Lauren told Anna as they met on the stairs. "I told them to look around a bit, you know, to get the feel of the place and see if they really want to work here. But maybe I should get on with the interviews." She looked uncertain. "And if they seem like good kids . . . do you think I should just go ahead and hire them today?"

"I trust your judgment," Anna told her. It was something she used to say to Lauren a lot, back when she first started working at the inn, but she suspected Lauren might need it even more than ever today.

"Thanks, Mom. I appreciate that."

"You know as well as anyone that we need help. And you're a good judge of character." Anna glanced at the clock. "And if you get moving, they might even be able to help with lunch."

Lauren looked hopeful. "Wouldn't that be something?"

Anna didn't want to admit that she had ulterior motives or that having a couple extra workers would come in especially handy right now. She didn't even want Lauren to know what she was up to. Perhaps Clark could tell her . . . later. She found him down by the bathhouse, and as he hosed off the nearby patio, she explained what she'd discovered. "I want to go there," she said eagerly. "I think I can talk Sarah into coming home with me."

He frowned and turned off the hose nozzle. "I want Sarah to come home as much as you, but I don't want you going there by yourself."

"But you need to stay here to help," she told him. "And there's your mom. You can't just take off while she's still in the hospital."

"That's true." He coiled the hose, setting it off to one side. "Maybe you should take Lauren with you."

"I can't do that, Clark. She'll be needed more than ever here."

He rubbed his chin with a furrowed brow. "I don't want you going alone, Anna."

"I knew you'd say that. But I honestly think I'll have more success with Sarah if I go alone. I think she'll listen to me."

"But what about the people running the place? They might try to make trouble for—"

"Clark," she said slowly. "I will be very cautious. If anything seems amiss about any of this, I won't even go in. And I have no problem calling the police or someone from the city for help." She sighed. "I think I've spoken to about half of them already today. Some were actually helpful."

He put his hands on her cheeks, looking intently into her eyes. "It's just that if anything happened to you—I don't know what I'd do. I'm sure I'd do something completely crazy."

She forced a laugh. "Oh, Clark, really. What do you think they'd do? Take an old woman like me captive? And, even if they did, I expect you'd be there with a posse to rescue me."

He nodded. "You can count on that."

"I looked at a map, and I figure if I take off pretty soon, I should make Medford by this afternoon. I'll try to go directly to the commune, but if I have a problem getting Sarah to leave with me, I might spend a night in a hotel."

"And you'll call me," he told her.

"Absolutely."

"And you'll write down all the details of the location and everything?"

"Of course."

He still looked uneasy.

"And I will pray every step of the way, Clark.

I will ask God to lead me." She made what she hoped was a brave smile. "Really, I have a good feeling about this. I think Sarah wants me to come for her. It might convince her that she really belongs here with us . . . that we are her family and this is her home."

"And Lauren? What about their problems?"

Anna shrugged. "We'll figure it out in time. Maybe Lauren will have to move the office to Babette's house. And, right now, she's interviewing a couple of guys who seem to want summer work."

Clark looked relieved. "We could use some good help."

"I'm going to go pack some things. And I plan to stop by to visit your mom in town," she told him, "before I head out. I'll tell her hello for you. Then maybe you go visit at dinnertime. Although I'll have to take the car."

"No problem. I've got legs. I can walk. By the way, I gassed the car up last time I was in town, so you should be all set to go."

With Lauren occupied in the office with the two young job applicants, who sounded enthusiastic, Anna quickly gathered what she needed then hurried back out. Before long, she was on her way downriver and imagining Sarah's pleased surprise to discover that Anna loved her enough to make this effort to bring her home.

Anna didn't forget her promise to stop by to

visit Hazel, and, seeing that she looked better and was acting bored, Anna told her what she was planning.

"That sounds like an exciting mission," Hazel told her. "I wish I could go with you."

"I wish you could, too, but you need to stay put until the doctor says you're well enough to come home."

"Humph." Hazel frowned. "I think I'm well enough to go home right now."

Anna patted her hand. "Maybe you can have Clark speak to your doctor." Now she told Hazel about Lauren hiring some more helpers. "Hopefully life will slow down a bit for everyone."

"I plan to help out again, too," Hazel reminded her. "I love working with the girls in the kitchen. I miss it."

"They miss you, too."

"And I miss our sweet Sarah, too. It seemed she was barely back with us and suddenly gone. Like a little bird in flight."

"I just hope she'll want to come home with me."

"Tell her we need her," Hazel said. "Tell her the river needs her."

Anna nodded. "I'll do that."

"And tell her about the walk on the beach."

"My grandmother's story?"

Hazel plucked at the blanket with a thoughtful look. "Perhaps it's everyone's story, Anna."

"What do you mean?"

"Perhaps it's part of your family's heritage . . . at least the heritage of the women . . . the matriarchal society passing it on and on to each new generation . . ." She looked into Anna's eyes as if searching. "Perhaps all of you must walk your own trail of tears."

Anna sighed. "I've had that same thought before, Hazel. That exact same thought."

"If I were younger, I'd want to write a new thesis," Hazel told her. "On just that. I think I'd call it The Matriarchal Trail of Tears, a Story of the Siuslaw Women."

"Then why don't you?" Anna nodded eagerly. "You're not too old to write, Hazel."

She made a weary smile. "I think my writing days are over. That's a book someone else will have to write. Maybe you . . . or Lauren . . . or even Sarah when she figures things out."

Anna looked at her watch.

"Speaking of Sarah, you should be on your way, Anna. Go and get our girl. Bring her back to us."

Anna stood, leaning over to kiss Hazel's cheek. "Pray for us."

"I will. And send Sarah my love."

Anna felt torn as she left the hospital. On one hand, she was eager to be on her way to find Sarah . . . on the other hand, she felt worried about Hazel. Despite her bravado about wanting to come home, she still seemed tired and frail. And

164

it seemed doubtful that the doctors were keeping her there for their own amusement. But she and Clark had been so distracted by Sarah's disappearing act that they hadn't been giving Hazel or her physicians their best attention. Hopefully, Clark would have a long conversation with some of the medical staff later today. Surely, he would get to the bottom of it.

It was close to five when Anna made it to Medford. But with nearly four hours of daylight left, she decided to continue out to where the commune was supposed to be. It took a few wrong turns, but finally, she found the right road, and after several miles, she spotted the farm that fit the description the woman at the city had given her. But, of course, there was a gate across the entrance with a "no trespassing" sign on it. Fine, she decided. She would simply park the station wagon in front of the gate and wait. Wouldn't someone eventually come out to see who it was? Better yet, maybe Sarah would recognize the car and come to speak to her. That would simplify everything.

But an hour passed, and no one came her way. This was particularly aggravating because Anna could see people moving around and about the property. It appeared to be a rundown old farm with the usual main house, barns, and outbuildings. A few pieces of dilapidated farm equipment were littered about, as well as several newer-looking, but simple buildings. Intermixed with all this were a number of travel trailers and various-sized tents. The overall effect was that of a shabby carnival.

Occasionally a worker would pause and furtively glance in Anna's direction, before hurrying along. Both men and women were like something from a time gone by; the men were bearded and the women wore long dresses. They appeared to be doing chores. Finally, it was close to seven when the place got quiet, and she suspected they might be sitting down to a meal. Naturally, the thought of food made her stomach rumble, but she was determined to stay put. Surely, someone would get curious as to why her car was parked here and come to investigate. Hopefully, before it got dusky since she'd promised herself not to remain after dark.

Finally, it was nearly eight o'clock when a tall bearded man began lumbering toward her. He seemed in no hurry and in his long white robe looked like something out of time or maybe out of the *Ten Commandments* movie. "Can I help you?" he asked in a solemn deep voice.

"Yes." She made a nervous smile. "I'm here to see my granddaughter."

He frowned. "Your granddaughter?"

"Yes. Sarah Gunderson."

His brows drew together, but he said nothing.

"She used to live here, and I believe she's returned. I need to see her about something."

"The person you seek is not here."

Anna didn't believe him but didn't know what to say.

Without another word, he turned to leave.

"Wait!" she cried out desperately.

He turned and looked at her with slightly narrowed eyes.

"Have you seen her?" she asked.

He just looked at her . . . not speaking . . . but she could tell he was holding back the truth. She suspected he often held back the truth.

"Do you teach the Bible here?" she asked.

"We teach many things from many spiritual sources."

"Do you teach that it's a sin to lie?"

"Many things are sinful."

"I know she's here," Anna declared. "Please, just let me talk to her."

"I'm sorry . . . your trip was in vain." He turned from her and began walking away again. Despite her calling out, he continued walking.

"I might have to call the police," she finally yelled out. This stopped him. He turned and looked at her with what she felt were truly evil eyes.

"Call them," he said loudly. "We have broken no laws."

"Then let my granddaughter come out here," she pleaded. "Let her speak to me."

He just shook his head now. Holding up his

hands, he turned away once more. But she could sense by the way he walked that he was done here. And she knew he wasn't being honest with her and that he was playing some sort of game—one where he made the rules and controlled everything and everyone. Even his stride had a strange air of smugness in it.

She stood there watching as he disappeared into the shadows and around a building. She had no idea what she should do. As much as she wanted to march onto the property and find Sarah, she had a bad feeling about it. Something about the posted sign and the man's dark eyes suggested danger.

It seemed the only thing to do was to wait. And at the same time that seemed senseless—that is unless Sarah was somewhere nearby . . . perhaps watching . . . waiting for the right moment when she could come over here unobserved. Perhaps in the protection of the dusky shadows that were growing longer and darker, after the sun was fully down. Surely it wouldn't hurt to wait that long.

As she'd promised Clark, Anna prayed for God to guide her in this. She prayed for wisdom and grace. She didn't want to be foolish. But she didn't want to be a coward either, and waiting for dark seemed her best chance to rescue Sarah from this place. She got back in the car. With the windows cracked for fresh air and so she could hear if anyone approached, she waited for the sky's light to fade.

As her impatience grew, she thought of her ancestors, wondering how many of them had sat quietly like this, waiting for something . . . perhaps a deer or a fish or maybe a spirit quest. Waiting was probably good for the soul.

Her eyes adjusted to the dimness of her surroundings, and when she checked her watch, she was surprised to see that it was past nine now. This was one of the longest days of the year, and she could still see fairly well. Lights had gone on inside the buildings, making it easier for her to pick out people and shadows as they moved about.

Then, just as she was about to give up, she noticed something making its way through a grassy field toward her. At first she thought it was a deer but then realized it was a girl, hunched down, probably to avoid detection. As the girl got closer, Anna could see she was wearing a long dress, and at first she thought it must be Sarah, but then she noticed that the two long braids appeared lighter and the pale face, which looked pinched and frightened, was definitely not Sarah's. Even so, Anna quietly got out of the car, going over to the fence to meet the girl who'd positioned herself against a fencepost, probably to hide.

"Who are you?" the girl asked with anxious eyes.

"I'm Sarah Gunderson's grandmother," Anna said quickly. "Is Sarah here?"

"She was here."

"She was here? When?"

"Earlier today. She left with some others."

"Left?" Anna felt a rush of panic. "Where did she go?"

"I don't know." The girl looked over her shoulder. "I wish I'd gone with them."

"Do you want to leave?"

The girl nodded eagerly.

"Do you want to come with me?" Anna asked cautiously.

The girl put her balled fist over her mouth now, as if afraid or maybe uncertain.

"I'll take you out of here if you want," Anna said in a strong voice. "No one can keep you here against your will. You must know that. We have laws protecting people from that." Now Anna saw someone coming from the house, calling out for someone. "If you want to come with me, I'm going now," she said evenly as she walked over to the driver's side of the car, getting in. It seemed clear that it was time to go. She felt it in her bones. Then as she started the engine, the girl squeezed through the gate, dashed to the passenger side, and jumped inside.

"You better go." The girl ducked down. *"And hurry!"*

"Do they have guns?" Anna asked nervously.

"I think so."

Anna stepped on the gas, spitting out gravel behind her as she turned her car around, heading back into the same direction she'd come earlier. She sped down the narrow road, squealing her tires around a curve and finally turning onto the main highway to town. She glanced up at her rearview mirror and to her relief no one seemed to be following her. Even so, her heart pounded wildly and she wondered what a grandmother was doing out here like this. But at the same time, she knew that love made people do even stranger things.

15

Finally, safely in town, Anna pulled the station wagon into a brightly lit convenience market and turned to look at the frightened girl seated beside her. Petite and fair, she looked even younger than Sarah. "How old are you?" Anna asked in a gentle tone.

"Twenty."

Anna just nodded, not sure whether to believe her or not. "What's your name?"

"Jewel."

"Are you hungry?"

Jewel nodded.

"Well, I haven't had any dinner. Would you like to join me?"

"I had dinner already, but we were short on food . . . again."

Anna drove down the street to where she'd spotted a diner earlier. "Is this okay?"

"I don't have any money," Jewel said.

"That's okay." Anna reached for her purse.

As they went inside and were seated, Anna realized this was not going according to her plans. Not at all. Still, she would make the most of it. Jewel had to know something . . . something that would help her locate Sarah. But she wouldn't question the girl until she had a chance to eat.

And, judging by the way she packed down a cheeseburger, fries, and shake, she truly was hungry. And she did look very thin. Anna just hoped that she wouldn't get sick from the rich food. But to Anna's surprise, after she finished, Jewel still seemed hungry. So Anna encouraged her to order dessert. Then as Jewel ate a big piece of banana cream pie, Anna inquired about Sarah.

"Sarah showed up at the farm really early in the morning," Jewel explained. "I heard her telling Aaron that she'd gotten a ride down I-5 with a trucker in the middle of the night."

"Aaron?" Anna remembered that name. "Isn't that the guy who originally started the place? Aaron and Misty?"

"Yes." Jewel forked into the pie again. "They just stopped by the farm a few days ago. Of course, Daniel acted like they were welcome to stay with us, but we could tell he didn't want them there. Aaron and Daniel never got along."

172

"Was that Daniel who came out to speak to me earlier?"

She nodded, chewing a big bite.

"So Sarah got here this morning. But now she's gone?"

"She went with Aaron and Misty and some of the others."

"The ones you wish you'd gone with?"

"Yes." She set down her fork with a clank. "Aaron and Misty had come to tell us about this enlightened guru from India who was coming to start a new order. Aaron wanted everyone to come with them to join it. But Daniel said no way. And then there was this big fight because some of the family wanted to go with Aaron and Misty."

"When did this all happen?"

"Not long after Sarah got there. It was like her arrival set things off because she immediately wanted to go with Aaron and Misty, and Daniel put his foot down. But it was too late because the others started to speak up, too."

"So did they leave this morning?" Anna was trying to piece this together in her mind.

"Yeah. Aaron and Misty had driven this blue van. When they left, about six people, besides Sarah, snuck out to go with them."

"So Sarah arrived early this morning then left almost as soon as she got there?" Anna said slowly, fully grasping what this meant. A full day of travel perhaps, taking Sarah even further away.

"Yeah. Sarah was smart to go. I wish I'd gone with them too."

Once again, Anna felt a conflicting mix of emotions. On one hand, Aaron and Misty were supposedly "good" people. On the other hand, Sarah was gone again. "Do you know where they were going?"

Jewel sadly shook her head. "Some of us were talking about it . . . afterward. Some thought they were headed for Mexico. Some thought Canada. It could be anywhere."

"But you think they were leaving the country?"

"I don't really know, but I got the impression it was a long ways. Aaron was eager to make an early start on the road."

"So they could meet up with this guru?"

"Yeah. They were going wherever the guru was going. . . . Aaron said he was the real deal. Of course, that just made Daniel really mad."

"I can imagine." And she could.

"Thank you for dinner." Jewel wiped her mouth with the paper napkin. She looked tired and sad.

"Where will you go now?" Anna asked. "Do you have family nearby?"

She shook her head. "No . . . I'm from the East Coast."

"Do you want to go home?" Anna studied her. "I could give you bus fare."

"I don't really have a home. Not really."

"Then what will you do?"

Jewel's gray eyes filled with tears now. "I don't know, but I can't go back to the farm. Not after running like I did. Daniel would kill me."

"Really? Is he a murderer?"

"No, not like that. But he's mean. Really mean."

Anna wanted to question why Jewel had stayed with him at all then . . . if he was that mean. But she realized that probably wasn't going to help Jewel's current situation. "You could come home with me," Anna said suddenly. "I run an inn on the river. It's near the coast. And we actually need some workers." Anna wasn't positive they still needed workers, but she figured another pair of hands couldn't hurt.

"Oh, yeah, I remember Sarah telling me about that inn on the river." She looked hopefully at Anna. "Really? You would really let me come and work for you there?"

"Of course."

She narrowed her eyes slightly. "And this isn't a trick or anything?"

Anna sighed. "No, it's not a trick. Trust me, I have no need of tricks." She studied Jewel more closely. "Unless you're tricking me. Are you really twenty?"

"Almost." Now Jewel told Anna her birth date.

Anna looked at her watch and was shocked to see that it was past ten. "Well, it's too late to drive home and make it there at a reasonable hour. We'll have to get a hotel for the night."

Jewel looked worried by this. Now, Anna felt concerned, too, especially as she considered what Clark would say to Anna's taking in a stranger like this, which reminded her that she needed to call him. He'd probably point out that she barely knew this girl. And what if Jewel decided to beat and rob Anna in the middle of the night? Clark, as always, would be looking out for Anna's welfare.

"We'll have separate rooms at the hotel," Anna told Jewel as she set out the cash for their dinner bill. "And if you still want to go with me in the morning—if you still want to work at the inn—be ready to leave around nine. It's about a four-hour drive."

And so when Anna finally called Clark from her hotel room, she was able to reassure him that she was perfectly safe and that all was well, as she explained all the events of the evening. "I'm sorry to call so late," she told him. "It's just been a really long day."

"I'm just relieved to hear your voice," he told her. "But I'm sorry you missed Sarah."

"Yes . . ." She sighed. "But maybe Jewel can help us find her."

"Anyway, it sounds like Jewel needs a good place to land." He chuckled. "She couldn't have found a better person to take her home, darling."

"We'll see if she's still here in the morning."

"Oh, she'll be there, all right. I'd bet on it."

• • •

Clark was right. When morning came, Jewel was waiting for Anna in the lobby. "I was afraid you'd left without me," she said nervously. "It's past nine."

Anna glanced at her watch. "You're right." She paid the bill then turned to Jewel. "Are you hungry?"

Jewel's eyes lit up, and she nodded.

So they returned to the diner, and Jewel, once again, ate enough food to fill a logger. "I don't understand how you kids could work on a farm and not get enough to eat," Anna said as they were leaving. "Didn't you eat the food you grew?"

"We didn't grow that much food, and then we had to sell a lot of it, too."

"But I would think with that many people working together . . . in a commune situation . . . you'd be faring better than it seems you were."

Jewel shrugged. "I guess that's what we thought, too. And it was better . . . before Daniel took over. Everything changed then."

"So why did people stay on?" Anna started the car engine. "If it was so bad?"

"Some of us don't have a choice . . . and Daniel . . . well, he makes it hard to leave."

"Does he keep people captive there?"

"Not exactly." Jewel looked out the side window. "But he makes you feel like a real failure if you even think about leaving."

"Do you feel like a failure now?"

Jewel bit into the nail of her thumb like she was thinking about this.

"Did Daniel preach at everyone a lot?"

She nodded. "We had morning and evening sessions . . . they could last for hours."

"Do you know what Daniel's training was . . . or if he had any?"

"He seemed to know a lot about all the religions. He had lots and lots of books. And he's writing his own book, too. He made sure that he was being recorded when he preached and taught. Then someone would have to listen to the tapes and write it all out for him." She slowly shook her head. "He made me do it once, but I was so slow he got someone else." She turned to look at Anna. "Sarah was always really good at it. I think she'd taken typing in high school. That was one reason Daniel got so mad when she left."

"Oh . . ." Anna wasn't sure she wanted to hear too much. And yet she did.

"Did Daniel punish people when he got mad?"

"Oh, yeah. There are all kinds of punishment there. The most common punishment was to miss meals. But sometimes we weren't allowed to sleep either. And for really bad stuff, Daniel would have us beaten."

"You were beaten?"

"For things like lying, cheating, stealing. And

there are limits to how many times we could be hit. And everyone had to watch it."

Anna shuddered. "How could you stand to stay there?"

Jewel shrugged and looked down at her lap.

"I'm sorry," Anna said, "but it's just hard to comprehend why an intelligent young person would subject herself to that kind of abuse."

"My parents got divorced when I was ten," Jewel said quietly. "Before that they fought all the time, so it should've been better after the divorce. Except that it wasn't. My mom started bringing home boyfriends. My dad pretty much vanished. I couldn't wait to get away from home. If you could call it home."

"Oh . . ." Anna nodded, realization sinking in.

"I got into drugs . . . and a bad crowd of kids. We came out to the West Coast thinking we'd find something better out here. Then, we were at this free rock concert right here in Oregon, and it was so cool . . . I mean it felt like everyone loved everyone, and they were preaching about love and peace and a perfect world. And that's where I met Aaron and Misty. They had this idea about a bunch of us living together. Everyone helping everyone. We'd grow our own food and make things to sell. We'd be this big, happy family." She sighed. "It sounded like heaven on earth to me."

"Was it?"

"It was pretty good in the beginning. Aaron and Misty had found the farm to rent, and we all were happy to work it. We worked really hard at first. Aaron was against drugs, well, except for marijuana. That was okay if we used it to connect spiritually. He controlled the growing of it, as well as who got to use it and stuff. He was kind of like our spiritual dad. Aaron really cared about us."

Not wanting to sound judgmental, Anna just nodded.

"Sarah and Zane joined us early on. But Zane didn't like it. He didn't want anyone telling him what to do. But Sarah was a hard worker. She understood the importance of family. She fit in."

Anna thought back to how much Sarah loved her summers at the river. It was probably the most structure she experienced in her rather tumultuous family life. In some ways, Sarah's story wasn't all that much different than Jewel's. Anna realized that Jewel had stopped talking now. "Do you think Sarah will be happy going with Aaron and Misty?" Anna asked.

"Happier than she would've been if she'd been stuck with Daniel." Jewel shuddered. "And I hate to think of what that place is like today."

"Why?"

"Because Daniel will be so angry. He lost those other six members, as well as Sarah, and just after he'd been so glad that she'd come back.

Then he lost me, too. So that's a big part of the family gone. And the others will probably suffer for it. I'll bet Daniel preached all morning. Especially since he knew there were others who wanted to leave." She shook her head. "I feel sorry for the ones still there. With less people, they'll have to work harder than ever, and summer is the busiest time of year, too."

"And if they want to leave?"

Jewel made a sad sounding laugh. "It's easier said than done."

"But Sarah left."

"In the middle of the night," Jewel sighed. "And now Daniel will probably get guard dogs. He'd been talking about it. Acting like the dogs would be to keep people out, but I'm pretty sure it will be to keep people in, too."

Anna decided, then and there, that she would be calling the state police now. Even if Jewel was unwilling to speak to them, Anna would tell them about this and ask them to look into it. How could authorities sit by allowing a man to hold people there against their will? It seemed nothing short of kidnapping. She wondered why the local authorities had been so nonchalant about it when she'd called them. Maybe no one really cared. Whatever the case, she would at least try. For Sarah's sake . . . because some of the people still stuck on the farm with Daniel had been Sarah's friends . . . her surrogate family.

"I wish I knew where Sarah was going . . . ," Anna said absently.

"You really do love her, don't you?" Jewel's voice was filled with longing.

"I really do. I just hope that she doesn't forget that I do. I hope she knows she has options. And that she can come home anytime she wants."

"Sarah is really smart," Jewel said with conviction. "That's why Daniel was so furious when she ran away the first time. He knew how smart she was. I think he had big plans for her. And it enraged him when she ran off."

Anna didn't want to think about Daniel anymore. Just remembering last night and the dark expression on his face made her feel sick to her stomach. At least Sarah was away from him now. "Sarah *is* smart," Anna agreed. "Very smart. And I hope she'll figure out what she really needs in life."

16

Jewel seemed to fit in well at the river. She got along with Janelle and Diane and, for the time being, was using Sarah's room. But Anna hoped that would change, and, shortly after Hazel was released from her week at the hospital, Clark started work on the store as well as a couple of cabins. One of them would be a dorm of sorts, to house employees. The other structure, located off by itself near the river, Anna was calling "Sarah's Cabin." And Clark was of the same mind. Of course, they weren't saying this out loud because they knew the others were frustrated over losing Sarah again. Frustrated and sad and hurt.

The only consolation this time was that they were sure that Sarah was alive. And that she'd gone on her own free will. And every morning, when Anna prayed for Sarah, she also prayed for Aaron and Misty. She hoped they were truly the people that Sarah had believed them to be . . .and that they would take good care of Sarah.

"Do you have any idea where she is?" Hazel asked unexpectedly one morning. It had been about two weeks since her heart problems and the two women were shelling peas together in Hazel's little kitchen. Doing simple household chores provided a convenient way for Anna to spend time with Hazel while she regained her strength.

"What?" Anna looked up.

"Sarah. Do you have any idea where this new commune might be?"

Anna shrugged. "You mean besides on this continent? It could be anywhere between Canada and Mexico. Or anywhere in the world I suppose. But I'm sure she's having a great adventure." Anna had already told Hazel about the guru coming from India, and she knew that Hazel was worried about Sarah. As a result, and due to Hazel's health issues, Anna had been trying to play it down.

"I met someone during my last trip . . . he had just finished his thesis," Hazel said slowly, "it was about communal living in the past two decades."

"Oh . . . ?"

"I asked him for his phone number . . . because I still thought Sarah was missing then, and I thought he might be a good resource. Then when Sarah was home, I forgot all about him." She popped open a peapod, sliding the peas out with her thumb. "But I remember that he mentioned how Oregon had more communes per capita than any other place. He said it was because of the liberal political environment here."

Anna reached for more peapods. "I suppose that makes sense."

Hazel nodded. "And I suspect that Sarah is still in Oregon."

Anna dropped the shiny green peas into the metal bowl then stared at Hazel. "Really?"

"If I were a betting woman, I'd make a wager on it."

Anna considered this. "I hope you're right. It would be a comfort to think that she's not too far away . . . in case she decides to leave and come home to us."

"It might make it easier for you to find her if

she's in Oregon. That is if you plan to look for her . . . and I'm guessing you do." Hazel made a weary smile. "I can give you my friend's name, if you like. He could probably tell you the names and locations of the communes located in Oregon."

"Yes," Anna said eagerly. "I'd like that."

Anna spent the next couple of weeks going over the list she'd gotten from Hazel's friend. Combining his information with a map that she marked, she was getting a vague sense of how many communal farms were in Oregon. However, she soon discovered that some of the communes had broken up and some of them didn't have listed phone numbers. But many of them did and, as a result, it didn't take long for Anna to cross a number of them from her list. And she was pleasantly surprised at how helpful some of the communal members were.

"I've heard about that place," a guy told her after she described the commune Sarah and Jewel had been part of. "It sounded like a real mess to me. We're not like that at all here. Mostly we believe in group cooperation and utilizing our various individual gifts and talents. And, believe me, if someone's unhappy here, and it doesn't happen too often, they just leave. No questions asked." He chuckled. "In fact, we're usually glad to see them go."

"Too bad all communes aren't like that," she told him.

"Good luck finding your granddaughter," he said kindly. "And I'll be sure to ask around here, to see if anyone's heard anything about this guru guy you mentioned."

She thanked him and hung up, trying not to feel discouraged. At the very least, she was getting the word out, leaving her phone number, and narrowing her search. Of course, it was possible that Hazel's hunch was wrong and that Sarah was on the other side of the world by now. Still, Anna wasn't ready to give up.

"Any luck?" Jewel asked as Anna pored over her list and map. One of Jewel's chores was cleaning the main house, and she'd been dusting the bookshelf while Anna made her calls.

"Not yet," Anna admitted.

"I'm sorry." Jewel slid a book back onto the shelf.

Anna studied her for a moment. "So, tell me, how are you doing? You seem to be settling in just fine. And I know everyone's been pleased with your work. But are you happy here?"

"I love it here." Jewel beamed at her. "It feels more like a home than anyplace I've been."

Considering Jewel's history, Anna wasn't going to take this as too high of a compliment. "And you don't mind the work?"

"I love it. And Diane and Janelle have been so

cool." Now Jewel looked slightly nervous. "Are you happy with me? I mean am I doing anything wrong or—"

"You're doing just fine," Anna assured her. "And it's so helpful having an extra worker. It gives me more time to help with Hazel . . ." she glanced at her map, "and other things."

"Oh, good." Jewel looked relieved.

"And you don't mind having your room up here in the house?"

She shook her head. "Not at all. It makes me feel like . . . ," she paused as if embarrassed, "well, almost like I'm part of the family."

Anna wrapped her arms around the girl, pulling her close. "You are part of the family, Jewel. And if Sarah ever comes home, I'm sure she'll greet you like a sister."

Jewel looked at Anna with tears in her eyes. "I hope so."

As summer passed, the inn stayed busy, and Anna's search for Sarah continued. Occasionally, prompted by a good lead or just an intuition, Anna would drive out to visit a commune. But as Labor Day drew near, Anna's hopes for finding Sarah in Oregon dwindled considerably. Despite a fairly exhaustive search, none of them, not Sarah or Aaron or Misty or any of the other names Jewel had given to her, had been familiar to any of the contacts Anna had made. It truly felt like looking for a needle in a haystack.

It didn't help that Lauren was blaming herself more and more for her missing daughter. "If only I'd been more understanding," she said one afternoon when Hazel and Anna and Jewel were having tea together. "Or if I'd taken the office work home to do. If I'd just given Sarah more space, she'd probably still be here now."

"If you want to play the blame game, maybe I should buy a ticket, too," Hazel told her. "If I hadn't come home from my tour when I did, booting poor Sarah out of my cabin, perhaps she'd still be here."

"Oh, Hazel." Anna shook her head. "That's perfectly ridiculous."

"Or not." Hazel took a sip of tea. "Having a place to come home to is very important—especially to young people."

"That's true," Jewel agreed sadly. "I hate to admit it, but I worry a lot . . . that Sarah is going to come home and want her room back. Then I don't know what I'll do."

"You'll come live with me," Lauren assured her. "There's plenty of room at Babette's house, and I'd love to have you."

"And the new cabins are nearly done," Anna told them. "Really, we'll have no lack of space. And with the season drawing to an end, we'll have even more room. So, please, let's all stop blaming ourselves for Sarah's choices. It's a waste of time and energy. Instead of fretting over her, we should be praying for her and sending her positive thoughts, hoping that she'll remember the river . . . and us."

They assured Anna that they were doing this, and then Lauren cleared her throat. "While I have you together like this, I have an announcement to make."

Anna turned to look at her daughter, feeling almost surprised to see that Lauren's blond hair was now streaked with gray and that she had slight wrinkles fanning around her eyes. How was this possible?

"I've registered for classes," she told them.

"Classes?" Anna was confused.

Lauren looked at Hazel who nodded as if she was in on this. "Hazel has been encouraging me to continue my education for several years now. So I finally applied at a business college last spring. I didn't really know if I'd actually want to go, especially at my age, but there seemed no harm in applying. Then when I was accepted, I wasn't so sure. So I didn't say anything. But after all that's happened with Sarah, well, it seemed like a good idea for me to be gone. In case she returns. I think it will simplify things for everyone if I moved on."

"Moved on?" Anna felt alarmed.

"Classes start in mid-September," Lauren explained. "I plan to do a full year."

"But who will help me with the business?" Although Anna knew that she could easily take it over again, especially this time of year when it slowed down, she had loved having Lauren's help. And Lauren had been so good at it.

"I've been training Diane," Lauren told her. "She's a natural, and I think she can handle it. She really wants this opportunity, Mom."

"But Lauren, I rely on you for so—"

"I think this is wonderful news," Hazel told Anna in a firm tone. "Lauren is an intelligent woman. It will be good for her to continue her education. Don't you think?"

Anna didn't know what to think. It was hard enough to lose Sarah, but now Lauren, too. It seemed so unfair. And yet she knew Hazel was right. This was a big opportunity for Lauren. It was wrong to hold her back. Anna made a weak smile. "I think it sounds like a very wise plan, Lauren."

Lauren let out a relieved sigh. "Really?"

"Yes. I'm proud of you for doing this."

Lauren made a nervous smile. "Can you imagine me, a middle-aged woman, going back to school with a bunch of kids my daughter's age?"

"Or Jewel's age." Hazel nodded to Jewel. "And what about you, dear? Do you ever want to further your education?"

Jewel shrugged. "I don't know. It seems like an impossible dream to me."

"Speaking of impossible dreams . . ." Hazel looked at Anna. "I have a dream, too." Her pale eyes sparked unexpectedly, as if she were truly excited. "I want to create a Shining Waters scholarship fund." Now she started to describe how she wanted to set up an account that Anna would manage for her. "To help out inn workers who want to attend college but lack funds. Do you think that's something that would interest you, Anna, as their employer? Do you feel you could help me with it?"

"It's a lovely idea, Hazel." Anna nodded. "I'd be happy to help in any way I can."

Hazel pointed to Jewel. "And perhaps you'll want to apply for it, too." She looked back at Anna. "And, of course, Sarah would benefit from it . . . when she comes home."

Shortly after Labor Day, Anna and Hazel worked together with a lawyer to change Hazel's will as well as to create the Shining Waters Scholarship Fund. Then, just one week later, Lauren set off to college.

"One thing you can count on around here," Clark said as they were having coffee on the upper deck, "is it's always changing."

"And yet some things stay the same." Anna looked out over the river and sighed. "For that I'm very thankful."

"Jewel has expressed interest in working at

the store when it's finished," Clark told her. "I said she should speak to you about it, but I expect it to be ready to open by next week."

"I think that's a great idea. Working at the store might help her confidence. She seems so unsure of herself, and I know she can do more than just housekeeping. Not that there's anything wrong with housekeeping. I certainly did it for many years."

"And there's nothing wrong with your confidence," Clark said with a twinkle in his eye.

"But if Jewel takes on a new challenge and succeeds at it . . . maybe she'll want to take advantage of your mother's scholarship fund."

"You mean Shining Waters Scholarship Fund," he corrected.

She nodded. "You're right." Hazel had corrected her on this very thing more than once. "It's so generous of her to do this."

"She was a little concerned that Marshall and I would feel cut out of her will." Clark laughed. "I told her that we're both doing just fine and not to worry."

Later that morning, Anna stopped by Hazel's cabin and was surprised to see that Hazel was in bed. "Are you unwell?" Anna asked as she pulled a chair beside the bed.

"Just worn out is all."

Anna reached for Hazel's hand. "Your heart?"

Hazel just slowly closed her eyes, but Anna knew that meant yes.

"Should I get Clark to call the doctor or the hospital?"

"No." Hazel opened her eyes. "Not this time, Anna."

"What do you mean?"

"I don't want to go . . . like that."

"Go . . . ?" Anna felt a jolt of panic but tried to keep her face calm.

"I had a dream . . . last night." She paused to catch her breath.

"Do you need some water?" Anna asked.

Hazel just nodded, and Anna hurried to the kitchen then, returning with a glass of water, waited as Hazel took some slow sips.

"My dream," Hazel began again, handing the glass back to Anna. "It's preparing me to go."

"What do you mean?" Anna felt a lump in her throat as she sat down again.

"I was walking alongside a river of gold . . . sparkling gold . . . and it was so peaceful . . . so beautiful." She sighed. "I think it was heaven. God is preparing me to go home."

Anna tried to hide her sadness.

Hazel looked into Anna's eyes. "First I want to thank you, Anna."

"Thank me for what?"

"For allowing me to share this special place with you . . . for letting me be part of your life . . .

193

for how you help others to forgive . . . and your healing touch . . . for showing us how to live in peace . . . thank you."

Anna didn't know what to say.

"You've given many of us a home, Anna. Sometimes for a few days . . . sometimes for many more. You've created a place that feels like a small portion of the heavenly home that awaits us. For that, I thank you."

Anna took Hazel's hand again, gently squeezing it. "Then I must thank you, too, Hazel."

Hazel looked surprised. "What for?"

"For coming here and befriending me. It was a very fragile time in my life . . . that day I met you on the river. I had no idea that you held so many keys."

"Keys?" Hazel's brows arched with interest.

"The key to my grandmother's stories, the key to my past, the key to my future."

Hazel waved a tired hand. "Oh, you're wrong about that. You already had those keys. All you had to do was to follow your heritage."

"But you helped me see my heritage."

"It was already in you, Anna."

Anna shook her head. "Maybe it was there. But it was locked up. You had the key, Hazel. I thank you for that." Now she smiled. "Not only that, but you brought Clark into my world . . . how could I ever thank you enough for that?"

Hazel's eyes lit up. "Clark needed you, Anna.

I'm just thankful I happened by at the right time to find you."

"So am I." Anna clasped her other hand around Hazel's cool one, warming it between her own. "Sometimes I imagine that it was my grandmother who called you to the river. She was the one who arranged our meeting that day when I was in my canoe and you were exploring," she confessed quietly, "because Grandma Pearl knew how much I needed you."

Hazel's pale lips curled into a knowing smile . . . as if she'd had this very same thought . . . as if she knew, as Anna knew, their lives had always been meant to be linked. She wondered if Hazel and Grandma Pearl were soon to be linked as well. Anna believed in the goodness of heaven and the afterlife, but she was not ready to say good-bye to this dear friend yet. And she knew Clark wasn't either.

17

It was early October, one of those flawless autumn afternoons when the river ran blue as topaz and the sunlight felt rich and pure, and Anna was carrying a fragrant basket of Northern Spy apples to Hazel's cabin with the plan of peeling and paring them into pie filling for tonight's dessert. But Hazel, who had been surprisingly energetic these past few days, now appeared to be sleeping. Leaned back in the old wicker rocker in front of her cabin, a well-worn and faded quilt draped over her lap, one sewn by Anna's mother and dear friend Babette, Hazel looked perfectly peace-ful . . . and still. Very, very still.

Anna set the basket on the porch step and touched Hazel's pale cheek to find that it was cold . . . and she knew . . . Hazel was gone. Pulling a straight-backed chair next to the rocker with a loud scrape, Anna eased herself into it, bent over, placing her head in her hands, and quietly wept. This was how Clark found her . . . found them. Being Clark and a natural caretaker, he gathered Anna in his arms then walked her back to the house and to their room.

As she lay on the bed, still crying softly, she could hear him using the phone in the office, calling someone in town, making arrangements. Thankful for his strength, Anna allowed her tears to flow. She knew that death was simply a part of life . . . and that Hazel had lived a good one . . . but it was still hard to say good-bye. It always had been. Perhaps even more so as Anna felt the years accumulating in her own life . . . her own mortality looming nearer with each passing year. These were the times when Anna drew near to God . . . and when she felt him drawing near to her.

Clark was no longer in the house when Anna rose from her bed and washed her face with cool water. She smoothed her graying hair back into the French twist she'd made this morning then went outside just in time to see Greeley's delivery boat slipping into their dock. Johnny Johnson's boat was already docked there, and Anna suspected that Clark had called him to help. Johnny had become something of a regular at Shining Waters, and Clark and he were forging what seemed like a solid friendship. Anna watched from the stairs as Bobby Greeley and another young man were met by Clark and Johnny, and together, the four of them removed a simple pine box, unloading it onto the dock.

Blinking back fresh tears, Anna turned and went back into the house, and, closing the door, she noticed the basket of Northern Spies on the dining room table. Clark must've brought it in. She carried the basket into the kitchen where she stood by the sink and began to peel an apple. She was just finishing the last one when Jewel came in.

"I heard the news," Jewel said quietly. "I'm sorry."

Anna nodded. "We'll all miss her."

"Clark asked me to tell you that he went into town . . . with her." Jewel's eyes were filled with tears, and Anna set down the half-peeled apple then wrapped her arms around the girl.

"Hazel was a very good woman," Anna said quietly. "She lived a very good life."

"I know," Jewel sobbed. "But I just wanted more time with her—you know—to get to know her better."

"I know." Anna nodded. "So did I."

Jewel helped Hazel to make the pie filling. Enough for several pies. As Anna rolled out the dough, she remembered the recently created scholarship fund and decided to mention it to Jewel, reminding her of Hazel's firm conviction that higher education was important. "Not simply for career opportunities, but for quality of life," she said as she slipped a round of dough onto a pie tin. "And she hoped that you'd be one of the recipients," she told her. "Someday . . . when you're ready for it. Don't forget that, Jewel."

"Did you go to college?"

Anna sighed. "I started to . . . but marriage . . . life . . . interrupted."

"Do you wish you'd finished it?"

"I used to. But not now. I feel like I've continued my learning in other ways. Studying my heritage—thanks to Hazel—and learning how to run this inn . . . well, that's been an education in itself." Anna looked at the clock on the stove. "Speaking of education, I think Lauren will be out of her classes by now. If you can finish this for me, I'll call her to tell her about Hazel."

As expected, Lauren was upset by the sad

198

news. Anna tried to console her, reassuring her as she had with Jewel, that Hazel had lived a good life. "And on her own terms too, Lauren. Back in her day it was very unusual to be a single mom with a successful career."

"I remember when she told me I could do it, too," Lauren said sadly. "Back when I was pregnant with Sarah. If only I'd listened to her then."

"What's important is that you're listening now." Anna forced brightness into her voice. "Hazel was so proud of you for going back to school, Lauren. I think you were the inspiration behind her scholarship fund. And you know how happy that made her."

They talked a while longer, and Anna promised to call back with details of the funeral arrangements. "I'm guessing we'll have a service during the weekend . . . so that Marshall and Joanna can come."

"I wish Sarah could—" Lauren's voice broke.

"So do I."

"I just keep blaming myself," Lauren confessed, "for everything."

"Blaming yourself for everything? Whatever for?"

"If only I'd handled things differently with Sarah, Mom, she never would've have run away. Not the first time and not the last time." She sighed. "Believe me I've had time to think about her. And I know that if Sarah hadn't left, there would've been less stress on everyone—including you and Clark. And I know that Hazel felt really bad about Sarah taking off like that. Remember how she even blamed herself, thinking that if she hadn't come home and Sarah could've kept living in her cabin—and Hazel's health seemed to go downhill right at that time. So it only makes sense. All this sadness and loss is all thanks to me. If I'd just been a better mom, a better person, things would be different now."

"Oh, Lauren." Anna didn't know what to say. On some levels, this made sense, but it wasn't healthy for Lauren to obsess over it. "I think it's good to look at your choices and realize that you made some mistakes. But instead of beating yourself up, you need to simply learn from the mistakes and determine not to make them again. And I believe you're doing that. You're on a good path, Lauren. Focus on that."

"I'm trying to, Mom. But I just keep thinking there must be something I'm missing . . . something I can do to fix this."

"To fix what?"

"I mean with Sarah. And I've got an idea." Now Lauren told of her plan to use her weekends to search for Sarah. "If you can send me your lists and your map, I can take over where you left off, Mom."

"But what about your studies?"

"I do my homework in the evenings," Lauren

explained. "My weekends are long and boring."

"Then come home," Anna urged, "you know you're welcome here. Jewel is staying at Babette's house, and I know she'd love your company."

"I'd rather spend my time looking for Sarah." There was a firmness in her voice that told Anna she wasn't going to back down. "It would help if I could have your information."

"I'll send it to you tomorrow," Anna promised.

"And you don't mind?"

Anna sighed. "Not at all. As long as it doesn't interfere with your classes."

"Knowing that I'm doing everything I can to find her might help me focus on my classes, Mom. It might help alleviate some of this guilt."

"Forgiving yourself would help even more," Anna reminded her. "And remembering that God has forgiven you."

"I know, I know." Her tone grew impatient. "But until I get Sarah's forgiveness . . . I'm not sure I can forgive myself or that it would matter."

Anna wanted to tell her that it did matter, but somehow she knew Lauren wouldn't hear this at the present. "We'll get back to you about Hazel's service as soon as we know more," Anna said before they hung up. "I love you, Lauren."

"I love you, too, Mom."

By the time Anna hung up the phone, Jewel was putting the pies into the oven and Janelle and Diane were coming into the house, expressing their sadness and sympathy. Anna asked if any of the guests were concerned or disturbed by this afternoon's turn of events. "Is there something I should do to reassure anyone?" she asked Diane.

"No," Diane told her. "We've been explaining the situation. Everyone has been really sweet and understanding."

Later that evening, after dinner, Anna asked the entire staff to come up to the house for a meeting as well as for some apple pie. Clark explained to them that he wanted to hold the memorial service at the river. "It was her favorite place in the whole world," he told them. "It seems fitting that we should commemorate her life here."

"What about the other guests?" Diane asked. "Only about half the cabins and rooms are full right now, but we do have quite a few booked for the weekend. Will that be a problem?"

"Everyone will be invited to everything," Clark explained. "I think Mom would've liked that."

"I agree," Anna said. "Hazel was always a natural when it came to interacting with the guests. She loved meeting them and hearing their stories. And Hazel is a part of the history here. I would think most guests would appreciate hearing her story and honoring her memory."

With Diane acting as secretary, they went over the details, making plans for a real celebration of life that would begin with an afternoon service on Saturday, followed by a dinner, and finally a bonfire. "Mom always loved the bonfires," Clark said finally. "Hopefully there will be a lot of sharing and remembering on Saturday night."

Hazel would've loved her memorial service. Anna knew it. Not just that it was well attended and that her family and friends remembered her fondly. But something about the spirit of the day was so sweet and special—almost as if she had orchestrated it herself. Hazel would've been proud of how her son handled everything. Throughout the day, Clark had played the part of host with honor and dignity. Whether he was with a guest who'd never met his mother or with his grieving son, Marshall, Clark remained gracious and kind.

And later that evening, during the bonfire and after everyone else seemed to have finished sharing stories and memories of Hazel, Clark stood and told everyone about how his relationship with his mother had been less than ideal during his early years. He confessed that he'd sometimes felt neglected by Hazel's career and responsibilities when he was boy. "But I came to understand these things better as I grew older. When I became a parent, I began to realize why my mother did what she did, and I came to fully respect her for it. She was an amazing woman, and I'm extremely thankful she was my mother. I'm also very thankful for the time I got to spend with her these past twenty years. I realize the quality of that time had a lot to do with being here together on the river," he said finally. "Something about this place allows people to slow down and take time to fully appreciate life and relationships." He turned to smile at Anna as she stood beside him. "That is a very special gift."

"A gift that Hazel had a lot to do with," Anna continued. She swept her hands across the small crowd gathered around the fire. "I can honestly say that without Hazel's help and encouragement, The Inn at Shining Waters might have never been realized. This place, all it's become, all it will continue to be, is due in part to Hazel. I will be forever grateful for the part she played in my life . . . in all our lives."

Anna paused, watching as the bonfire crackled and snapped, shooting bright orange sparks into the ebony sky. And now, Marshall started strumming on his guitar, and he and Janelle sang Hazel's favorite hymn, "Amazing Grace."

18

It wasn't unusual for Clark to spend more time away from the inn during their off-season. In fact, it was something Anna had always encouraged him to do in previous years. It seemed only fair that after working so hard during the height of the season, and after finishing some building projects, that he should enjoy some free time to go fishing or crabbing or to just meet a buddy in town. Now, with some additional staff hired, plus the new cabins and store finished, there wasn't all that much for Clark to do around the inn.

But during the weeks following Hazel's death, Anna noticed that Clark seemed to be gone more than ever. Breakfast would barely be finished and he would be heading down to the docks, hopping into his boat, and heading downriver. At first she assumed this was his way of dealing with the loss of his mother. But as October drew to an end, she wasn't so sure. She began to notice that when Clark was around the inn, he seemed distracted or preoccupied. And sometimes he would sit at his desk for hours in the evening, but if Anna asked him what he was working on, he'd close his desk and say, "Nothing much."

When Anna asked him if he was grieving for his mother, he seemed uncertain. They would talk about it for a while and then he would assure her that he was handling it. But the next morning, off he would go again. Anna couldn't decide whether she was more worried about him or if she simply missed his company. But she was definitely disturbed by his absence.

It didn't help that she now missed Hazel as well as Lauren and Sarah. How was it possible that all the women had been removed from her life? And now, the man she depended upon seemed to be removing himself as well.

"Is something wrong?" she asked him one evening in early November.

He glanced up from a contractor's magazine he'd been poring over. "Wrong?"

She looked directly at him. "With us?"

He shook his head and set the magazine aside. "Not that I know of."

"Oh . . ." She closed her book.

Now he got up and threw another log onto the fire that he'd built earlier that evening, and coming over, he sat next to her on the old leather sofa. "Do you think something's wrong?"

"I don't know." She reached up to touch his gray hair, thinking that he was overdue for a hair-cut. "I just feel like, well, maybe we're drifting apart."

He looked slightly alarmed. "Drifting apart?"

She nodded. "You seem different, Clark. I thought it was losing your mother, but now I'm not sure. Is it us?"

He touched her cheek and smiled. "It's not us, not as far as I'm concerned, darling."

"What then?"

He made a mysterious smile and shrugged. "Maybe your imagination?"

"Or maybe I'm just lonely."

"Lonely?" he looked surprised. "But you're

always surrounded by people, Anna. Jewel and Diane and Janelle always seem to be coming and going up here. And there are the other workers. And the guests. It seems every time I turn around, one of them wants to speak to you. If anyone should never feel lonely, sweetheart, it's you."

Anna knew that was true. She did seem to be in constant demand at the inn. Even with the extra workers, it seemed she remained busier than ever. But that was partly due to Lauren's leaving. Anna had probably taken for granted how much Lauren's presence here helped. "I guess I'm just missing Lauren," she said sadly.

"Why don't you call her?"

"Because I know she studies in the evenings." Anna looked at the clock, surprised to see that it was so late and wondering if Lauren might still be up. "And then she spends her weekends searching for Sarah."

Clark frowned. "Any hope on that front?"

She just shook her head. "At least she is narrowing down the list. We know where Sarah *isn't*. And even though Oregon has more than its fair share of communal farms, there is a limit to them. So maybe we're getting closer."

"Unless . . ." He paused.

"Unless?"

"Never mind." He pressed his lips tightly together as if wanting to retract that last word.

"No, what were you going to say?"

He sighed. "Unless she's left the country."

Anna didn't want to think about that. She read the news enough to know there were many cults and groups moving about these days. Sometimes they'd arrive in this country only to get opposition from the government and then leave again. With all this coming and going, it would be nearly impossible to track someone down on an international level.

"Sorry, darling. I didn't mean to suggest that. And I doubt that's happened. It wouldn't be easy to get out of the country without a passport and money, which I doubt Sarah has."

"Unless someone with money and influence helped her," Anna said quietly.

"Sarah has a good head on her shoulders and a strong will. She won't let anyone take her where she doesn't want to go."

Anna wanted to believe that. On many levels she *did* believe that. But she also remembered Jewel telling her about how Daniel had recognized Sarah's intelligence and how he'd wanted to harness her spirit and energy for his own gain. What if another "spiritual leader"—perhaps someone more evil than Daniel—wanted to do the same?

Clark reached up to pull Anna from the sofa. "It's late, sweetheart, and you look tired. Let's say we call it a day." He kissed her forehead, inhaling the scent of her hair, just like he used to do when they'd first met. And, as small as that gesture was, it was reassuring. Perhaps they weren't really drifting apart after all.

Life at Shining Waters calmed down as mid-November approached. Anna loved this time of year—everything from the deep russet and golden-toned leaves to the musky earth smell of the river. This was a time of year for slowing down, contemplating, preparing for winter. Not that their winters were ever too difficult here. Sometimes in January, the temperatures would stay in the upper sixties, and it was hard not to believe it was June.

To Anna's dismay, Clark continued going his own way. Usually without saying much about where he was going or why he stayed away so long. It was some consolation to see that Johnny Johnson was often going with him. Perhaps Clark was simply trying to help a troubled friend. And, she reminded herself, she was the one who had brought Johnny into their lives. She had asked Clark to reach out to him.

To distract herself from feeling lonely for Lauren and Sarah and Hazel, Anna had taken up one of her mother's old hobbies. She was making a quilt. It had been Jewel's idea to start with when, while rearranging a closet at Babette's house, she'd come across a box of old quilt patterns and quilting tools. She told Anna about her find and asked if she could use them to make a quilt.

"I'd like to see these things myself," Anna said. "Perhaps we could make something together."

So Jewel had brought the box, along with another box of fabric scraps, over to the inn. And one quiet afternoon, the two of them sat down together to figure it out. Anna thought this might be a lovely way for them to spend time together. And she'd been missing Jewel since she'd relocated to Babette's house. And for a few days, they both thoroughly enjoyed the process of selecting fabrics and colors, of pinning and cutting out the various shapes. But it didn't take long for Jewel to lose interest.

Anna knew this was partially due to one of the guy workers hired last summer, a sincere young man named Skip Halverson. When Jewel realized that Skip was interested in her, her focus on quilting seemed to evaporate. And her spare time as well.

But Anna persisted with it. She found something very soothing about using a softly worn paper pattern to cut shapes of patterned fabric then using needle and thread to work these small colorful pieces into something larger. The process felt like a sweet metaphor about life and people and relationships, carefully positioned and stitched together. Besides that, it gave her a sense of control and well-being . . . and hope. And, inspired by comments from some of the guests who'd heard what she was doing, she decided to set up a quilting corner in the downstairs dining room. She repositioned one of the big wooden dining tables over by the woodstove, laying out a rainbow of fabrics as well as the necessary quilting tools, hoping to entice even more interest. It wasn't long before several of the female guests were joining her.

"I feel as if I've gone back in time," Mrs. Parrish said as they worked together one gray morning. "My husband is out fishing in the fog, and I'm here sewing by the fireside." She chuckled as she threaded a needle. "And to think I could be answering phones and typing transcriptions in the law office right now." The Parrishes were regular summer guests who had come to the inn for several days to celebrate their thirtieth anniversary.

"Does it make you want to live like this always?" a younger woman asked her.

Mrs. Parrish tilted her head to one side as if giving this careful thought. "I don't think so. Vernon loves practicing law, and I love assisting him. No . . . this is a nice change of pace for us, and it's always a good reminder that sometimes we all need to slow down. But, no, I don't think I could live like this always." She glanced at Anna. "I marvel that you and Clark can do it full time. That you've been doing it all these years. Do you ever miss things like theater, music, or the arts?"

Anna smiled. "I suppose my taste in those

things is rather simple. I can satisfy them here on the river and in town."

"But what about the pace?" the other woman asked. She and her husband were new to the inn. "Do you ever get bored out here like this?"

Anna laughed. "Not at all. In fact, Clark sometimes complains that it's going to be harder for us to keep up at this pace. Especially as we get older. Trust me, it's not always this slow around here."

"And if you don't believe her, you should see this place in the summertime," Mrs. Parrish told the new guest. "It's hopping. We've brought our kids here since they were preteens, and, oh, the memories we have here on the river. We plan to bring our grandchildren in July. It will be their first visit, and we can hardly wait to see what they think of it."

"Anna?" Diane called into the dining room.

Anna looked up from where she was stitching a triangle shape of robin's egg blue. "Yes?"

"Lauren is on the phone."

"Oh?" Anna looked at the big clock in the dining room as she stood. It wasn't yet ten o'clock, and since it was a weekday. Lauren should've been in class.

"She said it's important," Diane told her.

"Thank you." Anna made her way to the door. "Perhaps you'd like to put some tea on for the ladies. I was about to do that."

"I'm on it," Diane called as Anna went out.

Anna felt conflicting feelings as she hurried to the house. Was something wrong at school? Had Lauren gotten hurt somehow? Or, more hopefully, perhaps Lauren had some kind of good news.

"Hello, Lauren?" she said breathlessly.

"Oh, Mom!" Lauren sounded upset. "Have you heard the news?"

"What news?"

"About the tragedy in *Guyana? Jonestown? The Peoples Temple?*"

"No." Anna sat down. "What is it?"

Lauren's words came tumbling out, one on top of the other, something about a cult group that had left the United States, a crazy leader named Jim Jones, hundreds of followers dead . . . including children, poisoned Kool-Aid. Horrifying!

"What?" Anna felt her heart giving a lurch. "Poisoned Kool-Aid?"

Lauren was talking between sobs now. "Yes, that's what they're saying on the news, that this horrible man forced all these people—men, women, children—to drink *poisoned Kool-Aid,* and they found them there, and they were all dead. All of them!"

"Oh, dear." Anna felt a tightness in her chest. "Do you think? Do you know? Was Sarah among them?"

"I don't know, Mom. I'm trying to find out. I've called some numbers. The guy told me it's

213

going to take some time to sort it all out. I gave them my contact information. And yours, too, in case I'm not home. I hope that's okay."

"Of course." Anna took in a deep breath, trying to hold back tears. "But you don't really think . . ."

"I don't know what to think. But it's too close to home for us to ignore. The Peoples Temple was in northern California, Mom. They left from there to go to Guyana a few years ago, but it sounds as if they continued gathering members even up to fairly recently. And from what I've heard, they didn't sound that much different than the last group, you know, the one Sarah and Jewel belonged to. Do you think Jewel would know anything about the Peoples Temple or if that other commune had any connections to it?"

"I'll ask her."

"I'm sorry to call with such alarming news," Lauren said in a shaky voice. "But I didn't want someone to contact you with . . . bad news about Sarah . . . without you even knowing about this."

"You did the right thing to call." Anna tried to keep her voice even. "And I'll turn on the radio and see what I can learn. But you know how we are out here—we don't get the latest news like you do."

"I'll keep you posted. And maybe we should keep the phone lines free."

"Yes." Anna hated to hang up. "And I'll be

praying. I'll ask everyone here to pray. Not just for Sarah, but for all those poor people . . . and their families."

But before Anna could tell anyone else this gruesome news, she had to hear it for herself from a news source. With a trembling hand, she turned on the radio, hoping that it was all just a mistake. Perhaps some horrible mean hoax that a student had played on Lauren's college. Really, *poisoned Kool-Aid?* It sounded crazy, like something out of a horror movie. But when the hourly news came on, it was the first thing mentioned. And it was as bad as what Lauren had reported . . . and worse. It seemed a California congressman and a number of other delegates and newsmen had gone down there to help some members defect from what some considered a dangerous cult, and that they had been shot by Temple members. Some were injured, and some, including the congressman, were dead. The estimated toll of dead men, women, and children was mounting. More than four hundred bodies found so far. But that many, or more, were still missing. Most suspected to be Americans.

Anna fell to her knees on the floor by the radio and began to pray. With a sense of sickened shock and panicked disbelief, she prayed on behalf of all those poor lost souls . . . she prayed for their surviving families . . . and finally she prayed for Sarah.

• • •

News of the Jonestown disaster spread quickly around the inn. As did the fear that Anna and Clark's granddaughter could be amongst the dead. When Clark got home, shortly before dinner, Anna was still sitting in the living room, next to the phone, with the radio on. A part of her knew this was senseless. What was done was done, and there was nothing she could do to change anything. But another part of her felt paralyzed.

"I just heard about it," Clark said as he gathered her in his arms. "I'm so sorry, Anna. But, really, we don't know if Sarah was there or not. Maybe we should just hope for the best."

"And be prepared for the worst," she said quietly.

"Has Lauren heard anything?"

"She called about an hour ago. So far Sarah's name hasn't shown up on any of the records, but it's going to take time to sort it all out. Lauren is saying she wants to go down there."

"No," he said firmly. "If anyone goes down there, it will be me. Does Sarah's dad know about this?"

"Lauren said she knows he has to have heard the news. Who hasn't? But he hasn't called her. She figures he assumes that Sarah isn't down there."

"And he's probably right," Clark said solidly.

"I hope and pray he's right . . . but we don't

know." Anna pushed a strand of hair from her forehead and sighed.

"Don't forget how many communal groups there are in Oregon and California alone," he reminded her. "Chances are in Sarah's favor that she's still up here in one of them."

"Maybe . . ." Anna took in a steadying breath. "But we've contacted so many . . . and she's never found."

"But what about the guru from India?" he asked. "This Jonestown place didn't have a guru like that."

"You know how those cults and communes are," she said. "Kids come and go, traveling from one place to the next . . . searching . . . hoping to find that perfect utopia, that piece of their soul that's missing."

"Or to find a family," Clark offered.

"We are her family!" Anna exclaimed. "We love her, Clark! Why couldn't she see that?"

"You're exhausted from all this emotion and stress," he said as he walked her to the bedroom. "I want you to take a break. I'll sit by the phone; and I'll listen for news on the radio. And I'll have one of the girls bring our dinners up." He set her firmly on the edge of the bed. "You just close your eyes for a while. Sleep if you can. Pray if you need to. But do not get up."

She did as told . . . except that she could not sleep. Images of those lifeless people—children, mothers, and babies, all laid out across the Peoples Temple property just as the newscasters had described them today—seemed to be embedded into her mind. It was all she could think of . . . and so she continued to pray.

19

Anna knew from experience that *family* was more than just blood relatives. And the day following the horrific news in Guyana, she discovered a renewed sense of family in her staff and guests. Their concern and support was evident and encouraging. And it was a great comfort to know that many of them, like her, were praying.

"My nephew joined a commune about eight or nine years ago," Mrs. Parrish told Anna as several of the women gathered in the quilting area a few days later. "My sister told me that he even experimented with LSD." She made a grim expression. "But he only lasted about a year in that place. You'd never know it to look at him now. He cleaned himself up, finished college, got a good job and a nice wife—and they're expecting their first child in December." She smiled. "So, you see, these things can still end happily."

Anna nodded. "That's what I'm hoping for."

The women shared more stories about friends

and relatives who went through rough periods and how things eventually turned around for them. "And don't forget it's a difficult era for young people in our country," Mrs. Croft said thoughtfully. A former high-school teacher, she'd been a regular guest at the inn since the early days. "Going through the Vietnam troubles and then the Nixon scandals . . . well, it was demoralizing for everyone. But I feel especially sorry for the younger generation. It's so different from when we were young, during the Depression when we all worked together to get by. And during the war, we experienced a sense of patriotism and pride, followed by victory. This generation hasn't had that. Can you imagine how frustrated they must feel?" She sadly shook her head. "I witnessed so much apathy in my students . . . it made it easy for me to retire last year."

"Anna?" Diane called from the doorway. "Lauren is on the phone—in the house."

Excusing herself, Anna left and hurried with Diane toward the house. "Did she say anything?" Anna asked as they climbed the stairs. "About Sarah?"

Diane shook her head. "But I didn't ask."

Anna hurried to the phone. "Hello Lauren?" she said breathlessly. "Have you any news?"

"The number of victims increases daily. I think it's over 900 now. But Sarah's name isn't on the list," Lauren told her.

"So she wasn't there," Anna said in relief.

"They told me they can't guarantee she's not among them, Mom."

"But her name's not on the list." Anna wanted to hold onto this hopeful piece of information. "How did they make the list?"

"It seems that Jim Jones had confiscated all the members' passports and put them in a locked box. The authorities found them and made a list. Sarah's name wasn't on it."

"Then she wasn't there," Anna said again. "Sarah wasn't in Jonestown."

"I feel really hopeful, Mom." Lauren let out a choked sob. "But at the same time I'm still scared. To think someone like Jim Jones can control people like that . . . to get them to take their own lives . . . and their children's . . . it's so frightening."

"I know."

"I don't like this world we live in, Mom."

"That is not the world we live in," Anna said calmly.

"How can you say that?"

"That world—the one that Jim Jones created in Guyana—is not our world." Anna looked out the window toward the mist-covered river, now a silvery shade of gray, draped in the soft afternoon light. "Our world is where we live, Lauren. It's being with family and friends. It's doing our best. It's the beautiful world God created for us. The river, the trees, the sky . . . this has been our world since our ancestors walked here. It will continue to be our descendants' world when we are gone. Remember that."

Lauren exhaled loudly. "You're right. Thanks, Mom. I needed to hear that just now."

"We are going to believe that Sarah is all right," Anna said firmly. "And we will keep praying for her welfare and that she'll be returned to us."

"And I'm going to keep looking for her," Lauren declared. "More than ever now. As soon as finals week is over, I'll make it my full-time job. I'm going to find her, Mom. I just know it."

"Let us know if there's anything we can do."

"Keep praying."

"We will."

"And I have a feeling that there will be a lot of parents as concerned as we are now. Maybe we can help one another."

"Speaking of other parents . . . does Donald have any thoughts about this?"

"Donald is oblivious, Mom. That's the way he likes it."

"He's not concerned about his own daughter?"

"He acts like she's just going through a phase that she'll outgrow someday."

"Hopefully, he's right."

"Well . . . yes. But it might be nice if he wasn't so nonchalant about it. If he showed a little more interest in helping search for her—instead of being so wrapped up in his new wife and her kids. It's like Sarah and I were never part of his life. Like we never even existed."

Anna controlled herself from reminding Lauren that she had as much to do with their failed marriage as Donald, probably more so. That was water under the bridge now.

"I know . . . I know . . . Donald is just being Donald. After all I put him through, I shouldn't expect anything more. And if I really wanted his help, all I'd need to do is ask."

"Donald loves Sarah."

"I know. The truth is, I'm glad he's not involved. I couldn't handle that stress right now. I'd rather do this—search for Sarah—on my own. I feel like I owe it to her."

"And to yourself."

"Yes. I couldn't live with myself if I didn't at least try."

They talked a while longer, and when Anna hung up, she felt a wave of relief washing over her.

"Good news?" Diane called from where she was working in the office.

"Sarah's name wasn't on the list!" Anna told her. "I don't think she was there at all."

"Thank God!" Diane exclaimed.

"Yes. Thank God!" Anna smiled. "Now I want to go tell the others the good news." As she went outside to search for Clark, who had been staying close to home recently, she silently sent up a heartfelt prayer of thanksgiving. Sarah was alive! She just knew it.

News continued to trickle in about what was now being called the Jonestown Massacre, but none of the news involved Sarah. While this was a relief, it was still disturbing to read the various accounts of the tragedy in Guyana. And yet Anna felt compelled to follow this story and to continue praying for the surviving family members, as well as families with missing loved ones involved in other cults. Anna knew that Jonestown was a wake-up call of sorts, a startling reminder of how a "utopian" society could easily become a scary place—not to mention a lethal place.

One morning in early December, Anna woke from a vivid and frustrating dream. As she made coffee, she replayed what she could remember of it through her mind. The dream had started out pleasantly. It was a lovely sunny day on the beach. Her feet were bare and the sand was warm. It seemed like it was Heceta Beach, near the campground where she and her family used to visit when she was a child. A hotel had been built there recently. Big, fancy, modern—and totally unlike Shining Waters.

But on the beach in her dream, the hotel was missing. And Anna had been walking by herself in the sunshine when she'd found a wounded seal. She tried to help the seal, but then the seal turned into a dog and ran away. And for some reason that had made her sad, and she was walking down the beach crying. As she walked, the sunshine was being swallowed by a bank of fog and clouds, and her despair continued, along with an overwhelm-ing sense of loneliness.

Soon she saw someone walking up ahead and somehow knew it was Lauren. Although Lauren was dressed differently and her hair was in long braids, Anna knew it was her. She called out to Lauren, trying to catch up, but couldn't make it to her. And then, she saw another image which looked like Sarah. She, too, was wearing long braids, which wasn't so unusual, and a long dress that looked like something their Siuslaw ancestors might've worn.

Again Anna called out and ran but couldn't catch Sarah either. Still she could see the two women walking up ahead of her. But she could see they weren't walking together because there was a wide space between them. Anna kept trying to catch up with them, but it seemed hopeless. Just when she was almost there, close enough to see them and close enough for them to hear her, they didn't stop walking. And finally they both just vanished in the fog, and she woke up with tears running down her cheeks.

"What did it mean?" she said quietly to her-self.

"What did what mean?" Clark said from behind her.

With her hand over her mouth, she turned to see him. "You caught me talking to myself," she confessed.

"Anything I should be concerned about?"

"Just mulling over a bad dream." She reached for another coffee mug.

"So . . . what did it mean?" he asked as he waited for her to fill the mugs.

She told him the dream as they sat at the kitchen table with their coffee, finally asking him if he knew what it meant.

"I'm not much good at interpreting dreams." He scratched his head. "That's usually your territory."

"Usually. But sometimes it's hard to be objective —or maybe it's subjective—about your own dreams."

"I think I know what it meant."

She tried not to look too surprised. "Really?"

"Actually, it seems pretty obvious now that I think about it. I suspect your dream was telling you that you need to separate yourself from your daughter and your granddaughter."

"Separate myself?" Anna frowned. "Lauren lives two hours away, and I have no idea where Sarah is. How much more separate can I be?"

He shrugged then took a slow sip of coffee, and for a while they just sat there.

"You think my life is too entwined in Lauren

and Sarah?" she finally asked him. "I'm too emotionally involved?"

"Maybe."

She considered this.

"Or I could be all wet," he said lightly.

She smiled. "Actually, I think you could be onto something."

He looked hopeful.

"Your mother told me that she thought the women in my family—all the ones she knew of anyway—that we all had to walk our own trail of tears. Remember the long walk on the beach to the reservation?"

He nodded.

"And maybe my dream meant we all have to walk it alone."

"Is it like you used to say, about how everyone has to paddle their own canoe?"

"Probably so."

"Do you think you lost sight of that?"

She sighed. "When Sarah came home last summer, I thought everything was going to be so perfect. Finally, my family would be complete. We've been through so much. I thought we were going to move beyond it. I finally had Lauren and Sarah, and even Hazel came home. And, of course, there was you. What could be better? I felt so hopeful for us. But then, as fast as it fell into place, it all started to unravel. I lost Sarah . . . then Lauren . . . then Hazel . . ."

He made a crooked smile. "I'm still here."

"And I'm thankful for that. But in some ways you've been missing, too."

His smile faded. "Sorry about that. But, trust me, it's going to get better. I promise."

"Don't get me wrong. I like that you've been spending time with Johnny. And I know he needs your friendship." She made an uneasy smile. "But I still need you, too."

His face lit up. "I'm so glad you do, Anna. Sometimes you seem so strong . . . you help everyone . . . I wonder if you really do need me."

She couldn't help but laugh. "I know you're not crazy, Clark. But that's an insane thing to say. Of course, I need you."

"It's nice being needed."

"I'm sure I needed you more than ever with this whole Jonestown thing," she confessed. "And maybe that's why I needed that dream. I've probably been trying too hard to hold onto Lauren and Sarah since that scare. I needed to be reminded that they are both on their own journey and that I can't go on it with them."

"Makes sense to me."

She smiled at him. "Seems as if you're a pretty good dream interpreter after all. Thanks."

20

December was always a slow month for the inn. But over the years Anna had come to think of this as her time to gather and reflect. In the past she used to "gather" what she needed for the upcoming season in the way of supplies and improvements and to "reflect" on how the previous year had gone and what she could do to make the inn a more pleasant experience for her guests. But then, Lauren had stepped into the management role. Because she took over many of the practical aspects of the business, Anna was able to enjoy a more philosophical sort of gathering and reflecting. But with Lauren away at business school and Diane's recent decision to return to college for winter semester, Anna found herself back in that old management role again.

Still, she appreciated having this distraction. It kept her from worrying about Sarah or missing Lauren and Hazel. Anna knew her world was changing . . . constantly changing. It had been like this since the beginning of the inn. But it seemed the older she became, the more she wanted to resist the changes. Or perhaps they just seemed to come at her at a more rapid pace. As crazy as it sounded, Anna sometimes wished she could stop the clock . . . and take a break from change.

"I have good news," Jewel told Anna one morning as they were working in the kitchen together. During the slow season, Anna liked to move the cooking back into her kitchen in the house, serving the guests at the big dining table, just like they used to do in the old days. It wasn't as convenient or modern as the downstairs facility, but it was much cozier and homier. And the guests seemed to appreciate it.

"What sort of news?" Anna asked as she adjusted the gas and turned the fried potatoes and onions in the big cast-iron skillet.

Jewel came over and held up her left hand in front of Anna's face. On her ring finger was an interesting-looking ring of twisted gold vines and a glowing opal that reminded Anna of a summer dawn.

"Very pretty," Anna peered curiously at Jewel, noticing that her eyes were sparkling even more than the ring. Anna blinked as realization set in. "Is that an *engagement* ring?"

Jewel nodded happily. "Skip proposed to me on Saturday."

Anna didn't know what to say. This seemed so sudden. How long had Jewel known Skip? Just a couple of months? No, Anna remembered, they'd met last summer. Even so, they were so young . . . and neither of them had been to college or even had much employment history. And yet,

Jewel looked so incredibly pleased that Anna knew she couldn't spoil this for her. Anna set down the spatula and hugged Jewel tightly. "Congratula-tions," she told her. "Skip seems like a fine young man."

Later when Anna told Clark about this new development, he seemed indifferent. "You weren't surprised by this?" she asked him as they walked down to the dock together.

"Not a bit. All you had to do was see that boy's eyes whenever Jewel came around and you knew he was hooked."

"Hooked?" Anna frowned.

He chuckled. "All she had to do was reel him in."

"But they're so young, Clark. How will they support themselves?"

He shrugged. "Just like the rest of us, Anna, one day at a time."

She couldn't help but smile since this was exactly the kind of thing she would usually say to him. "You're right. But I suppose I feel protective of Jewel. She's been through so much and doesn't really have any family to speak of. Plus she's turned out to be such a good worker. I'd hate to lose her."

"I'd hate to lose Skip, too. I was so relieved when he decided to stay on for the winter. He really seems to fit in here. He's a great outdoorsman and the guests like him a lot. He's one reason I've felt comfortable being away so much this fall."

Anna wasn't sure that was such a good thing but didn't want to complain about it. Especially since Clark had been staying closer to home these past couple of weeks. His boat trips with Johnny were only a couple of times a week now.

"But we'll get by," he continued as he reached for the windshield cleaning bucket and a rag. "We always do. Someone goes off to school or marries, and then someone new comes along. It all works out."

"Remember when we hoped that Marshall and Joanna would want to stay on here with us? After they got engaged?" She was simmering on an idea now. "To continue helping us with the inn?"

"Sure. But that wasn't what was best for them." He began cleaning the windshield of Anna's boat.

"I know. And I understand that." She handed him the window squeegee. "But what if Skip and Jewel wanted to do something like that?"

His brow creased as he pulled the squeegee across the glass. "Interesting idea . . ."

"What if we worked out some kind of plan for them? We could offer them a cabin to live in, food, of course. And perhaps even health benefits as well as their salary."

He paused, holding up the squeegee like a torch. "I definitely think it's something we should consider. But . . ." He frowned as if uncertain.

"But maybe we shouldn't mention it to them right away?"

"Maybe not. I'm sure they have a lot going through their heads right now. After all, they've just gotten engaged. Let's give them some time to think about what they want and where they're headed."

"I just don't want to lose them," she confessed. Suddenly she was remembering all the employees, including family members, who had come and gone over the years. Usually it didn't get to her like this, but for some reason it made her feel lonely today. Or maybe it was simply the gray sky and the solemn steel-colored river. She hated to admit it, even to herself, but sometimes she wondered if she needed a break from the river.

Clark set the bucket back down on the dock and nodded. "I don't want to lose them either. But you know as well as I do that we don't have much control over that."

"I know." She shoved her hands into the pockets of her old Pendleton jacket and nodded. "But I can pray about it."

Less than a week after the engagement announcement, Jewel asked to talk to Anna in private. Anna wasn't sure what this meant since it seemed they were already alone in the laundry room, where Anna had just set down a basket of sheets. But she could tell by Jewel's expression that this must be something important. "Want to meet me for coffee in my office?" Anna suggested.

Jewel made a nervous nod. "Let me get these towels in the dryer and start those sheets and I'll be right up."

Anna tried not to feel worried as she went upstairs. And, as she poured them each a cup of coffee, adding milk and sugar to Jewel's, she braced herself for what she suspected would be Jewel's next announcement—that she and Skip would be moving on. Clark had mentioned a conversation he'd had with Skip just yesterday. Skip's father had a plumbing business in town, and after hearing about the engagement, he had invited Skip to become a partner.

Before long, Anna and Jewel were seated in the office, and Anna waited for the nervous-looking girl to begin. "I don't know how to say this," Jewel finally said, "but you have been like family to me. Both you and Clark." She sniffed as if she was holding back tears. "That night when you let me leave with you in your car . . . and the way you took me into your home, gave me a job . . . well, I don't know if I can ever properly thank you for that."

Anna smiled. "That's not necessary. You know how much I love you, Jewel, how much I appreciate all you do around here."

"And I love being here. I love the river." Jewel bit her lip. "It's been like home."

233

"I'm glad you've enjoyed it here." Anna sighed. "And Clark told me that Skip is considering going into business with his dad and we understand. It's a great opportunity for—"

"But Skip doesn't want to be a plumber," she said suddenly. "He loves it here, too, Anna. Do you think there's any way we can continue to live here after we're married? I mean I realize I'm only using Babette's house until Lauren comes back. After she finishes school. And it would be unfair to ask you to let us live there. But is there—"

"Don't be so quick to give up on that," Anna said. Now she told her a bit about what she and Clark had discussed. "We would love to have a married couple in our employ," she explained. "It would lend some solidity to the positions. But it would only work if the couple really wanted to be here." She explained about Marshall and Joanna and how they had decided it wasn't the right fit for them.

"But we both love it here," Jewel assured her. "Skip was just saying that going to work for his dad—after working here on the river—would feel like going to prison."

"Really?"

"And Skip really respects Clark."

Anna felt a wave of relief. Perhaps everyone wasn't leaving them after all. "Well, we should all four sit down together and discuss this."

"Yes." Jewel nodded eagerly. "Whenever you want."

By the end of the week, the four of them reached an agreement. First of all, Jewel would move into one of the cabins so they could close up Babette's house for the winter. Then, following their wedding, which Skip and Jewel wanted to have in February, the newlyweds would be allowed to live in Babette's house together. In the meantime, Skip and Clark would begin building an additional cabin for the couple's use. They would also have health-care coverage and some other benefits.

"You guys are the best," Jewel said as she hugged Anna. "Better than parents!"

Clark laughed. "Well, just don't let your parents hear you saying that."

"Speaking of parents," Anna said, "where do you plan to have your wedding?"

Jewel looked at Skip. "Skip's mom suggested their church."

"But I don't really want to be married there," Skip admitted. "I haven't gone there since I was a kid. Even my folks don't go anymore. It would seem weird."

"I wish we could get married here," Jewel said with longing.

"Why don't you?" Clark suggested.

"Really?" Jewel looked hopefully at Anna.

"If you'd like to," Anna told her. "We think this

is a great place for a wedding." She smiled at Clark. "It worked for us."

"And for Marshall and Joanna."

"And at least a couple dozen other couples," Anna said.

So it was settled. And when Anna went to bed that night, she felt more hopeful than ever. Perhaps not everyone was going to leave the river after all.

Despite being unsure as to who would gather with them this year, Anna was working on some simple Christmas preparations at the inn. No guests were booked until mid-January. And this wasn't unusual during the holidays. But Marshall and Joanna had taken an unexpected trip to the British Isles. And Skip and Jewel planned to spend Christmas with his family. Even Lauren was unsure where she would be since she was using her Christmas break in her ongoing search for Sarah.

"It might just be the two of us for Christmas," Anna told Clark just a week before Christmas.

He lowered his newspaper and frowned. "Really?"

She nodded as she removed her reading glasses, rubbing the bridge of her nose. "There's a slight chance Lauren will be here, but she doesn't want to commit just yet. When I spoke to her yesterday, it sounded as if she'd found a new trail. She thinks Sarah might be somewhere down in California and plans to spend the next few days down there. I told her not to feel like she must come home. The most important thing is finding Sarah. And if the trail is still warm . . ." Anna knew better than to get her hopes up.

"I wish we'd known about this sooner." He set the paper aside.

"About the warm trail?"

"No, that it would just be the two of us for Christmas. We could've made other plans."

"Other plans?"

"Sure. We could've closed the place up and taken a trip somewhere."

She considered this, wondering if that was even possible.

"Someday we're going to have to take some time for ourselves, Anna."

She smiled. "Maybe we'll do that when every-one is gone next week."

He grinned back at her. "Imagine that—the whole place to ourselves—what will we do?"

She laughed at the twinkle in his eye. "Oh, I'm sure you'll think of something."

Just then the phone rang, and, since she was closest, Anna answered it.

"Mom?"

"Lauren. Hello. How are you?"

"I found her!"

"Oh, my!" Anna nodded eagerly at Clark. "You found Sarah?"

"Yes. I can hardly believe it. But I found her."

"Where? Is she with you?"

"She's at a place down near the redwoods. In California."

"So she's still in the place? Not with you?"

Lauren made a loud sigh. "She refused to see me, Mom."

"Oh . . . well . . ." Anna wasn't too surprised.

"The people running the place actually seem okay, Mom. But they said that Sarah's been sick. They said she needs some medical help."

"Oh, dear. What's wrong with her?"

"I don't know. But I'm worried. We have to get her out of there."

"Maybe I can get her to come home," Anna said.

"Yes!" Lauren sounded hopeful. "I think she'd go with you, Mom."

Anna looked at Clark. "Maybe Clark and I can both drive down there together."

"Could you?"

"Let me talk to Clark," she said. "Can I call you back?"

"This is a pay phone."

"Then give me a minute," Anna said. Now she quickly explained the situation to Clark, and he immediately agreed that they should go together as soon as possible. "It's settled," she told Lauren. "We can come."

Lauren gave Anna the information about the location, and, after a bit more discussion about the situation, it was decided that Anna and Clark would leave first thing in the morning.

Anna was so excited and nervous she could barely sleep that night. They got up early in the morning, and, while it was still dark, Anna packed a box with blankets and pillows, as well as a picnic basket with food and drinks. She even made some teas and tinctures. Using healthful remedies that worked for simple ailments like colds and flu, she put them into canning jars and packed them carefully. Before they left, she wrote a note for Jewel and Skip explaining why they were gone.

By the time the sun was coming up, they were already down the river and traveling south on the coastal highway. As Clark drove, Anna told him more about the other time she'd attempted to rescue Sarah, the time she'd come home with Jewel instead. Last summer, she had attempted to spare him because she knew how it would've disturbed him to think she'd been in any danger. Now she spared no details.

"I had no idea it had been such a frightening experience," Clark said in an alarmed tone. "If I'd known that, I would've insisted on going with you. That Daniel sounds like he could've been dangerous."

"But Lauren said this new place—where Sarah is now—is fairly friendly. The people she spoke to were helpful. And she doesn't expect us to have any opposition. It sounded as if they were eager to have her go."

"I'd think they'd be happy to have her leave if she's really ill." Clark sounded concerned. "Do you have any idea what's wrong?"

Anna just shook her head.

"Well, hopefully it's nothing too serious."

"Hopefully, it's serious enough to make Sarah want to come home," Anna added. "Sometimes we have to get knocked down in order to get picked up."

"Will Lauren meet us there?"

"She felt it would be best for Sarah's sake if she stayed out of the picture," Anna explained. "She asked us to call her at the motel she's staying in to let her know if we get Sarah out safely."

"Safely?" Clark frowned.

Anna smiled nervously. "Well, you know."

"Then what will Lauren do?"

"I told her to go on home . . . I mean to the inn."

"Do you think that's a good idea? What about Sarah?"

"Lauren offered to stay at Babette's house," Anna explained. "In case it's awkward." Anna wondered how many other families had problems like this during the holidays . . . or was it just them?

It was almost three when they were finally going down the private gravel road at the location Lauren had given her. "It's a relief to

240

see it's not all fenced in here," Anna observed.

"It's certainly pretty." He slowed down for a curve that wrapped around a mammoth redwood tree. "These trees are amazing."

"Is that it up there?" Anna pointed through the trees to where several cabinlike buildings were clustered around a lodgelike building.

"Looks like it."

Anna leaned forward and blinked at the attractively landscaped area. Such a contrast to last summer's commune, this place suggested that someone cared. The neatly cut lawns and stone borders around weed-free beds gave it a parklike appearance. "Does it remind you of anything?"

He nodded slowly. "Except . . . the river is missing."

"And the trees are much bigger." She felt a rush of nerves as she realized what they might be getting themselves into. Lauren had said the people seemed friendly, but from what Anna had read about Jonestown, it had been described as friendly, too. The congressman and others had received a very congenial tour, just hours before total chaos erupted and everyone was killed.

And yet something about this setting comforted Anna as she tried to see it from Sarah's eyes. Had Sarah felt a sense of familiarity here? Perhaps she'd been longing for home. Anna could only hope. As Clark parked the station wagon next to an old blue pickup in front of the biggest building, Anna said a silent and slightly desperate prayer. She knew they would need divine help today.

21

Clark and Anna walked tentatively up to the large door of the big building. "Do we knock or just go in?" Anna asked quietly.

But before they could decide, the door opened. "Hello?" A tall bald man with a red beard peered curiously at them. "Something I can help you with?"

"We're here to pick up our granddaughter," Clark said in a firm but friendly voice.

"Yes," Anna said eagerly. "Our daughter called and told us that she's here. And, oh yes, her name is Sarah—"

"Oh, yes. Sarah." He nodded, letting them inside a large windowless meeting room with metal folding chairs arranged in rows. "Let me find someone to help you. Please, have a seat." He headed toward the back of the room, going out a side door.

Anna and Clark glanced at the metal folding chairs, but neither of them sat. "He seemed fairly normal," Anna whispered.

"We don't appear to be in any imminent danger." Clark gave her hand a reassuring squeeze.

She made a nervous laugh then glanced around to see if anyone was lurking in any of the dark corners of the large room.

"Hello there." A young woman with curly blond hair emerged from the same side door. "Thomas said you're Sarah's grandparents?"

"That's right." Anna explained.

"I'm Danielle, and I'm in charge of the women. I'll take you to see Sarah now. I'll ask you not to speak while we're outside. This is a quiet hour."

Anna felt a surge of fresh hope as they followed Danielle out of the large building. Was it possible they were really going to see Sarah, that they would be able to bring her home? They walked in silence down a neatly groomed trail and past several other cabinlike structures. It was uncanny how much this place reminded Anna of Shining Waters. Well, except as Clark had pointed out, there was no river. And something else felt different, too. Perhaps it was simply the spirit of the place, or Anna's imagination, but she got the feeling that there was some kind of suppression here.

Finally, they were taken into a narrow dormitory building, where talking seemed to be allowed.

"She's down there." Danielle pointed to the end of the room where there did appear to be someone in bed.

243

Anna hurried down the aisle. But she gasped to see Sarah. Lying on a narrow bunk, her face looked pinched and thin and her skin sallow. The worst part was the sad and vacant look in her dark eyes. Almost as if she didn't recognize Anna or Clark.

"Sarah," Anna said gently as she reached for her hand. "It's Grandma."

Sarah barely registered acknowledgment, and Anna glanced at Clark with a frightened expression.

"Hello, sweet girl," Clark said in an easy tone. "Want to go home with your grandma and me?"

Sarah's eyes flickered with recognition. "Grandpa?" she said in a hoarse voice.

"We've got the car," Anna told her. "The old station wagon. Do you feel like you're able to travel?"

Sarah let out a shallow sigh then closed her eyes as if in pain. Her thick black lashes fluttered over the dark shadows beneath her eyes, and her breaths seemed shallow and labored. Anna touched her forehead to find that it was a bit too warm.

"Clark," Anna whispered. "Do you think she needs to see a doctor first?"

"No." Sarah started to sit up.

"You've been very sick," Anna said sadly. "We want to help you. Your friends think you should go home with us, but you seem so weak."

"Home." Sarah's weak grip tightened slightly on Anna's hand. "I want to go home."

Anna and Clark exchanged glances.

"Yes," Anna told Sarah. "We want you to come home, too."

Without Sarah seeing him, Clark mouthed the word "Lauren" to Anna then held his hand up like a phone receiver. Anna nodded, and with that, Clark leaned down to tell Sarah he was going for the car and would be back shortly.

While he was gone, Anna helped Sarah slip a raggedy-looking green and orange hand-knit sweater over her thin cotton dress, slowly buttoning it up to her chin. Then, just as she was helping her into some thick socks and a worn pair of brown clogs, Clark returned. "I pulled the car up to the back of the building," he said. "I left it running."

"We have blankets and things in the car," Anna said as she helped Sarah stand, with Clark on the other side so they could both support her. "And I brought some food and drinks."

"I packed Sarah's things for her." A girl carrying a limp brown paper bag joined them. "I hope she gets better."

Anna smiled at the girl as they slowly walked Sarah toward the door. "Don't worry. We *will* get her well again," she declared.

It took all three of them to get Sarah out to the car and into the backseat where Anna sat with her.

With the blankets and quilts tucked snugly around Sarah, Anna tried to make her as comfortable as possible. But as soon as the car started to move, Sarah was clearly in pain. She seemed to feel every bump and rut in the rough gravel road and at each lurch or turn would let out a little groan.

Anna had placed a down pillow in her lap to cushion Sarah's head. And knowing lavender was a natural soothing herb, she'd even tucked a sachet inside the smooth linen pillowcase early this morning. As she cradled Sarah's head with the fragrant pillow, Anna wished for a stronger way to buffer this ride for her.

Sarah's features twisted as they hit another lumpy part of the road.

"Maybe we should take her to the hospital," Anna said quietly to Clark.

"No," Sarah said in a weak but firm voice. *"Home."*

As encouraged as Anna was to hear how badly Sarah wanted to go home, she wondered if the sick girl could possibly make the almost eight-hour trip. This wasn't just a bad case of the flu. Sarah was seriously ill. Not only that, but also it would be the middle of the night by the time they reached town and the river, and they'd still have the boat ride back to the inn. And once at the inn, the doctor and the hospital would be nearly an hour away if they needed medical assistance.

"Clark?" Anna put a hand on his shoulder. "What do you think?"

He didn't respond as he continued driving down the graveled road as carefully as possible. The main road was in sight now, but Anna could tell by the angle of Clark's head and the way he was rubbing his chin that he was probably trying to decide what was best.

"Home," Sarah said again.

"It's a long trip," Anna told her. "You're very weak."

"I think Sarah's right," Clark finally said, "we'll keep heading for home. I'm not the least bit tired of driving, and if we need to stop somewhere between here and there for help, we will, but the sooner we get her home, the sooner you can make her well again. If anyone can make her well, Anna, I believe you can."

Anna wasn't so sure about this, but it did remind her of the basket she'd packed with this in mind, and once Clark was on the smoother highway, she began trying to coax Sarah to drink some of the cool tea she'd poured into canning jars last night. Infused with chamomile, lavender, and catnip herbs, it was sweetened with clover honey. She even packed some straws. Sarah could only manage a few sips at a time, but after about an hour on the road, she seemed to be resting better. Or else she was going into a coma.

Stroking Sarah's hair, Anna prayed silently for

her granddaughter . . . prayed for them to make the journey safely and quickly . . . and prayed that whatever was ailing Sarah would be treatable without hospitalization. Anna felt relatively sure that Sarah wasn't with child. This had been her concern earlier when Lauren had called with the news that she was sick. Anna had instantly flashed back to the time when Lauren had seemed so sick . . . but had simply turned out to be pregnant . . . with Sarah.

Anna studied Sarah's profile in the dusky light. The sallow tone to her skin suggested vital organ trouble—perhaps liver or kidneys—and Anna knew that was serious. Very serious. Sarah was even thinner than the last time Anna had seen her. Her fragile wrists looked like that of a young child. But the length of Sarah's dirty fingernails gave Anna a smidgeon of hope . . . perhaps it hadn't been that long since Sarah had been working, which would suggest she'd only gotten sick recently. So perhaps her malady, whatever it was, wasn't too far along.

No one at the commune had seemed to know exactly when Sarah had become ill or what was actually wrong with her. Danielle had claimed that Sarah had been sickly from the start and that they were concerned that she might be contagious. Not that any of this mattered so much to Anna. Mostly she'd just wanted to get Sarah away from there. And now she only wanted to get her home. And get her well. Hopefully they would make it there in one trip.

Anna knew that it was only God's grace and the soothing help of the herbal concoctions that got Sarah safely home to the river in the wee hours of the morning. But as the sun was coming up, Sarah was finally resting relatively peacefully in her old bedroom in the main house. Anna had coaxed Sarah to sip some chicken broth and apple cider and now felt like she could finally relax some herself. Clark had long since tumbled into bed and was fast asleep.

Thankful that no guests were with them, Anna explained the situation to Jewel, who had waited up for them. "Would you mind handling the cooking for tomorrow," Anna asked as she put some things away in the kitchen.

"No problem. And I can use the kitchen downstairs," Jewel assured her. "So it will be nice and quiet up here."

"Good. Did you hear anything from Lauren?" Anna wasn't sure if she was still in California or at Babette's house.

"She called earlier this evening. She plans to get here tomorrow."

"Well, you better get some rest." Anna let out a tired yawn.

"Is Sarah going to be okay?" Jewel asked with concerned eyes.

Anna sighed. "I think so, but I'm afraid it might be serious, Jewel. I can tell she's very sick."

"Oh, no." Her hand covered her mouth.

"Pray for her," Anna said. "And we'll do the best we can for now. But I plan to call the doctor tomorrow." She shook her head. "I mean today."

"You should go get some rest," Jewel told her. "If you like I can sit with Sarah while you sleep."

Anna considered this. She really hadn't wanted to leave Sarah alone. "You don't mind?"

"Not at all. I fell asleep on the couch for several hours while I was waiting for you guys to get home."

Anna thanked her, gave her some instructions about keeping the fluids going, and then went off to bed.

The next morning, Sarah seemed about the same, and Anna knew that she needed to get some professional medical attention for her. But the idea of loading the poor girl back onto the boat and then the car again seemed like cruelty. Anna remembered the days when Dr. Robertson used to make house calls. Unfortunately, he had long since retired. Since then, Anna and Clark had relied on Dr. Albers for their medical care. And he was a nice fellow and even enjoyed fishing with Clark occasionally, but Anna doubted that he or anyone else made house calls anymore.

Even so she called his office then waited on

hold to talk to him personally. After initial greetings, she began to explain the situation, going into detail over Sarah's symptoms and yesterday's difficult journey.

"I'm so glad to hear you found her," he said. "I'd heard you folks were looking for her again. How fortunate to have her home in time for the holidays."

"Yes, we're relieved to have her back with us, but I'm terribly worried about her, doctor. You know I believe in herbal remedies, but this seems very serious."

"Yes, it does sound like liver or kidneys. She needs to be seen, Anna."

"I know. But the trip will be hard on her. And she is so adamant about not getting medical attention." Now Anna explained some of Sarah's strange beliefs. "I suspect they're things she picked up at the communes."

"No doubt." Now he asked her to hold.

While waiting, Anna tried to decide what to do. What if Sarah's illness was life-threatening? Wouldn't it be better to force her into a hospital than to respect her wishes for natural treatments?

"Anna?" Dr. Albers interrupted her thoughts. "How about if I come out there?"

"A house call?" Anna was stunned.

"I just checked with my nurse, and I only have two more appointments today. I could come out there this afternoon if you like."

"You would do that?"

"Sure. That is if Clark can pick me up."

"He'll be happy to."

"Tell him to meet me at the dock at two."

She thanked him several times then hung up and ran to find Clark.

"I'm going to owe him several fishing trips for this," Clark told her.

"I'd gladly take him myself," Anna said.

It was close to three when Clark returned with Dr. Albers, and by that time, Sarah was starting to feel much worse. Thankfully, this reduced her resistance to Dr. Albers. She was in too much discomfort to protest.

Anna tried to busy herself in the kitchen by making ginger snaps and a fresh pot of coffee, but by the time Dr. Albers emerged from Sarah's room, Anna was on pins and needles.

"Something smells good out here," he said.

She offered him coffee and cookies, and as they sat down at the kitchen table, she asked how Sarah was.

His brow creased slightly. "You're right, she's in bad shape. I want to send some samples to the lab, but I'm fairly certain she has a kidney infection." He pulled a packet of pills from his jacket pocket and handed them to her. "These are samples of an antibiotic I brought along just in case. I already started her on them, and I'll have my nurse call in a prescription for you to pick up tomorrow."

Anna felt relieved. "So that's all then?"

He shook his head. "No, I don't think so. I suspect she has hepatitis as well."

"Hepatitis?" Anna wasn't sure of all the ramifications, but she knew this was not a simple diagnosis.

"Yes. I hope I'm wrong. But she has all the symptoms, and based on how she answered some of my questions and her life these past couple of years, well, I think it's highly likely." He frowned. "It's not uncommon in some of these communes. Poor health standards and whatnot."

"Oh." Anna sighed. "What does that mean? What's the treatment?"

He explained that there wasn't medication for it. "Mostly you treat the symptoms. You try to keep the patient comfortable. And usually they improve over time with plenty of rest and a healthy diet. Lots of clear fluids to help the liver repair itself."

"Herbal teas?"

"Yes. I'm sure you have some good ideas for that." Then he went over a list of things she shouldn't have. "Also, I told her, and you need to know as well, that she needs to be very careful of hygiene, and you can't allow her to work for the inn until she's completely recovered. Hepatitis is contagious, but if she's cautious, it should be no problem. However, if word got around that she has it . . . well, you know, it could hurt business."

Anna nodded. "We'll keep that in mind."

He smiled. "But, really, if Sarah gets plenty of rest—and no strenuous exercise—and wholesome food and lots of fluids, she should be back to normal by, say, springtime."

"That long?"

"The liver takes time to heal, Anna. And having the kidney problem on top of this." He reached for another cookie. "Well, it's a good thing you called, Anna. That girl could've very well been hospitalized if a few more days had gone by without antibiotics. The combination of hepatitis and kidney infections, well, it could've turned lethal. I told Sarah she's lucky she didn't end up in the hospital, and if she doesn't take care, she will yet."

"Will she feel better soon?"

"She should start feeling better in twenty-four hours. But keep those clear fluids going." He listed off some juices that might be helpful then held up a cookie. "And get some good food into her as soon as her appetite returns. The poor kid looks half-starved."

Anna walked him down to the dock where Clark was working on a boat engine. "I don't even know how to thank you for coming out here like this," she said.

"Well, it's Christmas." He shrugged. "Besides it's always fun to come up the river and see this place." He looked around. "You and Clark sure have the good life."

Anna laughed. "It didn't feel too good yester-day."

"No, I expect it didn't. Just be glad you got her out of there when you did."

"We are." She paused on the dock and thanked him again.

"And like I told Anna," Clark said as he joined them. "I expect that besides your bill, I will have to take you on a few deep-sea fishing trips."

Dr. Albers grinned. "Sounds like a deal to me."

Clark asked about Sarah, and they filled him in. Then Anna hurried back to the house to check on her. She knew that, despite the doctor's visit, Sarah was not out of the woods yet. Jewel met her at the foot of the stairs. "Is she going to be okay?"

As they went upstairs, Anna told Jewel about the diagnosis and recommended treatment. "And Sarah isn't supposed to help with the inn for a few months either," Anna said as they went inside, explaining about the contagious factor. "The doctor let her know, too. Mostly she'll just need to rest and recuperate." Anna filled another glass of apple cider and put a couple of still-warm cookies on a plate. "I want to check on her now."

"Do you want me to call Lauren?" Jewel offered. "I know she's anxious to hear."

"Yes." Anna nodded. "I completely forgot. And tell her I'll call her later with more information."

"Should I invite her to come for dinner?"

Anna considered this. It seemed unlikely that

Sarah would leave her room today. "Yes," she said. "I think that will be all right." As she opened the door to Sarah's room, it hit her—how quickly things had changed again. One day, she and Clark plan to spend Christmas alone, the next day they have both Sarah and Lauren back with them. But these were good changes . . . or at least they would be good . . . eventually.

22

The days before Christmas were quiet and subdued at the inn. Although Sarah was somewhat improved after a day of antibiotics, she was still in need of round-the-clock care. Between the pain, bouts of nausea, and mood swings, she was at best unpredictable. For that reason, the three women—Anna, Jewel, and Lauren—split Sarah's days into three shifts. Anna took the first shift, then Jewel handled the late afternoon into evening, and then around midnight, after Sarah was asleep, Lauren would step in.

"She opened her eyes and saw me last night," Lauren told Anna as they were fixing dinner together. "The full moon was coming through the window, and I'm sure she knew who I was." It was Christmas Eve and Sarah was finally starting to show signs of being able to come out of her room.

"Did she react?" Anna paused from mashing the potatoes.

Lauren shrugged. "She just kind of moaned then rolled over."

"She hasn't said anything to me . . . to hint that she knows you're here." Anna dropped a clump of butter into the potatoes, then continued mashing.

"But when she does?"

"We'll deal with it."

"I wish there was something I could do," Lauren said sadly, "to change how she feels about me. I love her so much, Mom. I know what a failure I've been as a mom. I know I let her down a million times when she was growing up. I want to make it up to her. But I just don't know how."

"Just keep doing what you're doing, Lauren. In time, Sarah will figure it out."

"I don't know . . ."

"It's going to take time," Anna told her, "but eventually, she will come around."

"I want to believe that, but it's hard."

Anna knew it was hard. She knew it was taking a toll on Lauren. She would see Lauren out walking by the river in the early-morning fog sometimes. She would raise her arms up and down as if she was having a conversation—perhaps she was praying—and then eventually, she would get in a boat and head on back over to Babette's house, where she was living all alone. It made Anna sad. And yet what could she do?

Christmas came and went, and when Sarah finally became strong enough to venture from her room, and no longer seemed to need round-the-clock care and supervision, Anna encouraged Lauren to return to her apartment in Eugene. "At least you have friends there," she told her. "You're so isolated here. And Sarah isn't ready . . . yet."

Lauren nodded. "And I decided I should look for a job for next semester."

"A job? But you have the scholarship money to live on. Why do you need a job?"

"Because I need something to do," Lauren said in an aggravated tone. "The classes are good, but I have too much spare time, Mom. I need something to occupy myself. I spent so much time looking for Sarah last semester. I'll go crazy with nothing but classes and homework."

Anna smiled. "Well, it seems you have it all figured out, darling. And it sounds like a good plan."

Lauren looked relieved.

"I'll keep you apprised about Sarah."

Lauren thanked her. And the next day, Lauren was gone. And Anna was thankful that Lauren had figured something out to fill her time and her days. Anna felt badly for her daughter, and a part of her wanted to reach out and help her, to fix it somehow. But another part of her knew she needed to keep letting go. Lauren needed to paddle her own canoe.

As Sarah's health improved, she became more bored and wanted to talk. And yet, her energy was so depleted that she couldn't even talk for long without tiring. So it was that Anna began telling her stories. First she told her the old story of how Grandma Pearl and her sister had been forced to walk north up the beach with the rest of the Siuslaw Indians.

"At least they had each other," Sarah said from where she was resting on the sofa with an old quilt over her legs.

Anna considered this. "You know, you're right. I never quite thought of it like that. I've always thought of the hardship and deprivation . . . and how unjust it was to drive them up there like cattle . . . how so many of them died."

"Well, that was wrong." Sarah frowned. "I wasn't saying . . ."

"I know." Anna nodded. "But you do raise an interesting point. At least they had each other." She sighed. "I think that's what I was missing this past fall."

"What?"

"Each other." Anna set down the patchwork piece she was working. "It felt like everyone had left. First you . . . then Lauren . . . and then Hazel."

"I still miss her." Sarah looked close to tears now.

"She lived a good life. And one of the last

things she told me was that she hoped you would get her cabin. Grandma Pearl's cabin."

Sarah's eyes lit up. "Really?"

"And it's yours . . . if you want it."

"All mine?" Sarah's voice sounded almost like she was twelve again. "Really? I don't have to share it with guests or anything?"

"It is all yours," Anna assured her. "One hundred percent. You can even change the locks if you like."

Sarah laughed. "No, I don't have to do that."

"But back to what you said, Sarah. I think that's a problem in our world today. We don't have that sense of family . . . of community . . . of tribe . . . not like they used to have back in the old days."

"But you have your friends on the river—and guests at the inn. They love you, Grandma."

"And I love them. But they constantly change . . . coming and going."

Sarah seemed to consider this.

"I suppose I hoped for more from my own family. Then I realized I had to let them go, too. I can't control you . . . or Lauren." Now Anna told Sarah about what Hazel had said about the women in their family, how they all had their own trail of tears to walk. "In fact, I remember the day Hazel told me to tell you about that."

"Really?"

Anna tried to recall. "I was on my way to get

you from that commune down by Medford, and Hazel was encouraging me. But you weren't there."

Sarah sighed. "Yes. Jewel filled me in on that. I'd left with Aaron and Misty and the others."

"Where were you going?"

Sarah bit her lip.

"I know you'd planned to meet up with some guru from India," Anna supplied.

"That was the original plan. But he never showed up at the place."

"The place where we got you in California?"

"No. Another place. A house down in the Bay Area. We waited there for several weeks. But we were running out of food and money. We found out the guru was still in India. It kind of started to fall apart then. Some of us were panhandling to get by. Then I got too sick to even do that. Some of our group was approached by the Peoples Temple. They were getting ready to go down there to work on the farm in Guyana."

Anna's stomach clenched. "Some of your friends joined the Peoples Temple?"

Sarah nodded. "I think so. I was going to go with them, but I started getting sick, and they wouldn't let me go. Aaron and Misty heard about this other place—where you and Grandpa got me—they took me up there. But I just got sicker."

"So, because of your illness, you were unable to leave the country?" Anna tried to keep her voice even. "Which is why we were able to find you?"

"Yeah. Maybe it was a good thing."

Anna took a deep breath. "Yes . . . maybe so." She could tell that Sarah had no idea of what had happened in Jonestown. And maybe she would tell her someday. But not now. There was no point in upsetting her about this now. Sarah wondered which of Sarah's friends had gone down there. Aaron and Misty?

Later that day, she considered mentioning this to Jewel but, worried that Jewel might become upset and spill the sad news of Jonestown to Sarah, decided not to say a word. As a result, she told only Clark. He simply shook his head and sighed. "But by the grace of God," he said sadly.

A few days after Christmas, Anna and Sarah were sitting together in the living room. Sarah was occupied with a book of short stories, and Anna was working on her current quilting project, but she could hear Jewel in the kitchen, getting an early start on dinner. It was one of those cozy afternoons, with a crackling fire in the fireplace and outside, sheets of rain pelted against the windows. The forecast was for gale force winds, and Clark and Skip had gone down to the dock to "batten down the hatches" and make sure the boats were secured.

"What are you making?" Sarah asked Anna.

Anna held up the quilt pieces she was stitching together and smiled. "It's kind of a surprise."

"Is it a quilt?"

"Sort of."

Sarah gave her a puzzled look.

So Anna pulled out a couple of the other pieces she had already stitched together and held them up.

"It's pretty, but what is it?" Sarah closed her book. "Some weird-shaped quilt?"

When Anna had unpacked Sarah's few items of clothing last week, removing things from the brown paper bag to put in the laundry, she'd noticed that Sarah's beloved patchwork dress seemed to be missing. However, the old Bible was there at the bottom of the bag. And that gave Anna real hope. She had no idea where that patchwork dress had gone or why it had been replaced with a couple of drab-looking muslin dresses, but she wondered if Sarah missed her favorite garment. And that's when she got an idea.

"Well," Anna began slowly. "I was hanging your dresses in your closet, and I saw that bag of fabric pieces and ribbons and laces—remember last summer when we got them?"

Sarah's eyes flickered with recognition. "Oh, yeah. I was going to make some clothes."

"I hope you don't mind that I used them for this."

"That's okay." Sarah studied the piece in Anna's hand. "I like those colors together. And it's cool the way you have that ribbon and lace worked into the pieces. You're really good at it."

"I'm still a novice," Anna admitted. "But it's been fun doing projects with the guests these past few months. And it was good therapy, plus I discovered I really enjoy piecing fabric together, but I don't really need anymore quilts. So I got to thinking, what if I made patchwork clothes? It didn't seem like it would be too difficult since I already know how to sew."

"Is that what you're doing now?" Sarah got up from the couch, coming over to look more closely at it.

Anna got up, too, and, on the dining table, she spread the oddly shaped pieces out to make sense. "See these are the sleeves." She fit them onto the bodice that she'd been working on then laid out the skirt so it resembled a dress. "What do you think?"

"Wow. It's going to be beautiful."

"I'm making it for you."

Sarah turned and looked at Anna now. "Really?"

Anna smiled. "Yes. Do you like it?"

"I love it—thank you!" With shining eyes, Sarah hugged her and, to Anna's surprise, started to sob.

"What is it?" Anna asked as she held her.

"It's just that—I don't deserve this. None of it."

"Yes, you do."

"But I've been so awful, Grandma." Sarah stepped back now, looking directly at Anna. "I've hurt you and Grandpa so much. I don't deserve you being kind to me—or that beautiful dress. Why are you being so good to me? Especially after I've been so bad?"

"Because you're my granddaughter and I love you." Now Anna couldn't hold back her own tears. It seemed she'd been holding them back for days . . . maybe weeks . . . and months. She hugged Sarah again. "I'm so glad you're home, Sarah. So very glad." Now she held her at arm's length and just smiled at her. "I missed you so much."

"Grandma," Sarah said solemnly. "You know you saved my life. I honestly don't think I'd be alive if you hadn't come for me . . . brought me home."

Anna pulled a handkerchief from her sweater pocket, using it to wipe her eyes, and then handed it to Sarah. "Not just me, sweetheart. We all worked together to help you. Your grandpa, Jewel, Dr. Albers . . . even your mom."

"But it was really *you*," Sarah said with conviction. "You were behind it all, Grandma. I wouldn't be here without you."

Anna considered pointing out the important role Lauren had played, too, but she realized Sarah was still in a fragile place. If she needed to think that it was Anna alone who had saved her, maybe that was best for now. Anna didn't want to do anything to upset her or set her back. Someday Sarah would learn about Lauren's part in this, how she hunted the place down and got the wheels in motion.

Instead, Anna told Sarah how much she loved her. "You are part of me, Sarah. And I felt like something in me was broken when you were missing. It was as if a part of me was gone."

"I'm sorry." Sarah sniffed. "I know I hurt you, Grandma. And, really, I'm sorry. Really, really sorry. I wish I could go back and do it differently."

Anna smoothed Sarah's hair back away from her face and smiled. "There's no going back . . . only forward. I'm just glad you're home—and that you're getting well. And I hope you realize that *this is your home.* You will always have a home here on the river. And we will always love you, Sarah, no matter what you do or where you go. You will always be part of us and we'll be a part of you. Even if you choose to live somewhere else, you must always know you have a home here. No matter what. Please, promise me that you'll remember that—that you'll believe it."

Sarah nodded. "I do believe that . . . and I'll remember it, too."

"Good." Anna wanted to ask her why Sarah didn't believe this before but then thought better of it. No going backward. "Do you want to help me with this?" Anna held up the unfinished piece for the bodice, and Sarah nodded eagerly.

"Can I?"

"Sure."

Together they worked on the dress . . . and by New Year's Day it was finished and Sarah wore it all day. Anna even got out her camera and took several pictures of Sarah. With the sallowness gone and the roses returning to her cheeks, Sarah looked prettier than ever. After Anna got the photos developed, she would send some to Lauren so that she could see how Sarah was improving.

Sarah continued getting better and stronger, and after a month, they all decided she was well enough to move into Grandma Pearl's cabin. It was one of those rare January days that felt like summer. Anna had asked Jewel to give the cabin a thorough cleaning and to box up and remove all of Hazel's personal items to make room for Sarah's things. However, there were still a lot of Hazel's things in the cabin.

"Would you like me to clear the cabin out for you?" Anna asked her as she walked out to the cabin. Anna was carrying a box of Sarah's clothes.

"Clear what out?" Sarah asked.

She told her what Jewel had done. "But Hazel's books and things are still in there."

"Do we have to clear all her stuff out?"

"Well, no. But it's a small cabin. You might need more space."

"Is it okay if I figure it out?"

Anna sighed. "I'd be glad if you did." She paused by the porch. "But only if you promise not to overdo. Remember what Dr. Albers said."

Anna had just taken Sarah to his office for a follow-up appointment the day before yesterday. While he said she was making marvelous progress, he still reminded her to take it easy and that she could still regress.

"I won't do too much," Sarah promised as they went inside. "I just want a chance to save things that are special. I loved Hazel, too, you know."

"I know. And I know you have great respect for old things." She smiled at her. "Just remember to pace yourself. And don't lift anything heavy. I know some of Hazel's thesis papers are in boxes, and we can store those in the attic. I don't feel comfortable throwing anything away just yet. Even though she made copies."

"Don't worry, I wouldn't dream of getting rid of any of that."

"Good. Those papers are precious to this place. That's our heritage she's recorded."

"And I really liked reading some of her notebooks last summer. I plan to read some more when I go through it." Sarah pulled a book from the shelf and opened it. "Maybe I'll become an expert on Siuslaw history, too."

Anna set the box on the wooden kitchen table. "That would make Hazel so happy, Sarah. In fact, I'll bet she recorded those stories more for you than any of us."

"Why for me?"

"Because it was the tradition of our people to

pass stories down to the next generation." Anna smiled. "That would be you. And we expect you to pass them along to your children . . . and your children's children."

Sarah wrinkled her nose. "I don't think I ever want to have children, Grandma."

Anna just nodded. "Well, not now anyway. You might change your mind someday." At least Anna hoped she would. For now, she would let it go.

23

Anna could tell by the tone in Lauren's voice that she was lonely. She had called to thank Anna for the photos. "Sarah looks so good," Lauren told her. "And she almost looked happy too."

"I think she is almost happy," Anna assured her.

"Does she still have those strange beliefs? Like she did last summer?"

"I'm not sure. I think being so sick might've taken some of that out of her." Anna looked out the front window, out over the river. The sun was just starting to shine through a hole in the clouds, making the surface of the water to shimmer like diamonds just as Sarah was paddling the canoe up to the dock. "I wish I had my camera right now," Anna told her. When Lauren asked, Anna described the scene out her window.

"Oh, I wish I was there!"

"Then come," Anna told her.

"No . . . I don't think so."

"Why not, Lauren? Just come for a weekend. You can stay in Babette's house. Sarah doesn't even have to know you're here."

"I have to work this weekend."

Anna knew that Lauren was working at a coffee shop on campus. "How is that going?"

"Okay."

"Will you come for Skip and Jewel's wedding?" Anna asked hopefully. "On Valentine's Day?"

"I don't think so, Mom."

"But Jewel wants you to be here," Anna told her.

"Yes . . . but Sarah doesn't."

"Sarah is going to have to accept that you are part of this family, Lauren."

"Maybe someday. But not yet. I don't want to push her, Mom. She needs time."

"But you need to come home, Lauren. I can hear it in your voice."

"No . . . I'm fine. Really, I am."

"But I miss you, sweetie." Anna sighed. Why was it that she couldn't have both Lauren and Sarah at the same time? Would she ever?

"I miss you, too, Mom. And, you're right, I do miss the river." She laughed at herself. "Whoever would've thought? Remember how I used to tell you I hated it?"

"Yes . . . but you grew up."

"And now I feel like I'm banished."

"Oh, Lauren."

"I'm sorry, Mom. I didn't mean to say that. And I know you didn't banish me. I've banished myself. But hopefully it's just temporary."

Anna changed the subject to Lauren's classes, inquiring how she was doing, and Lauren's voice cheered up a little. But when Anna pressed Lauren to consider coming home for spring vacation, Lauren shut down again. "I plan on working that week," she said.

"What about summer?" Anna asked hopefully. "I really could use your help during the big season."

"Didn't I tell you that I plan to take classes this summer? I'm hoping to finish this degree by fall."

"Oh . . . I didn't know. I thought you were coming home . . ."

"Sorry. You'll have to get someone else to help manage. What about Diane? I don't think she was going to take summer classes. And she was really doing a great job before."

"Yes." Anna sighed. "I'll check to see what her plans are. Hopefully she's coming to the wedding. I know Jewel asked Janelle to be a bridesmaid . . . along with Sarah." Anna chuckled. "And me. Do you think there's ever been an older bridesmaid?"

"Make sure Clark takes lots of photos."

"Yes. And we'll send some to you."

Anna knew that Lauren had been cheered up a

bit by the time they ended the call, but she also knew this was hard on Lauren. And it hurt Anna to think that Lauren no longer felt welcome in her own home. Still, she told herself it was just a matter of time.

In the meantime, Anna had her hands full doing the tasks that Lauren would normally enjoy doing. The goal was to get all the cabins fully equipped kitchens so that when the inn began cutting back on meals in the dining room, the guests would be well set up to do their own cooking. This meant buying pots and pans and utensils, and Anna was constantly making and remaking lists. Also, she wanted to make the dining hall kitchen more welcoming to guests for their own use. And they needed to plan for a well-stocked store. Anna knew these were tasks Lauren would've loved being involved in . . . but Lauren was not here.

Jewel made a very pretty bride. Sarah and Anna had made her dress for her. Using several different kinds of white fabric and a variety of white lace trims and ribbons, they had created a patchwork sort of bridal gown with three tiers to create the full gathered skirt. Then Sarah had made a wreath of flowers for her hair, with lots of white ribbons trailing down the back like a veil of sorts. The total effect was sweet.

Sarah, the maid of honor, wore her pretty

patchwork dress, Janelle wore a rose-colored long dress, and Anna wore a light blue dress. Clark, looking handsome in his dark gray suit, played the role of father, walking Jewel down the aisle. To everyone's surprise, Jewel's mother had made the trip all the way from New Jersey. But it was obvious to Anna that Jewel and her mother's relationship was strained at best. Even so, Anna did all she could to make Virginia at home.

"When Jewel told me about the wedding, I assumed she was living at another one of those crazy communes," Virginia confided to Anna after the wedding. "But this seems like a pretty nice place." She looked around the dining hall where they were holding the reception. "I guess she's lucky to have a job here."

"I feel lucky to have her," Anna said. "And Skip."

"He seems like a nice boy." Virginia looked over to where Skip and Jewel were visiting with Johnny Johnson. "I guess she could've done worse."

Anna had to bite her tongue as she wondered if Virginia had any idea what kind of place Jewel had been living at before coming here. Perhaps it didn't matter.

By the end of the day, Anna was reassured to know that both Janelle and Diane wanted to return to the inn to work for the summer. "But this might have to be my last year," Diane told her as she held up her hand to show off a diamond ring.

"You're engaged?" Anna looked at the young man Diane had brought as her date.

Diane giggled. "Surprise!"

Anna congratulated them both but immediately began to wonder who she would get to replace Diane next year.

"You seem deep in thought," Clark said as they sat down to eat a piece of wedding cake together. "Remembering the day when we did this?"

She chuckled. "I should be. That would be better."

"Better than what?" He peered curiously at her.

She shrugged. "Oh, I was just thinking about how the staff keeps turning over." She told him about Diane. "I'm happy for her. But sometimes I just wish I could freeze everyone and every-thing." She laughed at her silliness. "No, that's nonsense. Just like the river has to go and flow . . . I need to let my workers go, too. It's just not easy."

He leaned over and kissed her cheek. "At least I'm still here."

She smiled at him. "Yes, and for that I am eternally grateful."

Even though Anna knew Clark was "still here," she couldn't help but notice he was starting to go out in the boat with Johnny more often again. She couldn't really complain since this was still the slow season. But when he was gone two days in a row during Jewel and Skip's honeymoon, she had to question it.

"We're a little short-handed," she pointed out on a Friday morning. "And we have guests coming in at noon."

"Right." He nodded. "How about if I make a short day of it."

"Of what?"

He gave her his usual mysterious grin. "Just river stuff."

She frowned.

"Johnny and I will be back by two, okay?"

"I guess it's okay."

"And I'll ask Johnny to stick around and help," he promised. "Will that make up for it?"

"And you'll bring home some fish for dinner?"

"Of course." He nodded eagerly.

Well, at least that was something. She wasn't sure how they'd turned into such good fishermen, but they never came home empty-handed. Whether it was salmon or trout and sometimes crabs and clams, they always had something to contribute to the menu. And she had to admit, the guests really seemed to appreciate it. Not only that, but also it had been fun to see Johnny happy again. It seemed that Clark was truly good medicine for him. That was worth a lot.

Johnny wasn't the only one experiencing a renewal and healing. To Anna's delight, Sarah really seemed to be settling into life on the river again. She'd already made some changes to the cabin, including new curtains and a couple of patchwork throw pillows. Also, she was helping out more at the inn. Not in the dining room, since Anna still had concerns about the contagious factor. But Sarah had taken over the laundry room and seemed to love taking care of the linens. Also, as spring came on, she asked if she could start to work in the garden.

"As long as you don't overdo yourself," Anna reminded her.

"But I'm perfectly fine," Sarah assured her.

"Yes, I know you feel fine. But you need to keep building your strength up slowly. Give yourself time. It hasn't even been three months yet."

Sarah rolled her eyes but agreed to take it easy. Even so, Anna kept a close eye on her, and if it seemed like Sarah was pushing herself too hard, Anna would encourage her to go take a reading break. Fortunately, Sarah's love of reading had returned in full force. She seemed to be working her way through Hazel's library.

"I was talking to a guest," Anna told Sarah one afternoon in late March. "She told me her daughter took a GED test."

"Oh?" Sarah stood up from where she'd been thinning a row of carrots in the garden.

"I wondered if you'd like to get a high school degree. So that you can go on to college. Well, some colleges anyway. I guess not all will accept a GED. And, according to the guest, you'd still have to take SATs and a college entrance exam."

"That sounds hard." Sarah frowned.

"But you've always been an excellent student," Anna reminded her.

"But that was years ago."

"Yes, but you've been reading a lot lately, Sarah. Including some college-level books. You have a good brain." Anna decided it was time to tell Sarah about Hazel's Shining Waters Scholarship Fund. "And you were the main reason she established it."

Sarah squinted in the sunlight. "Really?"

"Hazel hoped you'd come home someday and want to finish your education."

"But that would mean having to leave." Sarah frowned. "I don't know if I can do that."

Anna put a hand on her shoulder. "And no one will make you do it. You'll have to figure that out for yourself. But in the meantime, it probably wouldn't hurt to look into a GED. Wouldn't it be nice to feel like you finished high school after all?"

She shrugged. "I guess so."

So it was that Anna started asking around town and was given the phone number of a retired teacher who sometimes tutored students in preparation for taking a GED test. Mrs. Smyth turned out to be a sweet old lady who lived less than a mile downriver from the inn. When Anna asked her if Sarah could come down to her house, Mrs. Smyth said she would rather come to the inn to give her lessons.

"That's not too much trouble for you?"

"I've always wanted an excuse to come there," Mrs. Smyth told her. "It looks like such a pretty place when I pass by. I've admired it for years."

"You should've come by," Anna told her.

"Oh, I didn't want to intrude. Not without an invitation."

"Consider yourself invited."

After a month of tutoring, Mrs. Smyth was so impressed with Sarah's intelligence that she requested her school records from her old high school. Then she spoke to the local high school, inquiring to the possibility of Sarah attaining a diploma from there. Thanks to the help from some of Mrs. Smyth's teacher friends, Sarah was allowed to join some classes and turn in some work and take some tests, and, by the end of May, Sarah was invited to graduate with the other high school seniors and receive a high school diploma.

"I can't believe it," she told Anna that evening. "I thought it'd be pretty cool just to get a GED, and now I get a real high school diploma instead."

"That's because you've worked hard, Sarah, and because you're so smart."

"Thanks for believing in me, Grandma."

Because of Sarah's studies, and because the inn was getting busier, Anna had decided to hire a couple more workers. This way they would be trained before summer when the inn was booked full for three months. She also began to plan a surprise graduation party for Sarah. This meant inviting Sarah's father and paternal grandparents. Anna considered calling Donald but wasn't eager to speak to him since the last time she'd called, to let him know that Sarah had been found and was living at the river. Donald had seemed uninterested, or maybe he was simply distracted by his new family.

Whatever the case, it had hurt Anna—or perhaps she'd simply been offended for Sarah's sake. Anyway, it had taken her several days to get over the sting. But she eventually forgave him, reminding herself that Donald's life wasn't exactly a happy one. Instead of calling him, she decided to send out invitations with an RSVP. That should keep everything slightly formal and as a result more comfortable. But first, she decided to call Lauren. Lately, they'd had a prearranged phone call appointment every Wednesday afternoon, while Sarah was taking classes in town, and Lauren was finished with her last class of the day.

"I told you about how Sarah gets to graduate with the senior class in town," Anna reminded her. "But I thought we should use this as an excuse to celebrate." She told Lauren of her idea about how she planned to send out invitations. "Please, tell me, you'll come."

"I don't know, Mom." Lauren's voice got that flat sound to it again.

"You have to come," Anna urged her. "You're her mother."

"But I'm pretty sure Sarah doesn't want me there."

"Don't be so sure."

"Did you ask her about this?"

"I wanted it to be a surprise."

"Then maybe you should ask her how she feels about me, Mom. If she's still angry at me, I don't want to come. It wouldn't be any fun for me, and if it spoiled it for her . . . well, I just don't want that."

"All right," Anna agreed. "I will sound her out on it. Okay?"

"Thank you."

Anna told her more of the latest news, not that there was much, but Lauren always seemed eager to hear everything.

"And now I have some news for you," Lauren announced.

"What?" Anna asked eagerly.

"Well, it's not really news . . . but I met a guy, Mom."

Anna could tell by Lauren's voice that this was more than just an ordinary guy. "Tell me about him."

"Well, he's just very nice. A very nice man."

"And . . . ?"

"And that's all there is to it, Mom."

"Are you seeing him?"

Lauren giggled. "I see him whenever he comes into the coffee shop."

"But you haven't gone on a date?"

"No. I wouldn't even know what to do on a date, Mom." She laughed. "Do you realize how long it's been? Even back when Donald and I were dating, it didn't last for long. And then we were married." She let out a little groan. "And pregnant. What a stupid way to start a marriage."

Anna chuckled. "Well, hopefully you won't make that same mistake again."

"Oh, *Mom!*" But Lauren was laughing even harder now. And Anna couldn't believe what a relief it was to hear her daughter happy again. Maybe this fellow was good medicine.

"I wish I could meet him, Lauren."

"Well, don't hold your breath. He may never even ask me out. Although I do know he's not married."

"Did you ask him?"

"Of course not. I got someone else to sleuth on him for me."

Anna laughed. "Good for you. Now you better keep me posted on him. And if it begins to develop into something, maybe I'll have to think of an excuse to run on over to Eugene . . . and check him out."

"*Please,* Mom." Lauren actually sounded worried now.

"I'm just kidding, dear. I wouldn't do that. But perhaps you could bring him out here to the graduation party with you."

"Oh, I seriously doubt that will happen."

Still, after she hung up, Anna said a prayer for Lauren's mysterious fellow. She didn't even know his name, but she hoped he was a good guy . . . someone who would be good for Lauren. Because, really, it had been so encouraging to hear Lauren's voice laced with happiness again. It gave Anna hope.

24

A few days before Sarah's graduation, Anna still hadn't heard from Donald. Did he not care that his only daughter, after all she'd been through, was about to get her high school diploma? Didn't he want to see her? Finally, Anna could stand it no longer, and while Sarah was busy in the dining hall, Anna called Donald's number and, after a formal greeting, asked if he'd received the invitation.

"Sure, I got it," he told her in an offhanded way.

"But you didn't respond . . . I still don't know if you're coming or not."

"Can't see any reason to come."

"Because she's your daughter?"

He made a harrumph followed by a long pause. "Sarah wrote me off a long time ago, Anna, back when she took off with her no-good boyfriend. As far as I'm concerned I have no daughter."

Anna felt a ripple of rage surging through her, but instead of speaking her mind, she took in a slow deep breath.

"I'm sure you think I'm a monster," he continued. "But Sarah's got her life, and I've got mine. I don't wish her any ill . . . I just don't want to be involved. It's not worth it."

"Not worth what?"

There was another long pause then Donald cleared his throat. "Here's the deal, Anna. Sarah and I used to be close. Remember back when Lauren was a useless mess. Well, Sarah and I got by. We helped each other, and, despite her lousy excuse for a mother, Sarah was doing all right. But then she took off like that . . . and, well, I just don't need that."

"I see . . ." And Anna did see. "Sarah has hurt you, Donald."

He coughed in a way that suggested he was still smoking more than a pack a day. "I'm not saying she hurt me. I'm just saying I got my own life . . . my own problems. I don't need hers."

"I understand. But she is your daughter, Donald." Anna kept her voice gentle, hoping to

283

get to the heart of the matter. "Someday you might wake up and realize that she's your flesh and blood, and you might want to be part of her life. I hope you won't let her juvenile mistakes keep you from that. Remember you made a few mistakes of your own back when you were her age. We all did."

"Maybe so. Anyway, sorry we didn't get back to you on the invitation, Anna. Give Sarah my best. My supper's on and I gotta go now."

Jewel and Skip had been in their newly built cabin for several weeks now, and Jewel was as happy as a clam. Anna had hoped that Lauren would be back in Babette's house for the summer, but with her enrolled in summer classes, the little house now sat vacant. And so Anna decided to use it to house some of the female staff, this way they wouldn't have to go back and forth to town. She put Diane in charge of it and hoped that the old house was strong enough to withstand the energy of four lively young women.

If Lauren came for the graduation party, which still sounded uncertain, Anna planned to put her in the spare room in the house. That would put a little space between her and Sarah. But Anna hoped that space wouldn't be needed. Sarah was making such great strides, becoming more and more like her old self, it seemed reasonable to think she would be ready to move on with her relationship with her mother as well.

Anna had made Sarah another patchwork dress for graduation. Sarah had picked out the fabrics and trims, all in earth-tone colors, and when the garment was finished, something about it reminded Anna of Grandma Pearl. Apparently she wasn't the only one who thought this, because when they picked up Mrs. Smyth to go with them, her eyes grew wide. "You look like a Siuslaw princess," she told Sarah as Clark helped her into the boat. "A beautiful Siuslaw princess."

As they went downriver, Anna remembered her own graduation day more than forty years ago. How proud her parents had been of her. Especially her father who never graduated from high school. But she didn't think they could've been as proud as she was of Sarah right now.

It wasn't until they were seated in the bleachers that Anna spotted Lauren coming into the gymnasium. Anna stood and waved, making room for Lauren to join them. "I wasn't going to come," Lauren said as she slid onto the bench.

"Oh, I'm so glad you did." Anna reached for Lauren's hand, squeezing it. "You look so pretty. New hairstyle?"

Lauren patted her short coifed hair and nodded. "Like it?"

"It makes you look younger."

"My hairdresser puts a rinse on it," Lauren whispered, "to make the gray look like it's really blond."

Anna wanted to ask if the man from the coffee shop had asked her out yet, but the ceremony was starting. Both Anna and Lauren cried when Sarah went up to receive her diploma. Even Clark pulled out a handkerchief and blew his nose.

But when Sarah joined them afterwards, she became quiet and chilly when she saw that Lauren was there. She accepted Lauren's congratulations but then left with an excuse that she needed to use the restroom.

"I'm going to head back home," Lauren told Anna.

"To the inn?"

"No, I mean home to my apartment." Lauren's eyes were filled with sadness.

"What about the party?" Anna asked.

"My presence there would just spoil it . . . for Sarah." Lauren stood a bit straighter. "Really, I need to get back. I have homework."

"Oh, Lauren, one day won't—"

"Please, Mom. I'm an adult." Her tone sharpened. "I know what I need to do."

Anna just nodded.

"I'm sorry." Lauren pressed her lips tightly together.

"I'm sorry, too." Anna shook her head. "I wish this could be different."

Lauren shrugged then opened her handbag and fished out a set of car keys. "You've done a great job with her, Mom. She looks beautiful . . .

and healthy." Lauren's eyes were filling with tears now. "You're a much better mother than I could ever be."

"Oh, Lauren."

Lauren hugged Anna and Clark. "I've got to go." And then she hurriedly turned, pushing her way through the crowd.

As they went home, Sarah never mentioned Lauren. And during the graduation party, which seemed to be a surprise, Sarah never asked about her mother's quick departure. Anna decided to just let it go for now. Especially since Sarah was doing such a lovely job of playing both host and honored guest. She was mingling with everyone, acting so comfortable and natural that Anna could barely believe this was the same moody girl that had been here so briefly last summer.

Anna listened as Sarah enthusiastically thanked Johnny Johnson for his gift, a golden locket with her initials and graduation date engraved on the back. It really was thoughtfully sweet.

"Well, if I'd had a granddaughter, I would've wanted her to be just like you," Johnny said as Anna helped Sarah with the clasp, adjusting the small golden heart around her neck.

"You'd make a wonderful grandpa," Sarah told him. "And I only have one grandpa so maybe I should adopt you."

He laughed. "I'd be pleased and proud to be your grandpa."

"Then I say we should make him an honorary grandpa," Anna told Sarah.

Sarah nodded. "How about it, Grandpa Johnny? Do you agree?" She stuck her hand out and shook Johnny's.

"I accept." He beamed at both of them. Now Sarah excused herself and went over to speak to someone else, and Johnny turned to Anna. "Well, I already felt like you folks were kin, but I guess I'm really part of the family now."

"And we're happy to have you. Honestly, I don't know what Clark would do without you," she told him. "You guys are thicker than thieves."

He laughed. "Hopefully we won't end up in jail."

"Sometimes I wonder what you two are up to." She tilted her head to one side. "Tell me, do you really fish all day long? Or do you have a secret poker group in the back of Greeley's store?"

He laughed harder now. "We always bring home fish, don't we?"

Now Clark joined them, and he and Johnny started telling her fish stories and jesting about some of their recent wild adventures, and Anna truly didn't know if they were joking or not.

Then, just a week later, Clark came home with the biggest fish tale Anna had ever heard. Unfortunately, this one was true. A pod of sperm whales had beached themselves along the Florence beach. Disturbed by what seemed a hopeless situation, Anna and Sarah went with Clark, along with some of the guests who wanted to see this strange phenomenon for themselves. Hoping they could help, they went equipped with shovels and buckets and ropes, joining dozens of others down at the beach.

But what they saw was so disturbing . . . so sad . . . Anna could barely stand to look at the mounds of dark shining bodies. More than forty sperm whales of various sizes were lying motionless on the sand. To think that only yesterday they'd been swimming freely in the Pacific, and today they were trapped and dying on land . . . it was too painful to witness. They soon realized there was no way to save the enormous mammals. Anna felt sickened by it. Sickened and confused. How did this happen? Why?

But when Sarah burst into uncontrollable sobs, Anna knew she needed to remove her from the beach. "Come on," she told her. "There's nothing we can do."

"But it's so wrong!" Sarah cried. "Why can't someone help them?"

"It's impossible," Anna said as she guided her back to the parking lot. Away from the beach and the dying whales, Anna held Sarah in her arms and they both cried freely. Finally when they were both cried out, Sarah told Anna that it reminded her of what had happened in Jonestown.

"You know about that?" Anna asked.

"I found an old *Newsweek* magazine when I was cleaning a cabin," she admitted. "It had photos . . . really gruesome photos. I read the article and couldn't believe it."

"You never told me."

Sarah shrugged. "I don't think I knew what to say . . . what to think." She looked at Anna with sad eyes. "That could've been me."

Anna moved a strand of hair away from Anna's eyes. "Thank God it wasn't."

Sarah sniffed. "But seeing those whales like that . . . it's just so wrong."

Anna just nodded, but she could see the similarities of Jonestown and the dying whales today. Unexplainable sadness. Senseless waste. So wrong.

As usual, summer was busy at the inn. But this year was different in that the store was up and running and the only meals being served were breakfast and dinner. And breakfast was only offered five days a week and dinner was only served three. Plus they had a full staff of young people from town. Still, Anna felt like she was running herself ragged to keep up. Diane had been a good manager last summer, but this year she was distracted with her fiancé and making wedding plans. Sometimes Anna thought she'd be better off having Janelle in charge, but how could she change gears in mid-season.

One thing that was going fairly smoothly was the store. Sarah had asked to be in charge of it, and, although Anna had been unsure if it was too much, she was pleasantly surprised to see that Sarah was a natural. "You take after your great-grandmother," Anna told Sarah one afternoon. She'd brought a box of candy bars down that had mistakenly been placed in the house.

"Your mother?" Sarah paused from stacking the bars into the rack.

"Yes. She and my father ran the store, but my mother was really quite good at a lot of the details and bookkeeping. My father was great at socializing with the customers and that was important, but it was my mother who made sure the orders were made and the bills got paid. Without her, I'm sure my father would've been overwhelmed."

"Do you have any old photos of them?" Sarah set the empty box on the counter. "And the store?"

"Sure. There's a few of them. Do you want to see them?"

"I thought it would be fun to frame some of them and hang them in here." Sarah pointed to the wall behind the register. "Kind of a history thing."

"That's a wonderful idea." Anna nodded. "I'll see what I can find."

"Did you see Mrs. Smyth today?" Sarah asked. But before Anna could answer, a couple of young teen boys set bags of chips and soda cans on the counter. They were both looking nervously at Sarah, in the way that young boys sometimes do when around a pretty girl. Anna couldn't help but chuckle as Sarah rang up their purchases, pleasantly chatting with them.

After they left, Anna asked why she would've seen Mrs. Smyth today.

"She came by to tell me that I'd been accepted at the university."

"Really?" Anna blinked. She'd almost forgotten that Mrs. Smyth had been helping Sarah to apply to some local colleges.

Sarah grinned. "So I guess it's final. I'll be going to the U of O this fall. I think I want to major in anthropology or sociology . . . or something like that."

"Oh, sweetheart, Hazel would be so proud of you."

Sarah shook her head with an amazed expression. "It's still kind of hard to believe. I mean when I think about where I was at . . . just last fall. Pretty weird."

"You've come a long way."

She nodded, calling out a cheery greeting to an older couple who'd just come into the store. "What a trip, huh?"

Several more customers came into the store now, and Anna knew that Sarah needed to give them her attention. So, congratulating her on the college acceptance, Anna left. But as she walked up to the house, she felt an unexpected sadness come over her. Oh, certainly, it was bittersweet . . . but it was still there. Sarah would be leaving in the fall. Once again, she would be removed from Anna's life. And, really, Anna wouldn't have it any other way. Sarah was too brilliant not to continue her education. And to think she was interested in the same things Hazel had studied and taught, well, it was beyond wonderful. Still, it would be hard to say good-bye . . . again.

Even so, Anna put on a happy face when she told Clark about Sarah's good news that evening. Sarah had gone to town with some of the other workers, to take in a movie. Naturally, Clark was pleased to hear that Sarah wanted to follow in his mother's footsteps. "I knew she'd been reading Mom's work, but I figured it had more to do with your family's history. I didn't realize she was actually interested in the field herself. Good for her."

"It's going to be hard to see her go," Anna admitted.

He made a sympathetic smile. "Your old friend —change—is back again."

She felt silly. "I know . . . everything has to keep changing." She looked out over the river from the upper deck where they were having coffee. "Even this river, which I think of as changeless, is constantly changing. Otherwise it would become stagnant and sick. New water is always coming from the mountains and then off it goes out to the sea . . . never the same water . . . it keeps moving . . . keeps it healthy."

"Just like the workers and family and friends that flow through here," Clark said. "They come and they go."

She reached for his hand. "But you're still here."

He smiled, nodded. "You bet I am."

The next morning, Anna discovered another change was coming their way. "I think I'm pregnant," Jewel told her as they were cleaning up after breakfast.

"Really?" Anna turned to look at her.

Now Jewel began describing the symptoms she'd been experiencing, and Anna had to agree. "That does sound like pregnancy."

Jewel frowned. "It's not that I'm not happy to have a baby . . . I am. But Skip thinks this means we have to move into town and he'll have to go to work for his dad."

"Oh . . ." Anna closed the dishwasher.

"And after all you and Clark have done for us. And our precious little cabin—" Jewel started to cry.

Anna put her arms around her, holding her. "It will all work out, Jewel. And having a baby —oh, that is such a blessing."

Jewel nodded. "I guess so. I just feel kind of blindsided. I think I'm in shock. I mean we've only been married a few months. I don't feel ready."

"Well, just take it one day at a time. Enjoy your summer here and know that whatever comes, even if you must move to town, you and Skip will have each other and the baby, of course, and you'll be just fine, Jewel. You're on a good path."

Jewel seemed somewhat comforted, but as Anna walked to her office, her feet felt heavy. It had seemed so right to have Skip and Jewel as full-time employees, a perfect way to lighten the load for her and Clark, and now it appeared that was destined to end. Still, Anna tried to take her own advice—one day at a time . . . just enjoy the summer . . . don't worry about tomorrow. She still had two months left with Jewel and Skip . . . and with Sarah. Then, like the water flowing down the river, they would move on.

25

"We have an unexpected guest," Clark told Anna shortly before dinnertime. This was one of the days when the dining room was not serving meals and Anna had just put a salmon into the oven while Sarah was making a green salad. It would be just the three of them tonight.

"But we're full up." She wiped her hands on a

dishtowel. "Did they have reservations? Is there a mistake?"

Motioning Anna to come toward the door, Clark whispered, "It's Donald."

"Donald?" Anna thought she heard him wrong. "You mean Sarah's dad *Donald?*"

He nodded. "Do you want me to tell her that—?"

"Where is he?"

"Down at the boathouse."

"Oh . . . why didn't you bring him up?"

Clark shrugged then glanced toward the kitchen. "I didn't want to upset her. You know how it was when Lauren showed up out of the blue."

She nudged him toward the door. "You go get Donald. But take your time and stall a bit. I'll speak to Sarah."

"I can give him a tour of the improvements," Clark offered as he opened the door.

"Yes. Do that." Anna went back to the kitchen, and Sarah looked curiously at her.

"Did we overbook?" She frowned as she slid some sliced tomatoes into the salad bowl. "Do you need my cabin for guests?"

"No, of course not." Anna shook her head. "It's your cabin. I wouldn't dream of moving you out for a guest."

Sarah looked relieved. "Good because it's kind of a mess today. I was in the midst of a sewing project that's spread all over the place."

"Your dad is here," Anna said gently.

"What?" Sarah's eyes grew wide. "Dad is *here?*"

Anna nodded. "Clark said he just got here. I'm as shocked as you are." Now Anna told Sarah about how she'd invited him for graduation in June. "He couldn't make it," she explained, "but maybe he felt badly for missing it."

Sarah scowled. "I doubt that."

"Well, he's obviously here to see you, Sarah. Should we invite him for dinner?"

"Do what you like." Sarah's scowl deepened.

"What does that mean?"

She shrugged. "It means I don't care . . . whether he stays for dinner or jumps in the river. He's nothing to me. And I don't plan to speak to him." She set down the paring knife and removed her apron. "I'll be in my cabin."

"Do you want me to go tell him that you don't want to see him?"

Sarah turned to look directly at Anna. "Do you want to see him, Grandma?"

"Well, not exactly. But I hate to turn him away. That's not very hospitable." She tried to smile. "And I am in the hospitality business after all."

"So have him up here for dinner if you want. Just don't expect me to come." Sarah was nearly to the door now.

"What if your father wants to say he's sorry?" Anna tried.

"Then I might have to say it's too little, too late." But Sarah stopped and, standing there in the living room, let out a frustrated sigh then folded her arms across her front the same way she used to do as a little girl when someone was pushing her out of her comfort zone. "It's just not fair, Grandma."

Anna went over and put an arm around her shoulders. "What's not fair?"

"That he and mom let me down in so many ways . . . and then they think they can just show up and act like everything's okay . . . let bygones be bygones. Why can't they just leave me alone? Don't they see that they weren't there when I needed them and now I don't need them anymore? Why do they feel the need to force themselves back into my life?"

Anna considered her response. "Because, like it or not, you are a part of them, Sarah. Their blood is in you. And even though family can be exasperating sometimes, they are still family."

"Does that mean I owe it to them?" Sarah's eyes were defiant. "That I should just put my hurts behind me, pretend that they never let me down, and just act like everything's fine. Because I suppose I could do that." She took in a deep breath, tightening her hands into fists and holding her arms stiffly by her side. "If that's what you want me to do, Grandma, I can do that. Put on a big phony act."

Anna didn't know what to say.

"You say the word and I'll do it," Sarah told her. "I'll fake that everything is just peachy keen."

"No . . ." Anna said slowly. "I don't want you to put on act. If you can't speak to your dad because you want to speak to him . . . then I don't really see the point."

Sarah nodded. "Good. I don't either."

Anna thought for a moment. Was this something Sarah should be forced to handle on her own? But then Anna remembered less than a year ago, when a confrontation with Lauren had sent Sarah running. Could that happen again? Probably not. But even so. "Do you want me to tell him how you feel."

"Thank you." Sarah's eyes were brimming with tears now.

"But, for your sake, Sarah . . ." Anna sighed. "I wish you were able to forgive him . . . and Lauren, too. It's not good for you to be bitter."

"I know, Grandma." Sarah's hand was on the doorknob. "You've told me that already . . . lots of times. And if I was able to forgive them and move on I would." She shook her head. "It's just that I can't. I just can't!" And now she went out, solidly closing the door behind her.

Anna went back to fixing dinner, setting aside a plate for Sarah, which she would take down to her later. She understood Sarah's dilemma. It would've been false for her to pretend that there was nothing wrong. Still, Anna longed for her to get beyond it.

After about ten minutes, Clark came in with Donald, the two of them chatting like old friends, and Anna explained that Sarah had chosen not to join them for dinner.

"It figures." Donald grimaced. "I knew I was probably on a fool's errand."

"Then why did you come?" Anna asked.

"I was going through some old photos, and it just hit me—Sarah deserved better than she got from Lauren and me. She was a good kid. And I know she's had some rough knocks, but I'm proud of her for making a comeback. I just wanted to tell her that. Guess I should be on my way."

"Wait," Clark said suddenly. "I think Sarah needs to hear those things."

"You mean if she'd listen," Anna told him.

"Come with me," Clark said to Donald. "I think we can get her to listen."

Anna wasn't so sure but decided not to intervene as Clark took Donald back outside. After all, Sarah respected Clark. Perhaps she would listen to him. Anna closed her eyes and whispered a prayer, begging God to soften Sarah's hard heart toward her parents.

For the next hour, Anna kept the salmon warm and wondered if anyone was going to return for dinner. Finally, it was close to eight and Clark, Donald and, to her surprise, Sarah came into the house. She could tell by Sarah's expression that something had changed.

"Anyone hungry?" Anna asked as she removed the salmon from the oven.

They all said they were, and Sarah came into the kitchen to help by filling water glasses. "As usual, you were right, Grandma," she said quietly.

Anna peered curiously at her.

"I did need to forgive my dad."

"And did you?"

She nodded. "And it actually does feel better."

Anna hugged her. "I'm so glad."

"Well, it was easier to forgive him when he admitted that he'd blown it. He seemed genuinely sorry, too. He owned up to everything. So I decided I really had no reason not to forgive him. And it does kind of feel like a weight's been lifted." She smiled as she picked up two glasses of water. "Thanks."

As they sat down, Anna felt greatly relieved. She hoped that this might be Sarah's first step toward forgiving her mother as well. But she wasn't holding her breath.

Early one Saturday morning in late July, Lauren called and barely said hello before Anna knew something was going on. She could hear the excitement in Lauren's voice.

"His name is Brad Stapleton, Mom."

"Your coffee shop man?"

"Yes. We had our first date last night."

"Really?"

"Yes. And he's absolutely wonderful. We talked and talked for hours. And it felt like I already knew him. There was this weird familiarity. I can't even explain it. Except that I never felt like this around a guy before. Not even back in the early days with Donald. Do you think I'm crazy? Or falling in love?"

Anna laughed as she sat down on the sofa. "I think you sound happy."

"I *am* happy. I got up with the sun this morning. And I've been singing!"

"So tell me about this Mr. Wonderful."

"I can do better than that," Lauren said, "I told him all about you and the inn and he really wants to come out to see it."

"Oh, darling, that'd be lovely."

"Except for one thing . . ."

Anna knew Lauren meant Sarah. And so she told her about Donald's recent visit and Sarah's unexpected turnaround. "So maybe she's ready to forgive you too, Lauren."

"I hope so, Mom. I want that more than any-thing."

"So when can you and Brad come out?"

"He suggested the weekend after next. And I think that's a good idea . . . we can have a couple more dates and make sure we're not rushing things."

Anna chuckled. Their first date last night and he was ready to meet the parents . . . that sounded a bit quick to her.

"And I know you'll be booked up so we'll just come early on Saturday and stay for the day."

"We are booked, but the spare room in the house is available. You could stay there if you wanted . . . that is, if your friend wouldn't mind getting a room in town."

"I'll ask him about that."

"And I'll try to warm Sarah up to the idea of your coming."

"Thanks, Mom."

However, later in the day, when Anna mentioned the upcoming visit, Sarah turned frosty. Anna decided not to pressure her. Then at dinner, Sarah announced that she wanted to visit the U of O campus before school started. "Do you think that would be okay?"

"I think it's an excellent idea," Anna agreed.

"I thought I could figure out where things are and look at the dormitory." Sarah frowned. "But I know this is a busy time of year. And I don't drive."

"When did you want to go?" Clark asked.

Of course, Sarah wanted to go to Eugene on the same weekend her mother had proposed to visit. Anna knew this wasn't a coincidence. Even so, she reminded her. "And I'd really like to meet him." Anna smiled at Clark. "Lauren sounds so happy. I think this guy must be pretty special."

"I'd like to meet him, too," Clark said.

Sarah got quiet now, looking down at her plate.

"But I'd be happy to drive Sarah to see the U of O," Clark told Anna. "Although I don't like being away for the whole weekend. Not this time of year when we're so busy." He turned to Sarah. "How about if we made it just a day trip? Maybe on a weekday."

"But I wanted to be there on Saturday so I could see Saturday Market, too. I went to it years ago, and it was so cool."

Clark looked stuck. "Well, I don't mind going on a Saturday. What do you think, Anna?"

She smiled. "I think it sounds like fun. I wish I could go, too."

"Then do come," Sarah urged her.

Anna laughed. "I can't very well take off when Lauren is bringing her friend to visit."

"You think I'm rude, don't you, Grandma?"

Anna studied Sarah, trying to think of a kind way to put this. "I just think you're still hurting, and, well, I wish you could move past it. For everyone's sake."

Sarah pursed her lips.

"Some wounds take more time to heal," Clark said gently.

"You're right," Anna agreed. "I just look forward to the day when we can all gather happily together."

Now Clark changed the subject, telling them

about how Johnny Johnson had made a woman friend in town. "She works at the café, and I could tell she'd caught Johnny's eye from the get-go. Her name is Margie, and she's got bright red hair, you know the kind that comes from a box. But she's pretty nice and seems to like Johnny. Problem is if we're anywhere near town, Johnny will suddenly get the urge for a piece of chocolate cream pie."

Anna resolved herself to Sarah and Clark being gone on the Saturday when Lauren and Brad were scheduled to come. The upside was that since Clark left the boat in the dock in town, Lauren and Brad were able to take it upriver with them. They were supposed to arrive at the inn just in time for lunch. And since it was such a nice day, Anna decided to serve lunch on the upstairs deck outside. Thanks to Clark and Johnny, she had made a big Crab Louis salad and was just setting a vase of wildflowers on the table when she heard the boat coming into the dock.

Anxious to see Lauren and curious about her new friend, Anna hurried down the stairs to greet them. Lauren was beaming and looking better than ever as an attractive man with longish straight hair helped her off the boat. Dressed casually in jeans, a faded Hawaiian shirt, and sandals, he seemed comfortable in his own skin. Lauren quickly introduced Anna to Brad; and

Anna could see why Lauren thought he seemed "familiar." With his dark hair and eyes, he could easily pass for Anna's son. In fact, he looked more like Anna than her own daughter did.

"This is a beautiful place," he told Anna as they walked up to the house. "It's no wonder you're fully booked."

She thanked him. "And I'm sure Lauren will give you the full tour after lunch."

"You should've seen this place before Mom and Clark went to work on it," Lauren said as they went upstairs. "It's been an amazing transformation over the years." She grinned at Anna. "It just gets better and better."

"This is great. Really pretty." Brad nodded at where the lunch table was laid out with the good china, linens, silver, and flowers. Now he turned to look at the river. "What a view!"

"Brad is an artist," Lauren said proudly. "A very talented bronze sculptor." She went on to tell about some impressive places where his pieces were being shown.

As they sat down, Anna asked about the subject of his sculptures.

"Nature," he told her. "Mostly animals. A few people."

"Brad's mother is Native American," Lauren told Anna.

"I wondered about that," Anna admitted. "Do you mind if I ask which tribe?"

"She's mostly Paiute. She grew up in Warm Springs," Brad explained. "But she moved off the reservation when she married my dad. I used to feel cheated by that—not living on the rez, I mean."

"How so?" Anna passed Lauren the salad.

"Well, Mom would take me to visit sometimes. And she has all these relatives and the kids there seemed to have so much freedom and there were horses to ride and the river and streams. I'd have such a great time that I was always unhappy when it was time to go home, back to our cracker box house in the 'burbs."

"I can understand how you would miss that sense of community," Anna said.

"I did."

"But you could live there now if you wanted, couldn't you?" Anna asked. "On the reservation?"

"I actually tried it for a while when I was in my twenties. Turned out it wasn't the same. A lot of good folks there, but some sad dysfunctions, too. I'd moved there thinking it would be idyllic . . . an inspiration for my sculptures, but I found I got distracted from my art when I was there. I'd get caught up in some of their problems . . . and then I started drinking and that was a disaster."

"I see." Anna passed the basket of rolls to him.

"I finally realized that for my own health, as well as for my art, I had to leave. But I go back to visit sometimes. And I've taught workshops at the school." Now he asked Anna about her own family and the Siuslaw heritage. She could tell he wasn't just making small talk but that he was genuinely interested.

"My stepfather's mother saved a bunch of our stories," Lauren told him. "You still have them, don't you, Mom?"

"Of course. And you're welcome to take copies if you want to read them." Anna smiled, thinking of how little interest Lauren used to have about these things.

"I'd love to read some," Brad told her. He gazed out toward the river and just shook his head. "This is really a magical place. I can feel it." He turned to Lauren. "I can understand why you miss it so much."

"It took me a long time to fully appreciate it," Lauren admitted. "But it really is special."

After lunch, Lauren gave him the full tour, and they even took out a canoe. Brad seemed to be even more enchanted when they went down to the dining room for dinner. "I think I could live here," he told Anna.

She smiled. "Well, you're seeing one of our best days. The weather isn't always this spectacular. We get a fair amount of fog and clouds . . . and then there's the rain. Some people can't take the wet gray days."

"It's not any grayer than Eugene," Lauren told her. "Trust me, I know."

"Good point." Anna agreed.

"The weather here on the coast seems to blow away and clear out better," Lauren told Brad. "Whereas the valley seems to trap the clouds."

"And the smog," he added.

Lauren sighed. "See why I miss it so."

Anna thought of Sarah and Clark now. Were they having a good visit in Eugene? Was it smoggy there? Did Sarah feel any remorse for dragging Clark away from his opportunity to spend time with Lauren and to meet Brad? More important, would Sarah ever figure out how to forgive her mother? Would they always be passing like two ships in the night? Carefully avoiding each other—going their separate ways? And if they did, how would Anna manage to accept it?

26

As usual, Anna had mixed feelings when Labor Day arrived. On one hand, she was relieved that their busiest time of year was coming to an end, but on the other hand, it was hard to say good-bye to another summer. And it had been such a pleasant one—not only because of Sarah's being with them, but the weather had been delightful, too. Sunny and mild besides that sorrowful time of the dying whales in June, it had been a perfect summer.

Even so, the hardest part about seeing it end was knowing Sarah was about to leave for school. Sometimes Anna wondered how many more partings she could bear. Oh, certainly, it was a part of life . . . but why was it that it seemed to grow more difficult as one grew older? Was this how her mother had felt when Anna had married and left so many decades ago?

Not for the first time, Anna wondered about how it had been a hundred years ago . . . or back before the white man came. Back in a slower time. . . when families and communities stayed together, helping one another, living peaceably alongside the river . . . and no one left. Was that what she was always longing for? That sense of connectedness . . . of being part of something bigger?

And she knew that, in some ways, she provided that for the guests who came to stay at the inn. They would settle in, make new friends, connect with old ways, experience the peace of the river, and perhaps even experience some form of personal healing. Or so she was often told as guests were departing, going back to their faster-paced citified lives.

But what if what she offered was only a temporary comfort? She tried not to think about it too much, but what if it was only a placebo? Or, even worse, what if she was some kind of charlatan? Pretending to have answers, feigning a place of healing . . . but it wasn't lasting or real? These were questions that sometimes bothered her in the middle of the night.

And yet, she knew that her motives were genuine. She wanted to share with others what she'd experienced on the river. As fleeting and confusing as that sometimes felt, she wanted others to know the peace and the wholeness to be found here. And at the same time she was tired . . . she was growing weary of all the coming and going . . . most of all the leaving.

Besides Sarah going off to college, both Diane and Janelle had announced this was their last summer to work for her. Diane was getting married, and Janelle was moving to New Zealand, of all places! Not only that, but with the expectation of their first child, Jewel and Skip seemed to be up in the air. One day they would want to stay here at the inn indefinitely. The next day, Skip would be talking to his dad about becoming a plumber. Nothing seemed to remain the same.

However, Anna continued to find comfort in the constancy of the river. Oh, yes, it was constantly changing as well. Always renewing itself, never running dry, it kept on flowing. Even after a long, warm summer, it didn't run out. Going and flowing, the Siuslaw rippled past the inn, shimmering like diamonds during the high tide, always finding its way out to the sea. She could count on that. In the same way that she could count on God's grace to continue to flow through her life, she could count on the river to keep flowing to the sea. And that was a comfort!

These were the thoughts Anna comforted herself with after they dropped Sarah off at college. She and Clark had driven her there, carrying in her boxes and bags and seeing her safely settled into the big brick dormitory. Sarah's roommate, a petite blond named Susan, had seemed sweet and smart and already knew where the best deli was located. And so, Anna had hugged her dear girl and parted ways.

She'd hidden her tears as she and Clark walked back to the station wagon. Really, they were tears of both joy and sadness. When she thought of where they'd all been just one year ago, she knew that she should be exceedingly happy. And she was. It's just that she was sad, too.

"I thought we should stop by Lauren's coffee shop," Clark said as he drove away from campus. "I found it when I was here with Sarah that weekend. I told Sarah it's where her mom worked, and, of course, she wanted nothing to do with it. But I know where it's located."

"Do you think Lauren would be there?" Anna asked. "I didn't even call her to say we were bringing Sarah. I didn't want to make her feel bad."

"Doesn't she usually work weekends?"

"That's what she said."

As it turned out, Lauren was there. And she was thrilled to see them. Anna quickly explained that they'd brought Sarah to school then just as quickly changed the subject to inquire about Lauren's classes.

"I'm taking a lot of hours this fall," she told them. "But I decided to go for my associate's degree." She swiped the counter and looked around the nearly deserted coffee shop. "I'm not even sure what I'll do with it, but I suppose it can't hurt."

"Are you still seeing Brad?" Anna asked.

Lauren smiled and nodded. "We're going out tonight. Maybe you guys could go with us." She looked at Clark. "You haven't met him yet."

"And I've heard he's quite a guy."

"How about it?" Lauren asked.

So it was that the four of them went to dinner together. And Anna was pleased at how easily Clark and Brad connected. She could tell that Lauren was relieved, too. "Maybe you two can come visit us on the river again," Clark told them as they were going their separate ways. "We're not fully booked now."

Brad agreed to this, and, before Anna got into the car, she hugged her daughter tightly. She wanted to tell Lauren that since Sarah was now going to school, Lauren could consider moving back to the river, but she knew that Lauren was making her own way, carving her own path, and

Anna wouldn't be surprised if Brad was going to be a part of those plans. For Lauren's sake, she hoped so.

Fall came gently, and Anna and Clark fell into a slower speed. And to Anna's relief, Jewel and Skip continued to postpone what seemed to be the inevitable—moving to town. The baby wasn't due until after Christmas, and Jewel seemed determined to hang on at the river for as long as possible.

"I love Skip," she confided to Anna one morning, "but his mother is insufferable."

"But you won't be living with his mother," Anna pointed out.

"Ha!" Jewel shook her head dismally. "Skip's parents want us to live in his grandma's old house. She's moving into a retirement center. But her house is right next door to Skip's parents. It'll feel like we're living with them."

"Oh . . ." Anna reluctantly recalled her years of living too close to her first mother-in-law. While she didn't want to plant any more worrisome thoughts in Jewel's head, she hoped that Jewel wasn't about to get into something like that.

"I wish we could stay here."

"You know you're more than welcome," Anna assured her. Of course, they'd already made this clear to both of them—although they weren't trying to influence them one way or the other.

This decision belonged to the young couple. "We'd love having a baby around," she reminded Jewel. "And even if you do move to town, I hope you'll come out to visit sometimes."

Lauren called Anna in October to share her good news. "We're engaged!" she cried into the phone.

"That's wonderful," Anna told her. "I'm so happy for both of you!"

"He's my soul mate, Mom. I just know it."

"He seems like a wonderful man, Lauren."

"I told him I want the wedding to be at the river. Is that okay?"

"It's more than okay, Lauren, I'm thrilled. Have you set a date?"

"We thought sometime after Christmas. So I can be done with my classes. Or maybe New Year's Eve. That would be fun."

"Well, either time is fine around here. You know how slow things are during December. We'll have plenty of room. And I assume he'll have family that will want to come."

"Yes. We'll make a plan and let you know."

"I'm really happy for you, Lauren. Brad is a good guy. Do you know where you'll live?"

"Brad has this really great house on one of the south hills over here. It's got vaulted open-beamed ceilings and lots of windows. You'd love it, Mom."

"Hopefully I'll get to see it someday."

"Someday soon!"

They talked a while longer, and Anna tried not to let the sadness she felt creep into her voice. She truly was thrilled for Lauren's sake, and she knew Lauren was over the moon with happiness. But she also knew this meant that Lauren would probably never move back home again. And, really, Anna should've known better than to expect that she would. Grown children weren't supposed to move back home. They were supposed to create their own way . . . and yet . . . Anna had hoped.

With Thanksgiving approaching, Anna longed to gather her family together and was delighted to hear that, besides Marshall and Joanna joining them, both Sarah and Lauren planned to come home as well.

"I want to stay here, too," Jewel told her as they were folding towels together just a few days before the holiday, "but Skip thinks we should go to his sister's."

"Well, know that you're welcome," Anna said. "The more the merrier."

"I'll try to talk Skip into it." Jewel rubbed her enlarged midsection. "I can always tell him that I'm too tired to go to town and back." She giggled. "Might as well use this while I can."

Anna laughed. "It would be fun to have you and

Skip, too. I thought maybe we'd all play games. I want to keep things lively so that Sarah and Lauren are too busy to worry about old baggage."

"I don't see why Sarah has such a problem with Lauren. I mean my mom wasn't the greatest, but we're okay."

Anna wasn't sure how much Jewel knew about Lauren and wasn't sure how much to tell her. "Well, it's complicated," she said.

"It's not like Lauren was a drug addict or anything." Jewel laughed.

"Actually . . ." Anna cleared her throat. "She was."

"Oh?" Jewel's eyes got wide. "I had no idea."

"Yes, well, it's not something I usually share. But Sarah has been through a lot. Lauren was never much of a mother. And Sarah's dad wasn't much better. I guess we shouldn't have been so shocked when she ran away at sixteen."

"She was only sixteen?"

Anna nodded as she placed a towel on the growing stack. "In some ways she seemed much older, but she was only sixteen."

"Wow, that is hard. I didn't realize. I was out of high school by the time I ran off. And that was hard enough for my mom." Jewel rubbed her belly again. "Man, I hope my kid never does anything like that to me."

"Hopefully, you'll be a good mother and your kid will never want to run away."

Anna had already gotten groceries, baked some pies, and was planning on a full table of family for Thanksgiving when she got Sarah's call on Wednesday morning. It seemed that Sarah had run into Lauren at the bookstore and consequently discovered that Lauren was coming for Thanksgiving, too.

"So I think I'll just stay on campus," Sarah said casually, "I'll catch up on my studies as well as my sleep."

"But I want to see you," Anna said.

"I promise I'll come home right after finals week," Sarah assured her. "That's only three weeks off."

"But it's Thanksgiving," Anna told her. "It would be so nice to be together."

"I'm sorry, Grandma. But, really, I think it's best. The truth is I'm kind of stressed out over school. I took some pretty hard classes, and I want to make good grades."

Anna tried to talk her out of it, saying that a break might do her good, but Sarah could be awfully stubborn when she wanted to.

"Well, if you change your mind, you are more than welcome to join us, Sarah. You know that."

"I know." She apologized once more then said she had to go because someone else needed to use the phone.

It wasn't until that evening that she heard the

rest of the disappointing news. "Lauren called this afternoon." Skip told Anna as he stood just inside the door. The rain was pelting down behind him. "Jewel took the message and forgot to tell you. Anyway, Jewel said that Brad's got a bad cold so they won't be coming tomorrow."

"A bad cold?" Anna was skeptical.

"That's what she said." Skip shrugged. "Sorry to be the bearer of bad news."

Clark stood up from where he'd been reading the newspaper and came over to join them. "That reminds me." He grimaced. "Although I'm sure you won't want to hear my news now."

Anna frowned. "What is it?"

"Marshall and Joanna can't come either. Marshall said his mom was pressuring him to spend a holiday with her."

Anna sighed. "Well, I can't blame her for that."

"The upside is that Marshall said this gives them the green light to spend Christmas with us. And they really want to be here for Lauren's wedding."

"That'll be nice." She forced a smile and turned to Skip. "So how about you and Jewel? Have you changed your plans too?"

"Well, my mom is pretty peeved at me for turning down my sister's invite." Skip shook his head. "Seems she was planning to make it part Thanksgiving and part baby shower for Jewel. As a surprise, you know? But no one told us."

"Maybe you should join them," Clark said.

"Yes," Anna agreed. "I hate to think of Jewel missing out on a baby shower. And it's not as if there will be much going on here . . . not now that everyone has cancelled."

"You really don't mind?"

Clark assured him that it was fine, and after Skip left, Anna went to give Lauren a call. Maybe she could entice her to come now that Sarah had backed out. But Lauren didn't seem to be home.

"I guess it's just going to be you and me tomorrow," Anna told Clark as they were getting ready for bed.

"Are you terribly disappointed?"

"A little, but I'll be fine." She continued braiding her hair, trying to act as if it didn't matter although she felt it deeply. "And we'll have lots of leftovers."

"Leftovers are good."

"Say, do you think Johnny Johnson would like to come over?" She tied off the braid and stood.

"Johnny's been invited to have dinner in town with Margie." Clark took her in his arms and looked into her eyes. "But I don't mind having a nice quiet Thanksgiving for two, Anna. Think about it . . . just you and me. Might even be romantic."

Despite her sadness, she couldn't help but smile. "Leave it to you to see the bright side, Clark."

27

Jewel and Skip moved into his grandmother's house the week after Thanksgiving. Anna tried to be brave as she told them good-bye, but when she was alone she cried. She knew it was probably for the best—for Jewel and Skip and Skip's family —but Anna had longed to have them remain here on the river. She would've loved to have had a baby around again. Still, it wasn't her decision. And she knew she had to let go . . . again.

Lauren and Brad decided to get married on the Saturday after Christmas. "We want to keep it small and intimate," Lauren told Anna when they finally connected by phone on the week after Thanksgiving. "Just family and close friends. Brad wants it to be in the evening . . . illuminated with nothing but candlelight."

"That sounds lovely."

"Do you think there's any chance that Sarah might come?"

"She's promised to be home for Christmas vacation. So as far as I know she'll be here."

"But do you think she'll want to attend the wedding?"

"It's hard to say, Lauren." The truth was, Anna didn't want to say . . . because she was afraid

Sarah would probably concoct some excuse to get out of it.

"After what happened over Thanksgiving . . . well, I won't get my hopes up."

"I'll talk to her about it," Anna told her. "She'll be here the week before Christmas so I'll have time to work on her."

"And Brad and I thought we should probably pass on joining you for Christmas."

"But Lauren, we planned on having you. Marshall and Joanna will be here. And Jewel and Skip. Johnny is bringing his new girlfriend. And Mrs. Smyth and several others, too. I thought if we had a big crowd, it would make it easier on you and Sarah. Please, come."

"I want to, Mom. Believe me, there's no place I'd rather be. But I don't want to spoil it for everyone . . . especially for Sarah."

"We've got to get past this," Anna firmly told her. "Promise me that you and Brad will come, and I will promise to have a long, serious talk with Sarah. I have a feeling she's gotten stuck in the past . . . that she might need some gentle nudging to move forward."

"And you want to nudge her?"

"As a matter of fact, I do."

Anna could tell that Sarah was worn out from her first term of college and final exams. For that reason, Anna decided not to bring up the topic of

Lauren's wedding until Sarah had some time to relax and recover. For three days, she'd slept in past ten, but on the fourth morning, she got up before nine.

"You look like you're more rested," Anna told Sarah as she came over to the dining table where Anna was working.

"What are you making?" Sarah asked.

Anna looked up from where she was gluing dried flowers and twigs onto a base of wood. "Candle holders." She showed Sarah the little brass cups that would hold a taper candle once it was adhered to the wood. "See how it works?"

"Pretty." Sarah sat down at the table and, picking up a sprig of lavender, sniffed it. "Hmm . . . sweet."

"Do you want to help?"

"Sure."

Anna explained the process, and they worked together quietly for a while.

"Are these for Christmas presents?" Sarah asked as she picked up a fragile rosebud.

"No . . ." Anna considered her answer, wondering if there was a way to soften it and then decided not to. "They're for your mother's wedding."

"Oh." The dried rosebud crumbled in Sarah's hand.

"Yes, I figured you'd lose interest if you knew that." Anna looked evenly at her. "But there you have it. Your mother has met a great guy, and they are getting married on the Saturday following Christmas. The wedding will be here at the inn with a reception following. I expect you'll want to disappear throughout the whole thing." She sighed. "And that is your choice."

Sarah looked slightly dumbfounded.

"I left some oatmeal on the stove," Anna told her. "In case you're hungry for breakfast."

"Uh, sure." Sarah slowly stood, going into the kitchen.

Anna stared at the pieces of crushed rosebud. She had dried those roses in the late fall, hoping to find a use for them for Lauren's wedding. She had plenty more. But something about seeing it there got to her.

"Grandpa and I already ate." Anna knew that her voice sounded stiff and tight. And she was well aware that she wasn't treating Sarah with the usual soft kid gloves. But maybe it was time for Sarah to get a small dose of reality. Well, after she'd had some breakfast anyway.

As Sarah fixed herself a bowl of oatmeal, eating in the kitchen, Anna continued to sit at the dining room table, gluing flowers . . . and she prayed silently. She didn't want to lose all her patience with Sarah. But at the same time she didn't want to sit idly by or give the impression she was encouraging Sarah's stubbornness. Even the coldest winter had to end eventually.

"Are you mad at me, Grandma?" Sarah sat back down at the dining room table.

Anna looked directly into her eyes. "I'm not mad at you, Sarah. But I am worried."

With pursed lips, Sarah picked up a willow twig and, spinning it between her fingers, studied it.

"Do you know what that is?" Anna asked.

Sarah's brow creased. "Some kind of branch?"

"It's willow."

"Oh . . ."

"Do you know what willow is for?"

Sarah's expression showed she did not.

"Willow is for maturity and balance. My grandmother used to make willow tea for people who struggled with bitterness and selfishness. Willow was supposed to help bring a more positive attitude."

Sarah dropped the twig.

"Perhaps I should make you some." Anna's lips curved into a partial smile.

"Do you think it would help?" Sarah sounded sincere.

Anna shrugged. "I doubt it would hurt."

"Okay." Sarah nodded.

Anna was surprised. "Really, you want some willow tea?"

"Sure."

Now Anna didn't even know if she had any dried willow. But as she went to her jars of dried herbs, she was determined to concoct some kind of tea—even if it wasn't willow, it would be worth a try. Perhaps tea and sympathy would unlock something in Sarah. When she returned with two steaming cups of herb tea, a combination of chamomile, lemongrass, and mint, Sarah was back to working on the candleholders.

As they sipped tea and glued flowers and twigs, Anna told Sarah a bit about how Lauren and Brad met, how they chatted regularly in the coffee shop, but that it took months for Lauren to find out his name. Sarah listened with an air of disinterest, but at least she listened. So Anna continued, telling Sarah about Brad's sculptures. She even went to find the photos Lauren had sent her and showed them to Sarah.

Sarah nodded in an absent sort of way. "He's good."

"And he's Native American," Anna said finally.

Sarah looked up with a stunned expression. "Really?"

"Yes. His mother is part Paiute. She grew up on a reservation."

"Really?" Sarah looked skeptical. "My mom is going to marry a Native American?"

"She is."

"That's hard to believe."

"Why is that?" Anna paused to sip her tea.

"Because she's always been so . . . well, so . . . conventional." Sarah frowned as if that wasn't what she wanted to say. "Or to be more specific, she's been rather narrow-minded and bigoted. I find it hard to believe she's going to marry a Native American."

"That's because you don't really know her, Sarah. You know who she used to be. But she has changed—dramatically. She started to change when she came to the river after her marriage fell apart. She changed even more during the time when you were missing. It was hard on her not knowing where you were . . . it was hard on all of us. But your mother blamed herself for your troubles, Sarah."

"Well, she had a lot to do with it."

"And she realizes that. And I know she wants to tell you she's sorry. Except that you won't listen."

Sarah took a long sip of tea then peered down into the cup. "Does this stuff really work, Grandma?"

Anna sighed. "You tell me."

Sarah shrugged.

"What good does it do you to hold onto your bitterness against your mother, Sarah?" Anna set the candleholder down with a thud. "Can you tell me one good reason for withholding your forgiveness from her?"

She shrugged again.

"Does it make you feel good inside?" Anna persisted. "Does it bring you peace and joy and happiness?"

"No." Sarah rolled her eyes. "Of course not."

"Then why hold onto it?"

Sarah drank the last of her tea then sighed deeply. "I don't know. I honestly don't know. It's like I've been doing it so long that I don't know what else to do."

"Do you need to get some kind of counseling?" Anna asked gently.

Sarah's chin was trembling slightly. "I don't know."

"You are such a beautiful person . . . so intelligent . . . such a bright future . . . but holding in that bitterness could steal it all away." Suddenly Anna remembered her own mother. "I've seen it happen before." And so she began to tell Sarah about how Anna's mother resented her own mother for returning to her Siuslaw roots.

"My mother was ashamed of her Indian heritage, Sarah, so much so that she shoved her mother away from her. And it shut my mother down inside. I didn't understand it at the time, but looking back, I can see that's what it did. Her bitterness against my grandmother poisoned my mother. It hurt me, too. I suspect it hurt everyone around her. But I doubt she could see it . . . not when she was younger. It wasn't until she was around my age that she finally acknowledged her problems and began to change. But I'm sure that all that bitterness shortened her life." Anna sighed sadly. "Because she wasn't much older than I am now when she passed on."

"You think I'm like her?" Sarah asked in an offended tone. "You think I would've treated Grandma Pearl like that? I loved Grandma Pearl. I can feel her spirit in the cabin. I can feel her when I read Hazel's book. I would never be like your mother."

"I think your bitterness is similar to my mother's . . . and I don't want that for you, Sarah." Anna picked up a willow branch, bending it in her hands. "I want you to be strong and resilient like a willow. I want you to forgive and heal and move forward with grace and beauty. But you have to choose it for yourself, Sarah."

"How?" Sarah stood with a defiant look in her eye. "How do I *choose* it?"

"Well, first of all, you have to want it. And then, you might need to ask God to help you forgive. Did you ever read those Bible verses that I wrote down for you? The ones about what Jesus said about forgiveness? How we can only receive God's forgiveness when we're willing to give it to others just as freely as he gave it to us? Did you read that yet?"

Sarah shook her head.

"Then I suggest you read it. Perhaps we can sit down and read it together. But you have to choose to do it for yourself, Sarah. And then you simply move forward, one step at a time."

Sarah politely thanked Anna for the tea then headed for the door. Anna wasn't sure if she planned to go read the Bible verses or if she was angry at being pinned down like that. And, really, Anna didn't care if she had angered the girl. It was high time Sarah got beyond these rough waters.

28

Anna had just finished the last of the candle-holders when the phone rang. To her surprise it was Johnny Johnson, and he was out of breath.

"I thought you were fishing with Clark," she said.

"I'm at the hospital, Anna."

"Are you okay?"

"I'm okay. But it's Clark."

Anna's heart lurched. "What? What's wrong?"

"He's in the emergency room."

"Why? What happened?"

"He fell, Anna."

"But is he okay?"

"I'm not sure. But can you get down here?"

"Yes. I'm on my way." She hung up the phone and grabbed her jacket and hurried down the stairs, calling for Sarah as she ran to her cabin. She knocked loudly on the door, and when Sarah didn't answer, Anna opened it. Seeing Sarah wasn't there, she quickly wrote a note saying that

Clark had been hurt and was in the hospital and that she'd gone to town. Then Anna ran down to the dock, started the boat, and was soon racing down the river.

She could hear Clark's calm voice in her ear, saying, "Take it easy, Anna. Calm yourself. Be safe. Slow down." And so she slowed the boat down a bit and tried to take some long, deep breaths, steadying herself as she guided the boat down the center of the river, focusing on the glossy dark water, watching for any logs that might be floating below the surface, trying to remain calm.

Even so, all she could think was—*what would she do without him?* Of all the loved ones who kept moving and slipping away . . . always leaving her behind . . . Clark was the one constant she could always count on. *What would she do without him?* She couldn't bear to think of it. And so she prayed, begging God to please just spare her this one part of her life—he could take all else from her, even this beloved river . . . if only he would spare Clark. Oh, she knew it was futile to bargain with God, and, really, it wasn't what she was trying to do. But she knew in her heart, she would give up all else to keep Clark.

To her relief, Johnny was waiting for her at the dock. He secured the ropes and helped her from the boat. "I've got the car," he explained. And soon they were en route to the hospital.

"What happened, Johnny?" she demanded. "How did Clark fall while you were fishing? Was he on the jetty?"

"Something like that," Johnny mumbled. "It was about a sixteen-foot fall. He hit his head. He was unconscious."

"Oh, no." Anna took in a quick breath.

Now Johnny began talking about what a great friend Clark had been to him and how he helped Johnny to find the good in life and how he didn't want to lose him.

"Do you think that's possible?" Anna asked in a shaky voice.

"I don't know, Anna. It looked bad."

She stared at him now, noticing that he had tear streaks on his face, like he was just as frightened as she was, and, in that instant, it felt like someone had just set a bag of rocks on her chest, like she couldn't breathe. Closing her eyes, she leaned forward, praying desperately for God to spare her husband. Not only for her sake, but for Johnny's sake, too.

It was strange to see the cheerful-looking Christmas tree in the lobby. All thoughts of the upcoming holiday festivities had been obliterated from Anna's mind. All she could think of was Clark. Was he alive?

"He hasn't regained consciousness," the emergency room doctor told them. "We're monitoring him, and his vital signs seem to be stable."

"What does that mean?" Johnny asked. "Is he going to be okay?"

"It's too early to say. And we haven't ruled out a spinal injury yet," the doctor continued. "But our biggest concern right now is the injury to the brain. When a patient doesn't regain consciousness after fifteen minutes, it becomes more serious. Clark has been unconscious for more than two hours."

"What does *that* mean?" Johnny asked again.

"It means it's very serious. The longer a patient remains unconscious, the more likely it is they are sustaining brain damage."

Anna felt her knees getting weak. "Can I see him?"

"Let me check first."

Without saying a word, Johnny and Anna stood there waiting for what felt like an hour when finally a nurse came out and asked for Anna.

"Yes?" Anna eagerly went to her.

"You can see your husband now. But not more than ten minutes."

"Is he conscious?" Anna asked hopefully.

"No." The nurse solemnly shook her head.

Anna followed her back to where Clark was lying motionless behind a privacy screen. His face looked so pale and lifeless that she had to choke back tears. The nurse pulled a chair next to the bed for Anna. "Just ten minutes," she reminded her.

Anna sat on the edge of the chair and, reaching for Clark's hand, careful of the tube in his arm, entwined her fingers around his. "Oh, darling," she whispered, "please, please, come back to me. I love you so much. I can't go on without you. Please, come back." She continued talking like that, rambling on about how much she loved and needed him and then she began to pray. It wasn't until she felt someone tapping on her shoulder that she realized her ten minutes must've expired. She opened her eyes to see that Clark looked exactly the same.

"I'll be back," she told him. "Don't leave me now, darling." She bent down to kiss his cheek, feeling the stubble on her lips. "I love you."

Her tears were flowing freely when she returned to the waiting area. Finally, she got enough control to tell Johnny that Clark was still unconscious. "It's like he's not even there," she said with a fresh sob.

Johnny ran his hand over his forehead and moaned. "I'm so sorry."

Anna excused herself to the restroom where she cried some more then, splashing cold water on her face, dried her tears and blew her nose, determined to be stronger. For Clark's sake, she would keep herself together. It might look hopeless, but she still had prayer. And she could ask everyone else to pray as well.

"I forgot to tell you that Sarah called here at

the hospital when you were in there with Clark," Johnny told her. "The head nurse said she sounded pretty upset. You might want to give her a call."

Anna nodded. "I'll do that."

Sarah answered the phone on the first ring, and Anna, trying to keep her voice even, described the gravity of the situation.

"Oh, Grandma!" Sarah cried.

"Can you do something for me?" Anna asked.

"Yes! Anything!"

"Please, call Marshall and Lauren and anyone else who loves Clark enough to really pray for him." She took in a short breath. "Because prayer might be all we have right now."

"I'll do that, Grandma."

"Thank you."

"And I'm praying, too."

Anna thanked her again then hung up. She went back to the nurse's desk now, asking how often she'd be able to visit him. "I just think it might help for me to be there with him," she said urgently. "Maybe if he can hear me . . . maybe it will help him wake up."

"Let me check on that for you," the nurse said in a compassionate tone.

"Thank you."

To Anna's relief, the doctor decided that it couldn't hurt for Anna to sit with him. "And if he shows any sign of regaining consciousness, you can alert us."

"Yes," Anna said eagerly. "I'll do that."

Seated by his bed again, Anna began to speak to him like she'd done earlier. Only this time, she tried to keep her voice calm and even, tried to keep her tears at bay. She began talking about how she'd felt when they'd first met nearly twenty years ago. "I'd felt middle-aged and faded and sad and lonely . . . I felt all used up and worn out," she confessed, "until you looked at me that day, Clark. When I looked into those eyes—those river-blue eyes—well, everything changed then. You made me feel like a girl again. I was young and fresh and new. That's what you did to me, Clark. You still do that to me."

She continued talking, telling him how important he'd been to her, how she couldn't have done the inn without him. She told him how much she loved him, reminding him of all they'd done and built together and how they weren't done yet.

Every once in a while, she'd look up at the big clock on the back wall. Judging by what the doctor had told her, Clark had been unconscious for more than three hours now. She wondered how much the prognosis worsened with each passing hour. What if he never woke up? And so she returned to praying again.

With her eyes closed and her warm hand wrapped around his cool lifeless one, Anna prayed like she'd never prayed before. Then shortly after she'd peeked at the clock again, cringing to see another half hour had passed, she was surprised to feel a movement in her hand. Clark's fingers had tightened their grasp.

"Clark," she said hopefully. "Clark, are you there? Can you hear me? Oh, Clark, please, come back to me. I need you so!"

With her other hand, she reached to touch his face, stroking his forehead and his cheek, imagining she could see muscles twitching, hoping it was so—and then his eyes fluttered open.

"Oh, Clark!" she exclaimed joyfully. "Oh, darling!"

At first he looked bewildered, almost as if he didn't know her—and her heart gave a lurch—but then the corners of his mouth curved into a smile. "I'm in trouble now," he said in a rough-sounding voice.

"Of course you're not in trouble, Clark." She stood up and tenderly kissed him. "You're not in the least bit of trouble."

"What happened?" he asked with a confused expression. "Where am I?"

"In the hospital. You fell and hit your head while you were fishing today," she explained.

"Fishing?" His brow creased causing him to wince in pain.

"Let me run and get the doctor, darling." She hated to release his hand. "He needs to see you. I promised I'd tell them when you came to."

"Hurry back," Clark said weakly.

Anna ran out, calling for the doctor and nurse, excitedly telling them the good news. And Johnny, who was standing by the nurse's station, let out a happy hoot. Then Anna followed the doctor and nurse back and, waiting on the sidelines as they began to check him and ask him questions, said a sincere thank-you prayer. She couldn't hear everything being said but thought it was a good sign when the doctor and nurse both burst into laughter. Clark must've been clear enough to say something amusing.

Finally, the doctor just shook his head. "Well, maybe this is our Christmas miracle this year. But you seem to be just fine, Mr. Richards."

"Can I go home?" Clark asked.

"Not today," the doctor said. "That was quite a blow you took to your head. I'd like to keep you here to observe overnight. But if you continue to improve like this, I think we can let you go home tomorrow. As long as you promise you'll get several days of bed rest. You'll need to take it very, very easy." He chuckled. "And no more fishing!"

Clark held up his hand like making an oath. "You have my word."

The doctor laughed loudly, like this was a good joke. Anna didn't really get it. But she didn't care either. She was so happy to have Clark back that she just laughed along with them. Before long, Johnny came in to visit, too.

"I called Sarah and told her that you're going to be okay," he told them. "You really had us scared, Clark." He let out a long sigh. "I wasn't ready to lose my best fishing buddy yet."

"But the doctor made me swear off fishing," Clark told him. "Told me it was time to hang up the old fishing pole. And I think he's probably right."

"Aw, you don't need to go fishing no more," Johnny said. "We caught enough fish to last a lifetime." And the two men chuckled like this was still a very funny joke.

Anna tried not to feel left out. And, really, what did she care if they enjoyed their silly boyish humor, the important thing was that she had Clark back. What else mattered?

29

Busy taking care of Clark, Anna left the bulk of the holiday preparations in Sarah's hands. Sarah took these responsibilities seriously. She got a tree in place and decorated it. She did some baking. And she even took Anna's boat to town and did the shopping. But during this time, Sarah seemed somewhat distant and moody. However, Anna didn't have the time or energy to deal with it.

"Like I already told you," Anna reminded Sarah as they unloaded the groceries in the kitchen, "we can have a very low-key celebration this year. The most important thing is just being together." Anna hadn't brought up the subject of Lauren again. And since the wedding was to be a rather simple affair, there was no need to speak of it much. If Sarah chose to boycott the ceremony, so be it. Anna decided she no longer cared. Sarah would have to paddle her own canoe.

On the day before Christmas, Clark was finally allowed to get out of bed and move around some. But sore from two cracked ribs and the bruises incurred in his fall, he was moving slowly. But all things considered he was in rather good spirits. And when Skip and Jewel arrived, he perked up even more.

"We came early in order to ask you something," Skip told Anna and Clark.

"Go for it," Clark said as he reclined on the sofa with a cup of cocoa.

"We want to come back," Jewel exclaimed.

"It's not working out," Skip said, "living so close to my folks."

"It's awful," Jewel confessed.

"But it hasn't even been a month," Anna pointed out.

"Yeah, but it's really not good," Skip explained. "I hate working for my dad. I never wanted to be a plumber."

"We want to come back here," Jewel said again. "This feels like home to us."

Anna laughed. "Well, then by all means come back."

Clark patted his midsection which was wrapped in a stretchy bandage. "We need you more now than ever."

In response, Jewel patted her midsection which had gotten enormous and nodded. "And you don't mind that there will be three of us soon?"

"Not a bit," Anna assured her. "You know that I wanted that baby around here. I just didn't want to come between you and Skip's family."

"But you guys are my family," Jewel proclaimed.

Sarah came in with a hard-to-read expression as she set a plate of cookies on the coffee table. "You and Skip are coming back to the inn?" she asked.

"Isn't it great?" Jewel said enthusiastically as she reached for a cookie.

"Yeah." Sarah nodded. "I guess so."

It wasn't long before Marshall and Joanna and Lauren and Brad arrived. They had coordinated their travels in order to share a boat on the river. Anna got them settled into their rooms and cabins, and after a while, they all began to gather in the house upstairs. Everyone that is, except Sarah.

"It's so wonderful to have you all together like this," Anna said as they stood around the crackling fire. "It seems long overdue."

They visited and caught up as other guests,

including Johnny and Margie and Mrs. Smyth, began to arrive. Anna's plan was to serve a casual buffet and then play games and sing Christmas carols. But it bothered her that Sarah was missing. Still, she decided to do her best to ignore this. After all, she had told Sarah that it was up to her whether she participated or not. She had obviously chosen not to.

"Where is Sarah tonight?" Mrs. Smyth asked as they were eating.

"I'm not sure," Anna admitted. "Maybe in her cabin."

Lauren tossed Anna an uncomfortable look, but Anna just shrugged. Then, as the guests were beginning to enjoy dessert, Lauren excused herself. Anna was tempted to chase her daughter down the stairs and demand that she stay and participate in the celebration with them, but she knew it would be futile. Lauren's feelings were probably hurt by Sarah's absence. And, really, who could blame her?

Anna could see that Clark was wearing down. "I don't want to put a damper on the party," she told everyone, "but I'm going to have to insist that Clark call it a night." She smiled at him. "I know your doctor would back me on this."

He made a helpless look. "I suppose I better mind her. Otherwise, Santa might put a coal in my stocking."

To Anna's dismay, the rest of the party began to

break up after that. But as she got ready for bed, she decided that perhaps it was for the best since they still had Christmas day to spend together. And then there was the wedding. No sense in trying to do it all in one night. Seeing that Clark was already sleeping soundly confirmed that she'd done the right thing. It was ironic though . . . finally, she had her family here with her and she was content to just go to bed. Maybe she was getting old.

The next morning Anna got up early and was making coffee in the kitchen when she noticed two figures down by the river. It was hard to tell who they were since it was barely dawn and a thick blanket of fog had rolled onto the riverbank overnight. But they appeared to be embracing. Probably one of the couples sharing a Christmas hug. But then as the pair walked up to the house, Anna nearly fell over from shock. Blinking to see if her eyes were playing tricks, she realized it was really true—Lauren and Sarah, mother and daughter, walking side by side on their way up to the house.

Anna took in a deep breath and waited for the front door to open and then, trying not to look as stunned as she felt, welcomed them, casually offering them coffee.

"Oh, Grandma," Sarah said in a teasing tone. "Don't pretend you're not shocked by the fact that Mom and I are acting civilly."

Anna poured three cups. "Well, I'll admit you've caught me off guard."

"I went to talk to Sarah last night," Lauren explained. "But then, for some reason, I decided not to. Instead, I went to bed early. Then this morning, I woke early and went for a walk. When I saw Sarah down on the dock, I thought I'd corner her. I marched down there thinking I'd force her to listen to my full apology. Either that or she'd have to jump into the river." Lauren laughed. "But I'd barely asked her to forgive me and she said yes. Just like that!"

"Actually, there's a little more to it than that." Sarah took a cup and sat down at the kitchen table. "I was feeling guilty."

"Guilty?" Anna sat down across from her.

"Yes. I was thinking about Christmas—I mean that it's supposed to be the celebration of Jesus Christ's birth—and I remembered the Bible verses you told me to read, before Grandpa got hurt."

"About forgiveness?"

Sarah nodded. "I read them yesterday morning."

"Good for you."

"And I'd been thinking about them off and on all day. Then last night when everyone was having a good time together and I realized how miserable I was . . . that's why I left."

"So she could be miserable alone," Lauren said in a slightly teasing tone. Then she smiled apologetically at Sarah and sat down. "Sorry. But I'm glad you took the time to think about it. Not just for my sake either." She sighed. "When I think how long it took me to figure these things out—well, maybe I still am—anyway, you're way ahead of me."

Sarah looked at Anna with sparkling eyes. "So, I kept thinking about everything you'd said. And I read those verses again. It was around midnight when it started to make sense. I started to figure it out—and it just hit me. I finally got it."

"About forgiveness?"

"Yes!" She smiled happily. "I understood that I was blocking God from forgiving me when I refused to forgive my mom. I could see how I'd built this wall all around me. Each stone was like each time I chose not to forgive. I realized how this wall isolated me from God and from others— and that it was making me miserable. And I knew I needed to knock it down. And that's what I did."

"We both happened to get up early," Lauren told Anna. "To go for a walk." She winked. "Think that was a coincidence?"

"I think God planned the whole thing," Anna said with certainty.

"As soon as I saw Sarah, I started telling her how sorry I was about everything—but she cut me off. She didn't even let me apologize for all the messes I've put her through over the years."

Lauren shook her head. "And it was a long, long list."

"But I didn't really need to hear it anymore," Sarah confessed.

Anna could hardly believe her ears.

"Because I had already forgiven her." Sarah smiled at her mother.

"Good for you," Anna reached for Sarah's hand and then for Lauren's. "Good for both of you."

"I'll say." Lauren sighed. "What a relief."

"You were right all along, Grandma," Sarah admitted sheepishly. "And I feel so much better now. I don't know why I couldn't see it before."

"It doesn't matter," Anna assured her. "What's important is that you see it now. What a wonderful Christmas present for you, Sarah. And for all of us."

"This is the best Christmas present I ever could've received," Lauren proclaimed.

And it turned out to be the best Christmas as well. Anna was thrilled to have so many of her loved ones around her—and without any squabbles. She knew she couldn't expect every Christmas to be like this one, but she was determined to enjoy it to the fullest while it was here.

By Saturday, as they were getting ready for the wedding, Lauren asked Sarah if she would consider standing up with her. "I know it's last minute. I wasn't really planning to have anyone. But would you be my maid of honor?"

"Really?" Sarah blinked. "You'd want me? After all we've been through?"

"But it's behind us now," Lauren reminded her.

"What about Brad?" Sarah asked.

Brad came in from where he'd been visiting with his parents in the living room. "I think it's a great idea," he told Sarah. "Lauren already asked me about it, and I gave her two thumbs up."

"Okay then." Sarah glanced at Anna. "Do you think I should wear my graduation dress?"

"Oh, yes," Lauren told her. "Please, do. You looked so pretty in it."

And so later that evening, with about fifty candles burning in the handmade candleholders, and with Marshall playing classical guitar, and with Sarah positioned by the bride, and a small group of family and friends looking on, Lauren and Brad stood by the fireplace and repeated their wedding vows. Anna thought it was perfect.

Then, just before the happy couple was getting ready to make their exit on a riverboat the next morning, Lauren and Brad took Anna aside.

"We want to ask you something," Lauren began a bit nervously, "before we go, we wanted to hear your thoughts on this."

"On what?" Anna asked curiously.

"Well, Brad and I both love it on the river. And he can sculpt anywhere. And now that I have my business degree I'm ready to really manage a business."

Anna felt her hopes soaring. "Do you mean . . . would you want to come here to live?"

"Could we?" Brad asked hopefully. "I could probably help out with the inn, too."

"And we can take one of the little cabins," Lauren told her.

"You can have Babette's house," Anna told her.

Lauren's eyes lit up.

"Is that the little cottage you told me about?" Brad asked her.

She nodded happily. "We'll stop by and see it on our way out."

Anna hugged them both. "This is wonderful news!"

"We probably won't be ready to make the move until March or so," Lauren told her. "But I definitely plan to be back here before the summer season begins."

"I'm already looking forward to it," Anna told her.

Then, after they'd all waved good-bye to the newlyweds, throwing birdseed instead of rice, Anna hurried upstairs to tell Clark the good news.

"Do you know what this means?" she asked.

He grinned. "That you won't be nearly so busy this summer?"

"Yes. Plus I'll have Lauren nearby. And Jewel and Skip will be here, too. It's like everyone who'd been leaving is coming back again. Maybe Sarah will end up back here, too." She sighed. "But I won't pressure her."

"Maybe they're like the water in the river," Clark said thoughtfully. "It seems like it goes its own way as it passes to the sea, but eventually it evaporates from the ocean, turns to rain, and runs back down the river again."

Anna laughed. "You're right."

The wedding guests were coming back into the house now, but Anna could tell by the excited sounds of their voices that something was wrong—or as it turned out, something was right.

"Jewel is in labor," Janelle announced. "Skip is taking her to the hospital to have the baby."

"And Sarah went with them to help," Marshall explained.

Anna chuckled. "I'm not sure what Sarah knows about birthing babies, but I'm sure Jewel appreciates the gesture. Hopefully they'll get there fast."

"Skip asked for you to call his parents to meet them at the dock," Janelle explained.

Anna made the call and, later in the afternoon, was making plans to go into town herself, when Sarah called from the hospital. "Jewel had the baby!" Sarah said with excitement. "Practically as soon as they got here. It was so scary. I thought she was going to have it on the boat."

"But she didn't—and she's all right?" Anna asked.

"Yes. She and the baby are fine. Skip is a basket case."

"What was it?" Anna asked. "Boy or girl?"

"A girl. Seven pounds something. I can't remember for sure. But she had a lot of hair. And everyone is saying she's a really pretty baby, but she looks kind of red and wrinkly to me. Although Skip's mom says that's normal."

Anna laughed. "Yes. That's normal."

"But I think Skip's mom is a little mad at you."

"Mad at me?" Now Anna remembered that Skip and Jewel wanted to move back to the river.

"Because Jewel named the baby Anna."

"She did?" Anna laughed. "Well . . . I'll be."

"Anyway, I wondered if you want to come to town to see the baby, Grandma. Then you can give me a ride home."

"Wild horses couldn't keep me away," Anna told her.

It took Clark a few weeks before he was ready to get out and about very much. In the meantime, Johnny faithfully visited him almost daily. He came every afternoon right around four, and the two would play checkers or chess and catch up . . . Anna assumed on fishing.

It was early February when Clark finally proclaimed that he was ready to go out in a boat. Fortunately, it was a nice warm day. Anna assumed that he planned to go fishing with Johnny, but Clark firmly shook his head. "No. I'm done with that."

She felt slightly bad now. "But you guys had so many good times out there . . . I mean before the accident."

"I want you to come with me today. And I already told Skip and Jewel that we'd be gone for several hours. So you have no excuses."

She smiled. "I would love to go with you. Let me get my jacket."

Before long, they were chugging up the river and Clark was wearing the biggest grin she'd ever seen. "You're really happy to be out here again, aren't you?" she said.

He nodded. "Oh, yeah."

"Are your ribs okay?" she asked as they bounced on another boat's wake.

He grimaced slightly. "There's still a little pain. But not anything too bad."

"Because we could make it a short ride," she suggested.

He shook his head. "No, I'm fine."

She was surprised when he continued on past the docks in town, going right out under the bridge. "Clark," she said with alarm, "you're not going out on the ocean today, are you? Crossing the bar could be hard on your ribs."

"Don't worry." He continued heading down the river.

She didn't say anything, but she was worried. Even though it was a relatively smooth day on the river, the bar could be choppy and rough. And it looked like the tide was coming in. She glanced nervously at her husband, hoping that his previous head injury hadn't impaired his judgment.

But instead of heading out the river, Clark pulled up to a dock on North Jetty. It was a relatively new-looking dock and sturdy looking. "Whose is this?" she asked as he helped her out of the boat. And then she remembered something . . . something about this location was familiar.

"Come on," he said as he took her hand.

"Clark?" She tilted her head to one side. "Are you thinking about purchasing that lot again?"

"Nope." He shook his head. "Just come on." He led her to what looked like a recently built staircase. "Feel like a little climb?"

She shrugged. Whatever he was up to, he was certainly determined. And since this was the most exercise he'd had in weeks, she wasn't about to let him go up alone. But when they got to the top, she thought they must be trespassing. The house in front of them was new and beautiful and obviously someone's home.

"Clark," she said quietly but urgently, "whose place is this anyway?"

He reached in his pocket and pulled out a key. "Yours."

"What?" She looked at him then looked at the fabulous house. "That knock on the head must've done more damage than we realized."

He laughed. "This is the fishing trips, Anna.

Every day when Johnny and I said we were going fishing, we were coming up here to work on the house."

"You're kidding!" She felt slightly dizzy. "This amazing house? You actually built it? And you never even told me?"

"I wanted to surprise you, darling."

She stared up at the shimmering windows, the clean bold lines, the expansive observation deck that wrapped around the riverside. "Clark, it's beautiful."

"Come on inside," he urged. "I want you to see all of it."

Anna felt like she was dreaming as he took her on the full tour. With vaulted ceilings, wood floors, and enormous windows in all the right places, it looked like something she'd seen in a magazine. It felt spacious, but not overly big. The space was well used. And the kitchen was modern yet friendly. But it was the view that took Anna's breath away. "You can see both the river and the ocean," she said as she stared out.

"I call it River's End," he told her.

"River's End," she repeated happily.

"I thought that, if nothing else, it would be a place for us to escape to when the inn got too busy, or when it got too slow. A little getaway."

"It's a lovely getaway."

"But with Lauren and Brad coming to help. And with Jewel and Skip back. Well, maybe we'll want to spend more time here. Especially as we get older and don't have the energy to run Shining Waters." He slipped his arm around her. "I hate to admit it, but we are getting older, Anna."

She didn't say anything, just kept looking out at where the river met the ocean.

"Are you mad at me?"

"No, of course not."

"That's probably the biggest reason I kept it a secret. I was worried you'd get mad. Remember how upset you were that first day I brought you up here? And I did try to sell it to the other guy, but then Sarah went missing and I got distracted. Finally, I decided to just keep it. I started plugging away on it, but it was slow going. Then Johnny got the idea that he and I could build it together. It seemed impossible at first, but I subbed some jobs out, and it all just started falling into place." He looked at her. "You're really not mad?"

"No." But now she frowned. "Except that I don't like how you lied to me, Clark."

"Lied?"

"About going fishing every day."

"That wasn't exactly a lie. Either Johnny or I would run a line behind us as we ran the river. Sometimes we'd even catch something. And when we had no luck, we'd stop by the docks and do a little *fishing* from the local fishermen." He chuckled. "Those boys were always real glad to see us coming."

"Oh, Clark!" She playfully punched his bicep. "So, tell me, what happened the day you fell and hurt your head? I'll bet you weren't fishing then either."

"We were working on the dock steps. I wanted to get the railing up before I brought you up here. One misstep and I lost my balance and plunged down." He rubbed the back of his head. "Johnny kept coming up here. He's the one who finished it."

She looked around and sighed, wondering how she would've felt to know all this was going on. "Maybe it's a good thing I thought you were fishing."

"So, what do you think of it?" he asked hopefully. "Could you be happy here?"

She laughed. "I'm already happy here. I absolutely love it. Everything—the floors, the ceilings, the layout, the fabulous view. I love it, Clark!"

And she did love it. Even without a single stick of furniture, it already felt like home. She wasn't sure how much time they would be able to spend here, but she hoped it would be more than just a little getaway place. She could imagine a nice cozy sofa across from the fireplace. A breakfast table for two by the south window. A pair of rocking chairs out on the observation deck. It would be a lovely place, away from it all, for them to just to sit and relax together. And when they tired of each others' company, not that she expected to, they could run back down to Shining Waters and enjoy the hustle and bustle of the inn.

But Clark was right, they were getting older. The day would eventually come, maybe it was closer than she knew, when they would need to slow down. What better place to do it than here at River's End?

30

Summer 2010

An amazing fifty years had passed since Anna had returned to her roots along the Siuslaw River and the Inn at Shining Waters had been established. Hundreds of people had come and gone to the inn since those early days, many of them taking a piece of Shining Waters with them, and many of them leaving a piece of themselves behind. Anna had loved them all . . . guests and neighbors, friends and family . . . and, of course, her beloved Clark, who had passed on just two years ago.

Anna still missed Clark, still woke up early in the morning reaching for him . . . only to be reminded that he was gone. And with her ninetieth birthday nearing, Anna suspected it wouldn't be long before she joined him. But in the meantime, she intended to fully enjoy this day, and she would participate in the activities that her daughter and granddaughter had planned as much as these old bones would allow.

"Are you ready, Great-grandma?" Pearl called from the kitchen. Pearl was Sarah's youngest child. Sarah, despite her claim as a young person, had five children. Three boys and two girls. And Pearl had insisted on living with Anna this summer. Pearl said it was because she loved Babette's house, where Anna had decided to move last year when the long stairs to the dock became too much for her, but Anna knew it was because her family was worried about her living by herself. And, no matter, for Anna loved the company of the energetic twenty-year-old—and thought it no coincidence that she was named for Anna's grandmother because they shared the same spirit.

"I think I'm ready," Anna told Pearl as she reached for her old plaid Pendleton jacket. Like her, it was faded and gray, but the familiarity was comforting. And, according to Sarah, '49ers jackets were back in fashion again.

Anna touched the back of her gray hair. She'd tried to pin it into a tidy bun, but her shaky hands sometimes betrayed her. "Is my hair all right?" she asked Pearl.

Pearl looked and made some adjustments then nodded. "You look beautiful, Great-grandma."

Anna laughed. "Thank you, dear. But perhaps you should get your eyes checked."

"Grandma and Grandpa are down at the dock." Pearl hooked her arm into Anna's. "But they said not to rush you."

"I'm ready," Anna told her. And slowly they made their way down to the dock. Lauren, who still managed the inn, had sent out a couple staffers, two strong young boys from town, to make this walkway easier for Anna to use.

"Hello, Mom!" Lauren waved from the boat. Her hair was completely white now, similar to how Eunice's had been when she was that age. But Lauren's smile was sweet—and all her own.

"Ready for the big day?" Brad took her other arm, helping Anna into the boat, where she sat down next to Lauren and patted her daughter's knee. Lauren had put on a few pounds over the years, but it looked good on her.

"Yes!" she said eagerly. "Let the festivities begin."

Within minutes, they were pulling into the dock at Shining Waters. Like so many other things, the dock had been enlarged and improved. Clark had "supervised" the project, but, according to Lauren, he usually rolled up his sleeves and helped as well.

"Grandma!" Sarah greeted her from the dock. Her face was lit up with a huge smile, and as usual her long dark hair was pulled back in a single braid down her back, and for a moment, Anna thought someone had turned the clock back. Surely, Sarah wasn't turning fifty! But there she was with a little dark-haired bundle in her arms— and Anna knew that was Sarah's first grandchild.

"Come and meet your first *great-great-*grandbaby," Sarah said happily.

Anna knew that Sarah's oldest daughter, Silver, had given birth to a little girl less than a week ago. "I didn't think they'd be able to make it," Anna said as Brad helped her off the boat and she went over to see the baby. Anna touched the soft dark hair and sighed happily. "She's beautiful, Sarah!"

"They finally decided on a name," Sarah said as all of them began proceeding up to the inn.

"What is it?" Anna asked as she leaned on Brad's arm.

"Anna," Sarah told her.

"Oh . . ." Anna smiled. "Well, isn't that nice."

Now Sarah's husband Emery joined them, followed by their other children and their significant others. Everyone but Silver, who was resting, had come down. But it was a loud and boisterous crowd, and Anna marveled again that it was Sarah, the one who never wanted children, who had produced such a family. About halfway up, Jewel and Skip met her, along with some of their grown children and grandchildren. And then Marshall and Joanna and their children, along with a number of the other old staffers, joined the happy party. Everyone talked at once, exchanging greetings and hugs and slowly making their way up to the inn.

For a moment, Anna paused and, looking up at the clear blue sky, wondered how this happy procession might look from Clark's perspective. Because she felt certain he was watching . . . along with her parents and her sweet grandmother and all those who had gone on before.

"Are you okay, Mom?" Lauren looked at her with concern.

"I am perfectly wonderfully fine," Anna assured her. And then feeling like the queen of the parade, Anna led her tribe up to the inn, finally stopping at where a large number of people were already gathered around a large draped object out in front of the main building—the same building that was once a humble general store on the river.

"We have a chair for you here," Lauren told Anna, guiding her to an old rocking chair near the draped object. Anna suspected that her son-in-law, Brad, had something to do with whatever was under that big canvas tarp and that it was probably a bronze sculpture, but everyone had been very mysterious about it. As Anna sat down, she was surprised at how tall it was. Most of Brad's work was table-size, usually of wildlife, and always lovely, but this statue looked to be nearly six feet high.

"As you know," Lauren spoke loudly from the rustic podium that Clark had built decades ago for weddings, "we're here to commemorate the fiftieth anniversary of the inn. And we're all very happy you could join us today. Whether you're old friends or new friends experiencing the inn for the first time, *welcome!*" Lauren went on to tell a bit about the inn's history, as well as a bit about how their family acquired this land more than a hundred years ago.

"But to be fair, our ancestors—the Siuslaw—had dwelled along the river here for many, many generations, long before my great-grandmother and her sister filed a claim for this piece. And back in those days, before our history was recorded—other than in the storytelling tradition—our people didn't believe in ownership of land. The land was for everyone, and our people used it and shared it—living in peace." She turned to Anna. "And my mother understood this tradition. When she returned to the river about fifty years ago, she was determined to live in peace. It took some of us longer to learn how to do this, and some of us are still learning." Lauren smiled. "But over the years, my mother has taught us—in the same way her grandmother taught her—to live in peace amongst ourselves and with the river."

After Lauren's speech, Sarah came up to the podium. "I want to share an old story with you today," she said, "one that was passed down from my great-great-grandmother, Pearl. I lived in her cabin for years and I plan to live in it again when I come to live here full time next winter." She grinned at Anna. "Emery and I have decided to move home permanently in order to help with the management of the inn."

Anna nodded her approval. She knew that Lauren had been hoping and praying that Sarah and Emery would give up their demanding jobs of teaching college-level classes at the university and return to the river.

Sarah cleared her throat. "This is the story of *When the River Stopped.* Long, long ago, Otter and Bear lived by the River. Otter watched over the water, and Bear watched over the land; and they had enough, and they lived in peace. But Sun grew hot, and the River grew small until it was only a stream. And then it was nothing. Bear blamed Otter, saying, 'You did not watch River closely enough.' Otter blamed Bear: 'You were too greedy and drank too much.' Then Bear said, 'You stole River and took it to the Sea.' On they went fighting and fighting until Otter was close to death. And then Moon came out, and Otter and Bear heard Coyote laughing, laughing, laughing. Moon told Otter and Bear that Coyote and Beaver had built a dam and that was why the River had dried up. So Bear picked up Otter and carried him up the dried riverbed, up the mountain until they reached the lake that contained River. Coyote and

Beaver wanted to keep all the water for themselves. But Bear and Otter worked together and broke the dam, and River came rushing out, carrying them back down the mountain with it."

Sarah set the paper aside. "I believe that story is about forgiveness and grace," she explained to the listening crowd. "And my grandmother taught me long ago that forgiveness, like the river, must flow freely. I didn't understand it at first, and I selfishly held back my forgiveness. But like a river that's not allowed to flow, I began to dry up and die. It wasn't until I broke the dam holding back my forgiveness and grace that I began to heal." She put a hand on Anna's shoulder. "Thank you, Grandma."

Anna felt tears welling as she reached up to clutch Sarah's hand, but they were happy tears. Hadn't they all come so far! A few more family members and old friends got up to share words about the inn, the river . . . and how Shining Waters had changed them. And finally, it was time to reveal the statue. Anna watched eagerly as Brad pulled the cloth away. And what she saw took her breath away—a handsome Siuslaw woman wearing a cape that looked just like the one Grandma Pearl had given Anna long, long ago, and the beautiful young woman was standing proudly by a dugout canoe that looked just like Water Dove. Anna stood to get a better look, reaching up to touch the chin that was tilted up slightly.

"Beautiful," she told Brad. "Simply beautiful."

"You don't recognize it?" Lauren asked her.

"That looks like my grandmother's cape and the Water Dove." Anna tilted her head slightly. "Is it Pearl?"

"It's *you,* Grandma." Sarah pulled out a small black and white photo now. "I found this in the attic. Your father must've taken it."

Anna stared at the old photo then slowly nodded. "You're right. This is me. I remember the day this picture was taken." She looked back up at the sculpture, blinking to adjust her eyes and to see it better. "Perhaps it is me," she mused aloud. "Or perhaps it is all of us . . . it's Lauren and Sarah and Sarah's daughters . . . and even Baby Anna." Anna looked over to see the infant snuggled into the arms of an auntie. "Just as no one can own the river, perhaps no one can own this story . . . it is the story of all of us. It is our tale and our history . . . a story of love and heartache and grace and brokenness and peace. The traditions of our ancestors are being passed along to each new generation—both the good and the bad . . . but always, I pray, along with forgiveness and healing. This is the heritage of Shining Waters."

A Word from the Author

An interesting thing happened as I finished writing this book. My husband and granddaughter and I were staying at our beach cabin (near Florence and the same town that the Inn at Shining Waters books are set in). And as we drove past the airport, we discovered that biplane rides were being offered in exchange for contributions to a local charity. Naturally, we decided to enjoy a flight (although the granddaughter had to experience her first airplane ride in an enclosed plane). When my turn came to go up, the kind pilot (Sam Spayd) described points of interest to me. And as he flew over where our little beach cabin is located, by Heceta Beach, he showed me where the Siuslaw River was trying to return to its original course (the waters are sneaking outside of the massive North Jetty). I'd always been curious about what the river looked like before the jetties were built more than one hundred years ago. But I was pleasantly surprised to discover that river's original course to the ocean is right next to where our beach cabin is located! Our beach cabin is at the River's End! And like the house that Clark built as a getaway for Anna and him, my husband rebuilt this house as a getaway for us—and that's where most of this book was written and where I am right now—at the River's End.

Discussion Questions

1. Anna is in her late fifties at the beginning of this book and yet she still feels young inside. Why do you think that is? Describe your own attitude toward aging.
2. Anna's beloved granddaughter, Sarah, had been missing for two long years and for all they knew she could've been dead. Where do you think Anna found her strength in those two years?
3. Sarah's return to the river is a huge relief, and yet it comes with its own challenges. Describe a time in your own life when you received a mixed blessing and how you dealt with it.
4. Lauren has finally turned a corner in her own journey to maturity and yet she still struggles with parenting Sarah. Why is that?
5. Sarah had seemed like such a mature and responsible child. Why do you think she took the path she chose?
6. Were you surprised when Sarah decided to leave again? Why or why not?
7. Anna's "tribe" seems to be constantly changing, sometimes to her frustration, and yet good seems to come out of it. Describe what your "tribe" is like.
8. Clark and Anna almost seem to be drifting

apart at times. What did you think was going on when he was missing so much?

9. After discovering Sarah's new whereabouts, Anna sets out to bring her back. What gave her that kind of dogged determination?

10. Even after Sarah is rescued and nursed back to health, why do you think she hardens herself to Anna's encouragement to forgive her mother?

11. Sarah's presence at the river makes it too uncomfortable for Lauren to stay at the place she's finally claimed as home. And yet good seems to come of it. Describe a time when you were pushed out of your comfort zone but grew as a result.

12. Sarah is so hard on her mother, Lauren. What, if anything, do you think Anna could've said or done differently to bring Sarah around sooner?

13. What was your reaction when Clark got hurt? Were you surprised to find out what he'd been up to?

14. Anna had originally objected to the idea of a second home near the ocean. But when she sees what Clark has done, she realizes that it's perfect and just what they need. Have you ever opposed something only to find you were wrong? Describe how that feels.

15. The Siuslaw Indians are said to have been a matriarchal society. How would you describe

the heritage that was passed down from woman to woman in Anna's family?

16. What kind of heritage do you hope to pass down through your future generations?

Center Point Large Print
600 Brooks Road / PO Box 1
Thorndike ME 04986-0001 USA

(207) 568-3717

US & Canada:
1 800 929-9108
www.centerpointlargeprint.com